A Pride & Prejudice Reimagining

Fortune
Mi&sfortune

Pride, Prejudice, & New Adventures
Volume II

NEY MITCH

DEDICATION & AUTHOR'S NOTE

Hello Reader,

Welcome to the sequel to *Rapture & Rebellion*. This is the **second edition** of this work.

However, this book relies heavily on the story that took place in *Rapture & Rebellion*, which began in 1810.

Also, in regards to the content of the book, a significant portion of the story takes place in America when Mr. Darcy takes Elizabeth to Pennsylvania to meet some of his relatives. Also, with the character of Jane Bennet, she walks down a very different path than her sisters. While it may be surprising, as the series continues, her choices will become essential for the family. I hope you, the reader, enjoy it.

Reader, if you enjoyed *Rapture & Rebellion*, then I hope you enjoy this next installment, for I shall not deny that every time you all pick up one of these books, it means a great deal to me, and I dedicate this book to you all.

❦ I ❦

NOW AND FOREVER

I t's a fact, universally accepted, that a gentleman and a lady, when on the road to marriage and true happiness, by their will or not, find themselves to be the center of attention and news—both the good and the bad.

When Mr. Darcy paid a visit to Longbourn in February, asking for a private audience with Mr. Bennet, all the women in the household were sitting in earnest, waiting for the interview to be concluded.

However, I did not worry over the outcome of the meeting, for I knew how it would be. I simply just wished for my father, Mr. Bennet, to for once conceal his sardonic wit and be grave and gentle enough in attitude when hearing Mr. Darcy ask for my hand in marriage.

When last I unfolded the story of the day that Mr. Darcy had announced our engagement, the details of every moment were inconsequential to list at the time. Yet, as I search through my memories, I realize that those were some of my fondest moments. For, in truth, my father had doubts towards my finding happiness with Mr. Darcy, and I had to learn to help him relinquish his hesitation to accept my fiancé as my emotional equal. As such, here is the true and complete account of my time, my seconds, and moments of waiting outside of my father's study, for my fiancé to exit and tell me what my father had said.

However, the wait was not very long, and after Mr. Darcy had exited my father's study, he gave me a knowing look.

"What does that expression mean?" I teased.

"Are you your father's favorite child?" Darcy asked me.

"Possibly—I would reply in the affirmative, but I fear sounding too self-confident or smug."

"Well, I believe it, and that explains everything."

I cocked my head at him. "And what does it explain?"

"That I had to intimidate your father into giving me his consent for your hand in marriage."

At that I chuckled. "Mr. Darcy, please don't tell me you threatened my father with a pistol or blade of some kind, for I don't think I could look at you the same afterwards."

"Nothing so drastic, Lizzy, but I did give him my stare of doom."

"Ah, Mr. Darcy's infamous stare of doom and destruction. I would swear, if magic did exist in this world, when angry, you would have the ability to shoot fire from your eyes."

"Oh, that would settle all my land disputes in Kent quicker."

"Elizabeth!" my father called from his study. "Could you please come in here and close the door behind you?"

Mr. Darcy looked over my shoulder and saw my mother and three sisters Jane, Kitty and Mary looking at him from the sitting room—not to mention all the maids' eyes who were watching him from the crack of the doorways.

"I'm going to wait outside while you prove to your father that I am the best of men to marry."

"And what is so frightening about the sitting room, sir?"

"I'm outnumbered by four to one. A man can take a bullet, or a tragedy to befall him, yet one thing that a man cannot stand easily, is his future wife's mother."

"I heard that, Mr. Darcy!" my mother called from the sitting room, and it was quite comical to see Mr. Darcy, so great and strong a man, who had the sternest scowl that could be seen on any human, quake in his boots under the words of an older woman.

I grabbed Mr. Darcy's hand affectionately, and then moved past him and entered my father's study, where he remained sitting in his seat, looking as calm as always—yet I knew, despite his ease, that he was secretly unnerved.

I closed the door behind me, sat down before him, and awaited the confrontation of a man with his favorite child.

"I know that look, Father," I said, "and you can tell me, what are you really thinking?"

He sighed. "Lizzy, I think you are out of your senses."

🙢🙠

"Am I?"

My father's response then turned from one of complacency to one of grave anxiety, and I therefore felt sorry that I had put him through any sort of unease when I had always been the individual in the family who wished to be in harmony with him.

"Lizzy," he continued. "What are you doing? To be accepting this man? Have not you always hated him?"

"You knew of my dislike of him before now?" I said, startled. "I thought that I had been discrete with my temporary feelings of resentment toward him. And I had agreed to dance with him at the ball at Aginfield, and we had dined at his home."

"Yes, you did." Our father nodded. "Yet I am not an unobservant book, but rather I only pretend to be aloof. It helps me see more in earnest. You of all people should know that it is my natural inclination to see more than people assume that I do."

"The way that you saw it right for Lydia to go to Brighton?"

My father looked down at his hands and then turned and looked up at me.

"I have made mistakes, 'tis all too true, but those were ones made from carelessness, and that is not so with this case. When you came back to Steventon from Derbyshire, you were upset and spoke nothing of the name Darcy, and every now and again, there would be this look of resentment in your eye, one of anger—the same look of anger you had when Mr. Darcy slighted you at the assembly we had at the Red Lion when he refused to dance with you. Am I correct in assuming that?"

Then it was my turn to look down, feeling the embarrassment of being found out.

"Yes," I whispered, "that is correct."

"This means, that Mr. Darcy has hurt you in the past. This means that you hated him once, and you could always turn that way again."

I touched his arm with affection. "I can assure you that my feelings for him are so steady, and so much are my affections tied to his very presence. What can I say to you to assure you of the constancy of my affections for him?"

"Or in other words, you are determined to have him. He is rich, to be sure, and you may have more fine clothes and fine carriages than Jane ever could've gotten. But will they make you happy?"

"Have you any other objection," I replied, "than your belief of my making the wrong choice? Of my marrying with indifference and in consideration of only his station in life?"

"None at all. We all know him to be a proud, unpleasant sort of man; but this would be nothing if you really liked him."

"Pride," I replied. "That thing we see in so many others, and that I contained so often in myself. Yet Father, I have seen the good in him, and it far outweighs the bad. He has been wrong about things, erroneous to a fault, quite ill-behaved at times, but then who hasn't? I certainly have myself."

I paused a moment. "I do like him, exceedingly." Tears filling my eyes. "I love him. Indeed, he has no improper pride. He is perfectly amiable, and if you knew the extent of his goodness, you would not berate his character so."

"Lizzy, I have given him my consent. He is the kind of man, indeed, to whom I should never dare refuse anything, and in truth, he gave me this very *very* determined glare, as if he would try and melt me with his eyes if I decided to object."

I stifled a chuckle.

"And I should give it to you now. But I worry for you. Elizabeth, you know that I know firsthand the grief that comes from marrying someone who you cannot esteem or respect, and are you certain that you esteem him, you admire him? For if you don't, then I must suffer the tragedy of seeing you unable to respect the man you chose to spend the rest of your life with."

"But I do," I said, leaning forward. "And I always will, even when he makes mistakes, I will cling to him, and I already have so. Father, whether by heavens will or not, there is nothing that can take me from him."

"Well then," he said. "If this is the destiny you choose for yourself, then may fortune find you there. And I consent with all my heart."

My father smiled. I rushed up to him and kissed him on the forehead, and as I left, he called out to me.

"If any young men come for Mary or Kitty, send them in, for I am quite at my leisure to say yes to them, even if they were made of pine cones and tree bark!"

⚜

I walked out of his study and looked at my sisters and our mother.

"Where did Mr. Darcy go?"

"Where do you think?" Kitty laughed.

"He's walking by the rosebushes," Jane said.

"And he clearly thinks that I am intimidating," our mother said.

"You are intimidating, Mother." I chuckled, and then I rushed out of the house to the rosebushes.

There, walking amongst the green and the red, I found Darcy pacing back and forth. At first, I just stood there, watching him, looking stoic, but secretly nervous, and I wondered at the man who chose to marry me. How had I been so fortunate? How had providence found me, for to think that I, Elizabeth Bennet of Hampshire could be plucked from the multitude and selected to be loved by a man of such greatness, containing much sincerity and generosity—and a willingness to look past what he thought was integrity and find truth within it. A man who would face the censure of the world, all for the desire of pursuing me.

Mr. Darcy's greatness was not in his wealth, or his home, his imposing stature, or his regal appearance and graces. It was in his spark of life, his will to be the man he wanted to be rather than what the world restricted him —it was in his perseverance to be brave enough for many things, even the hardships of true love.

When he noticed me, he turned around and sighed out.

"Judging by that arched look on your face, I'd say that he has given you his consent as well."

"Did you ever doubt that I would not fight for you?" I asked.

"Never—though the long interview you had with him made me most anxious."

I rushed to him and he lifted me in his arms and twirled me around.

"So, we are free to fall in love now."

Darcy smiled. "Now and forever. Isn't it an amusing thing?"

"Very amusing."

We kissed once more.

2

THE NEWS THAT CAUSED A SENSATION

As you could imagine, it was not a moment too soon before my mother became filled with hysterics, not knowing how to take in her daughter's good fortune—especially since, out of all her children, I was the least dear to her.

And yet, at first my mother, Mrs. Bennet, was still when I had delivered the news, making it quite extraordinary...however I knew why. After I had been unable to lure Mr. Bingley into being in love with me, my mother secretly had begun to lose hope in me catching a husband.

Then, when Jane's and Kitty's prospects dwindled, she grew especially dejected. And the almost unfortunate fate of Lydia before her marriage to Wickham was brought about was especially trying to her *poor nerves*, making all appear as if the family of Bennets was forever to be ruined.

Therefore, to be standing there now, with one of her daughters marrying Mr. Darcy of Pemberly in Kent was too much good fortune for the woman who had succumbed to all her fears coming true.

"Good gracious!" she eventually exclaimed. "Lord bless me! Dear me, to think of such a thing occurring! Mr. Darcy! Who would have thought it! And is it really true? Oh! My sweetest Lizzy! How rich and how great you will be! What pin-money, what jewels, what carriages you will have! Lydia's fortune is nothing compared to yours! Nothing at all! I am so content—so happy. Such a charming man and as I had said when he came

7

to the first assembly we had here in Hampshire, he certainly is handsome! So tall! Oh, my dear Lizzy, pray apologize for my having not paying any notice to him so much before and I hope he will overlook it."

She paced before me. "Yet that is not my fault! He barely paid attention to you, and you know how I don't take heed to anyone who does not pay attention to my daughters. It wasn't until Lady Catherine came here that I knew that there might be a great chance with you and him. And now you shall have so much good fortune, a house in town! Everything that is charming! Two daughters married! Ten thousand a year! Oh, Lord! What will become of me? I shall go distracted!"

☙❧

"She really said all that?" Jane Austen asked after I was helping her and Cassandra wash clothes in their home.

After my mother ceased her effusions of joy of hearing my good fortune, I decided to pay a visit to the vicarage. There I would meet my friends to talk about my mother's new plans on the subject, while my mother would spend the day at our Aunt Phillips home, telling her all the news.

"Yes, Jane," I said, "she did."

"I'm surprised that she didn't wish to find a way for her to take credit for your catching Mr. Darcy."

At that comment, I nodded. "I believe that my mother would attempt to do so if there was a chance of it. Yet there is none, making it impossible to do anything else but realize that happy endings can occur in this world even without her schemes and machinations."

"I daresay that knowing even Providence is on her side," Cassandra Austen said, taking the wet clothes and wringing the water out of them, "must be a lot to her sensibilities."

I laughed. "It was at first, but I think she has grown to be flattered by the fact that harmony is in accordance with her will."

"I would be if I were her!" Jane Austen chuckled. "Though I am slightly disappointed."

"Why so?"

"Well, of all the things that I hoped you would tell me that your mother said after hearing news of your engagement, I was hoping to hear something more...spirited, such as her saying to Darcy, 'I knew that you would marry one of my daughters, for I knew that you could not be so handsome for nothing.'"

"Actually," I said, "that is a very good line, Jane."

"Is it?"

"I agree," Cassandra said. "It is a witty phrase."

"Then perhaps I will write that down."

"Yes, do that."

After we finished washing the clothes, we decided to go into town.

"So," Cassandra Austen asked as we walked. "What is it like?"

"What is what like?"

"To be in love, and have it returned?"

"Oh." I sighed, guarded, for fear that Cassandra was asking it from a place of sadness and from remembering a love that was lost. Yet I also realized that to not answer the question would not only be inconsiderate, but also would show her that I was thinking of something that was so intimate of hers that she didn't want me to perceive. "I daresay that love is different for all, for I have noted, love makes many girls smile, some it makes sigh, others it makes them proud, yet with me—it just makes me laugh."

"It made me laugh as well once," Jane Austen answered wistfully.

"Did it? I could see a man with the name Tom Lefroy doing that."

"And he did. He was funny, Elizabeth, so terribly entertaining, witty, and charismatic." Her expression was dreamy.

"And didn't your father always say that wit was the route of evil?" I grinned wickedly. "Even though I think it quite beneficial to have at times."

"As do I, yet I look back on my life," Jane continued, getting a faraway look in her eyes, "and, despite all logic, I cannot despise him still, to this very day. I can look at life and wonder what could have happened, but it would not change anything, nor would it answer any of the questions that I have.

"You see," she added, "that is the thing about love that is lost. You are left with many questions. Many questions, where there is no possible way to get answers for, and even if you get them, they are not the ones that you wanted to hear anyway.

"However, I must say, that if he did love me truly, would he have abandoned me so? Or did he love me, but he was pressured against his heart? What questions they leave us with. Now, on those constant notes of woe, I daresay that it's time for us to speak of brighter things because you are getting married to a man who has turned out to be as if he would only exist in storybooks. For he is flawed, yet he did right by the end."

"Indeed," Cassandra said. "After hearing the story of your romance with him, I was left with only one question in my mind: is he human?"

"He is an angel!" I exclaimed. "Never mind, that will not do! Angels can be so boring, and I wish to find that he is more interesting. Oh dear, I hope I don't get struck by a lightning bolt for my blasphemy."

"No," Jane said, "that would be too extreme. You are more likely just to step into a pile of horse manure."

"I think I would prefer the lightning strike."

⚜

We passed Lucas Lodge, which was where our good friend, once Charlotte Lucas, now named Charlotte Collins, stayed for a temporary visit. Though now married to Mr. Collins, who was the reverend of Hunsford, Charlotte still felt a deep connection to her home town and when I announced my engagement to Mr. Darcy, she asked her husband if she might remain in Hampshire while he had to return to Hunsford, so that she might be able to enjoy my news.

Mr. Collins at first was in a huff about this. But soon he saw the benefits of agreeing to his wife's whims, because now she would be the friend of the future Mrs. Darcy, and pleasing Mr. Darcy was one thing that Mr. Collins would have loved to do at all costs.

Therefore, he left for Hunsford Parsonage while Charlotte remained at Lucas Lodge, which suited me most. Charlotte was the better half of that married couple on many counts—some might even say on all counts—yet Mr. Collins was a naturally uncomfortable man to be around, and though his intentions always were to please, he often did not please anyone. And since my younger sister Kitty had rejected him, he would sometimes give me a look of apprehension or unease, as if because Kitty had rejected him, I was guilty by association. It was his reaction to my presence that made it even more obvious as to why Kitty had every reason to reject his hand in marriage and Charlotte had *no reason* to accept his hand in marriage.

When we came to fetch Charlotte, she and her younger sister, Maria, were available and met our invitation to walk into town with alacrity.

They expressed their congratulations of my good fortune and we spoke about our long memory of wedding gowns that we had seen in our time—and how we usually didn't think any of them were actually lovely. They were always said to be beautiful, yet they very rarely were, and were always less lovely than the common ball gown.

As we walked and Maria held the attention of Cassandra and Jane with news of a woman that one of her brothers was courting, I was able to converse with Charlotte.

⚜

"So," I began. "How do you find Hunsford?"

Our cousin Mr. William Collins was the reverend to Hunsford Parsonage, which was the church to Rosing's Park estate that was the seat of Lady Catherine De Bourgh.

Lady Catherine, who was a woman I met only once in my life, had ruined our relationship as quickly as it had begun. For her quickness to accuse me of seducing her nephew, Mr. Darcy, and then stating so boldly that I was not worthy of him had damaged any good opinion that I could have of her.

Such a proud and senseless woman, content to judge the world and think herself ill-used by those who stood up to her, Lady Catherine De Bourgh may be loved by the world, yet the first impression she gave me was of being a woman who did not deserve to be regarded as such.

Yet I turned my attention back to Charlotte as she continued to speak of her new life as *Mrs. Collins*.

"Lizzy, it is quite fortunate to run my own home. And my life is comfortable, complete and quaint."

"Comfortable, complete and quaint?" I sighed. "That sounds like a perfect match made."

Which I knew it wasn't, for my cousin, Mr. Collins, was quite possibly the most ridiculous man in all of England!

"Indeed, I suppose that my fortune when entering the marriage state was and is as lucky as anyone else can boast of when securing a match," Charlotte added. "For you see, Mr. Collins, if anything, is very good at being placed on a schedule and committing to it."

I angled her a glance. "Is he?"

"Yes, for you see, in the morning, we eat breakfast, then he spends the course of the morning after our meal working on his sermon for the next Sunday, then he spends time in his garden, tending to his beehives that he keeps."

She turned to look at me, her expression veiled. "I encourage him to be in his garden as often as he can. Then he also must visit his parishioners every now and again, and also he has to walk to Rosing's Park nearly every day."

"So often? Is that necessary?"

"Perhaps not, but I encourage him to do that as well. And I prefer to sit in the parlor, which I have told him that I use for my own particular use. Therefore, as you can imagine, Lizzy, sometimes a whole 24 hours can pass, and he and I have not spent more than a few moments in each other's company."

"I suppose you cannot include your sleeping quarters, for you both are not awake during the process," I answered with a wry smile.

"Oh, we definitely do not converse there, because we sleep in two separate rooms."

"Oh, really!" I replied, surprised. "I know that a husband and wife having two separate chambers is quite common, but it's not something that I think on often."

"Oh yes," she said knowingly. "I made sure to encourage that as well, for as I have often suggested to my husband, keeping separate rooms is more fitting for a clergyman."

"Especially one who has been fortunate enough to have received the attentions of Lady Catherine De Bourgh," I said sagely.

"Oh, especially so. Therefore Lizzy, I repent what I said before about being unhappy with my fate. And I find that I can bear the solitude that is my life quite cheerfully. I find myself quite content with my situation."

I knew that Charlotte was only speaking in half-truths. A part of her regretted her course of action in marrying my cousin, for she had confessed as much to me and the Austens. Yet she always had to tell herself to enjoy her fate, relish her fortune, and cling to every moment as one of contentment and triumph.

We entered Meryton and walked around. Everywhere that we went, people were expressing their congratulations to me on my upcoming wedding and, at first, I wondered how such news could have traveled so quickly. Then I realized that my mother was after all...my mother. And as I spoke with the townspeople of Hampshire, I so often heard so many sentences beginning with 'Mrs. Long heard from Lady Lucas, who heard from her servants, who heard from Mrs. Pratt's servants, who heard from Mrs. Shelby, who heard from your aunt, who heard from your mother that Mr. Darcy proposed to you!' so often that there was no room for confusion to still exist.

Over time it became very obvious that all of Hampshire had heard the story of Mr. Darcy's and my engagement, to which I was certain that they were beginning to create false tales of how our love could have possibly come about. Yet as long as that news did not fall into the lines of me drawing him in with my *arts and allurements* as Lady Catherine had said, acting as if I used witchcraft to seduce her nephew, then I could suffer any manner of falsehood.

Yet what was undeniable was that, in making no attempt to have a marriage that was something wholly splendid and worthy of everyone's notice, I had accidentally fallen into a marriage that was *wholly splendid and worthy of everyone's notice*. If happiness was meant to be found and obtained in irony, then mine was the most perplexing of all... and I welcomed it. I treasured it. Even though I felt all eyes on me and it unnerved me, I did not regret for a moment being a part of the news that caused a sensation.

❧ 3 ❧

LETTERS

M r. Darcy rode his horse to Aginfield, quite content with himself. When he approached the steps, dismounted his horse, then handed the reins to one of the stable hands, the door to Aginfield opened and Mr. Bingley emerged.

"Oh, look who appears content with himself," Mr. Bingley said. "And is smiling, even though smiling is one of his least favorite pastimes."

"I smiled often enough," Mr. Darcy objected.

"Did you?"

"Yes, I just made sure to never do it in public. So, what was so important that you couldn't even wait for me come inside?"

"You know me, Darcy, I don't believe in doing anything if I don't do it quickly."

"And I don't believe in doing anything if I do it moving faster than a snail."

"You just compared yourself to a snail." Bingley laughed, following Darcy inside the house. "That's a first."

"And it will be a last. And I should make a mental note later how I should organize and shape my metaphors and similes."

"I'll remind you if you forget."

"Thank you, but who is to remind you when you forget?"

"We must rely on the fact that you have a valet who somehow overhears everything that is said around you."

"Ah, which reminds me, where is Jefferson?"

"And that reminds me, weren't we talking about something?"

"I did ask you what you came to tell me, but you and your desire for afternoon witticisms distracted me."

"The afternoon is the only time that I can be witty, for in the morning, I'm not awake enough, and in the evening, I'm too much at my leisure to allow any strong thinking on my part."

"And as I asked before the wit of the world, what did you come out to ask me?"

"Oh, just to tell you that Jefferson was looking for you, for you have received some letters."

"Oh, that was it?"

"Darcy, they are letters. When is that ever it?"

※

Darcy walked through Aginfield and went to his bedroom to find Jefferson in there, packing his employer's clothes.

"Jefferson? You are packing my things? Am I going somewhere?"

"Yes sir, you are," was Jefferson's reply while he kept packing.

"Jefferson, I am your employer and I am still awaiting a reason for why you are packing my things."

"Because we must away to leave for town." He calmly continued his chore.

"Why must I go to London? I am getting married soon, and whatever the reason, London can wait."

"But it can't."

"Jefferson, you seem to be mixing up your idea of your station with mine and seem to be giving me answers with no explanation. I'm your employer and it's my job to confuse you with my strange demands."

"Forgive me, sir," Jefferson said, stopping and standing up. "You are correct, I am not giving you an explanation, but earlier you have received a series of letters."

"Mr. Bingley informed me of such. And I take it that they were of the sort that was general, and you could open."

"You gave me the permission to read all letters that are clearly invitations for parties and such."

"Yes."

"And I have just received a letter from Lady Dalrympe, congratulating you on your engagement to your cousin Anne De Bourgh, and that she wishes to throw a party for you at her townhouse in London."

"What!"

"Yes sir, the end has come."

⚜

"But," Darcy said, perplexed, "that is outrageous."

"And yet her invitation was most explicit and pressing," Jefferson said, packing away one of his master's cravats.

"Jefferson I can assure you that I did not tell anyone of those circles about my first engagement."

"I am certain you didn't, sir, but I am also quite certain that your aunt might've taken it upon herself to do so."

"There is no need to away to London simply because of an erroneous report, especially since my aunt has been talking of my engagement to Anne for years and nothing has come of it. Therefore, they must know that it is an event that my aunt wishes to take place, but never shall."

"Precisely, which is why I am worried."

Darcy studied his valet. "Beg your pardon?"

"For years, your aunt has been talking of your engagement to your cousin, Anne. Yet never has there been an invitation sent from any of the aristocracy to celebrate it...until now."

Darcy thought on Jefferson's words and then the implication finally came clear to him.

"You mean to say that even after I have removed my proposal from Anne, my aunt has still decided to tell everyone that I am getting married, in hopes of pressuring me into actually succumbing to her will."

"And she is perhaps using her friend, and I use the term of friend loosely here, Lady Dalrympe, to help pressure you into doing so. And even if I don't have full proof on the matter, the next letter supports my claim."

"There is another letter?"

"Yes sir, from your Uncle Earl of Matlock. Now I didn't read that letter, but something tells me that it is a response to what Lady Catherine De Bourgh is up to."

"It might simply be to tell me something about Richard."

Jefferson nodded. "I would agree, if it weren't for the next letter."

"There's another letter?" Darcy grew impatient.

"Of course, sir."

"Indeed, there always is."

"Yes, there is, and this one was from your cousin, Colonel Fitzwilliam. Now I didn't read that one either, for it is not my place to do so, however what are the chances that Lady Dalrymple, Earl of Matlock and Colonel Fitzwilliam will have written to you at the same time and not be speaking of the same thing, especially when Colonel Fitzwilliam's and Earl Fitzwilliam's letters were sent express?"

"Jefferson, where are the letters?"

After Jefferson informed Darcy that the letters were in the drawer, Darcy took them and went to the library for some privacy. He opened the first one that was sent from Earl Fitzwilliam and began reading.

Dear Fitzwilliam,

You must return to London immediately, for there is much spoken on your behalf that I am certain is neither correct nor for your benefit. Your Aunt Catherine came to London in a bitter state, angry about the wedding arrangements on your behalf and declared that she had work to do. She would not be very forward with me about her plans at first, nor about what she meant, which was quite strange for you know how your aunt loves to speak about everything and never listen, but she seemed determined. And then the next thing that I know, all of the aristocracy is planning on celebrating your 'official' engagement to Anne. Please either come to London immediately if this be untrue, or if you are detained somehow, please write a letter confirming or negating this report so that your aunt and I know how to act.

Sincerely

Your Uncle Fitzwilliam

PS-We have received word from medical experts that mercury is very much dangerous. Therefore, if you are ever ill, do not take mercury, for it has been deemed poisonous and more likely to kill you than cure you. Your aunt told me to include that in the letter, for she thought that you'd want to know that in case you were sick when you found this letter.

When done reading, Darcy closed the letter and then opened his cousin's which was a great deal briefer, for that was always Richard's way.

Dear Darcy,

I know that you are not engaged to Anne, and you know that I know, just like Lady Catherine knows that I know, just like I know that she knows that I know—yet more importantly, just like I know that Lady Catherine knows that you are not, yet she is doing this anyhow.

My father and mother believe that it is best for you to come to London, yet that is not what I find. If you were to come to town, then people might regard it as a confirmation of your engagement rather than a negation of it, but if you send a letter to Lady Dalrympe saying that you are not engaged, she will be angry because Lady Catherine made her look like a fool and then the truth would have no choice but to spread.

I am sorry that I cannot come down to meet your wife's family and there is still a great possibility that I won't be able to attend your wedding due to my company of soldiers marching to the peninsula, yet I am doing my best. Either way, this is the best advice that I can give.

Your fighting cousin,
Richard

PS-I heard about what my mother told father to write in his postscript, and I'm sorry about that. Though to be honest, it was wise for her to say, because mercury is in fact poison.

Darcy closed the last letter and sat there, wondering whose advice that he should have listened to. He saw the logic of Richard's advice and at one time in his life, he would have followed it. Yet too much of his past had been dominated by Lady Catherine's constant meddling in his life.

His devotion to his family always allowed him to overlook her incessant domination over everything, yet now it had all gone too far. He understood her feelings of betrayal, yet her reaction was inexcusable. His aunt should have confronted him for his breaking off his engagement, yet instead she confronted and offended Elizabeth—his Lizzy!

Therefore, though he wished to heed Richard's advice, he could not let such behavior stand. His Aunt Catherine, to be blunt, was a prig and a bully, and for too long she had her way and therefore was not in the habit of being spoken to in a way that upset her. Yet now that time had to come to an end. If he allowed Lady Catherine to let her tongue go unchecked, these attacks on Elizabeth would continue.

Darcy stood and walked back to his bed chamber and found Jefferson finishing up packing.

"Jefferson, have my horse brought round."

"I already have done so, sir."

Darcy realized that Jefferson had been one step ahead of him.

"I had assumed," Jefferson added, "that you would want to journey to Longbourn as soon as may be."

"Right." Then Darcy looked at the chests and suitcases that Jefferson had packed for him.

"Jefferson, perhaps it would have been preferable if I had journeyed to London by horseback and just changed horses at each inn."

"Oh, and by traveling from inn to inn, you mean that I should allow that thing that your father, on his deathbed, told me to do my best to dissuade you from doing."

"I loved my father," Darcy said, "yet my father also told me on his deathbed to marry Anne De Bourgh and look what happened?"

"Ah," Jefferson added with a smirk, "point taken, but this is something I agree on. Mr. Darcy, it's safer to always travel by carriage."

"I don't know about that, Jefferson, for I have seen some fairly fatal carriage overturns in my day."

"And I have seen many proud horsemen be thrown from their saddles."

"Very well," Darcy said, turning around. "I'll take a carriage. But don't think that you've won this argument or anything."

"Sir, I would never dream of thinking such a thing."

Darcy raised a cynical eyebrow in his valet's direction and went to tell the butler to inform Bingley that he was journeying to Longbourn.

"Lizzy," Hill, our maid called from the hallway.

I stood up and left my bedroom. "What is it, Hill?"

"Your father needs you in his study."

"Thank you, Hill."

I walked past her, went down the steps and knocked on my father's door.

"Is that you, Lizzy?"

"Yes, it is."

"Excellent, you may enter."

I opened the door and entered to see my father holding a missive in his hand.

"Come in, come in."

I closed the library door behind me and sat down, my curiosity heightened, knowing his reasons for wishing for me had to do with the contents of the letter.

"I have received a letter this morning that has astonished me exceedingly. As it principally concerns you, you ought to know its contents."

I perked up at his comment. "Who is it from?"

"I was thinking of making you take three guesses as to whom, but I realize that that wouldn't be enough tries. Then again, maybe all the guesses in the world wouldn't be enough for you to figure it out."

"Then that must mean that the letter comes from Mr. Collins."

My father's eyes shot open in surprise.

"And just how did you figure that one out?"

"The only supposition that I can give you is reasoning it out. You said that I would need all the guesses in the world, which meant that I would not be looking forward to hearing from the person, and the main person I could not think of looking forward to hearing from was Mr. Collins."

"Get better acquainted with the world, Lizzy, and I can assure you, my dear, you shall find people who you don't wish to see even more."

"I suppose you have a good point there, now what could he have to say to the sister of the woman who rejected him?"

"Ah, I still admire Kitty for having such a backbone. Yet with Mr. Collins, he says much both to the purpose and not to the purpose." My father settled back into his chair. "He begins with congratulations on the marriage of my youngest daughter, Lydia, but then afterwards, he writes to tell me that her behavior and very nature, which must naturally be bad, should be returned with utter contempt and that our entire family should shun her.

I gasped, truly shocked.

"Yes, Lizzy, that is the advice he gives as a servant of the church, which are his Godly words, while also claiming to be a man of the cloth who is supposed to teach mercy and benevolence."

Old memories of Wickham poked like thorns. "He knows about our misfortunes with Lydia's running away with Wickham."

"Of course, he does, probably due to the loose tongues of some of the good-natured but gossiping Lucases. I shall not sport with your impatience, by reading what he says on that point any longer, for we shall then have to consider who is worse: your sister for being loose, the Lucases for being loud mouths, or Mr. Collins for being Mr. Collins. Therefore, I shall skip ahead to the part of the letter that relates to you. Here I shall read it."

My father put on his glasses and began to read the missive.

"Having thus offered you my advice on how to handle your most unfortunate daughter Lydia, let me now add a short hint on the subject of another: of which we have been advertised by the same authority. Your daughter Elizabeth, it is presumed, will not long bear the name of Bennet, and the chosen partner of her fate, may be reasonably looked up to, as one of the most illustrious personages in this land. This young gentleman is blessed in a peculiar way, with everything the heart of a mortal can most desire—splendid property, noble kindred, and extensive patronage. Yet despite all these temptations, let me warn my cousin Elizabeth, and yourself, of what evils you may incur, by a precipitate closure with this gentleman's proposals, which, of course, you will be inclined to take immediate advantage of. At first, I welcomed their union, now I am suspicious of it—wary. My motive for cautioning you is as follows. We have reason to imagine that his aunt, Lady Catherine de Bourgh, does not look on the match with a friendly eye."

I grunted to myself.

"You are not diverted, Lizzy?"

"Of course not. Who is he to think his opinion will hold any sway over me and keep me from being wed to Mr. Darcy? As if I am so easily influenced or frightened."

"Well, it gets worse," our father said and then he read on:

"After mentioning the likelihood of this marriage to her ladyship last night, she immediately, with her usual condescension, expressed what she felt on the occasion; when it became apparent, that on the score of some family objections on the part of my cousin, she would never give her consent to what she termed so disgraceful a match. I thought it my duty to give the speediest intelligence of this to my cousin, that she and her noble admirer may be aware of what they are about, and not run hastily into a marriage which has not been properly sanctioned."

My father lowered the letter and looked at me over the rim of his spectacles.

"Your mother told me that Lady Catherine De Bourgh paid you a visit not so long ago."

"Yes," I replied, guarded. "She did."

"And how did the interview with her suit you?"

"It was...fine."

"Only fine? And yet why do I assume that it is less so? Lizzy, was Lady Catherine's coming here a sign of her happiness of you entering her family, or did she come to refuse her consent?"

"The latter, I'm afraid. She told me, with many insults placed at my feet, that I was not worthy of her nephew."

"So, she came all this way to bully you, show herself not worthy of the title she was given, and slighted you?"

I studied my hands on my lap. "All of my family. She slighted all of us."

"How delightfully absurd!" My father exclaimed. "Yet I am sorry that you had to experience that Lizzy. Though I must ask dear, for I have no choice. Does she hold any sway over her nephew? I just would not have you suffer the disappointment of a man proposing to you and then revoking it in the name of family and duty."

"Father, Mr. Darcy is not like that."

"Society has been known to make the strongest of men buckle under its weight."

I smiled. "And he is no longer as afraid of the world as others are. You know that, father."

"I want to know it. Well, then I have no choice but to trust him."

I picked up the letter and gazed at it.

"Why do we families in this world always have to have a Mr. Collins and a Lady Catherine de Bourgh?"

"Because absurdity is how the Holy Father amuses himself. That is the only excuse that I could make for it."

⚜

After I left my father, Kitty approached me with a letter that Lydia had sent her from Newcastle.

"Lizzy," Kitty began, "Lydia has just sent me this letter, and now Wickham is serving in a regiment in Newcastle, but part of it was addressed to you."

"If that is the case, then why didn't she just send me a letter separately?"

"You know Lydia," Kitty replied knowingly. "She probably didn't even think to do so, or she probably didn't wish to spend more money in sending another letter."

Kitty handed me the letter and I began to read the part that was addressed to me.

My dear Lizzy,

I wish you joy. If you love Mr. Darcy half as well as I do my dear Wickham, you must be very happy. It is a great comfort to have you so rich, and when you have nothing else to do, I hope you will think of us. I am sure Wickham would like a place at court very much, and I do not think we shall have quite money enough to live upon without some help. Any place would do, of about three or four hundred a year; but, however, do not speak to Mr. Darcy about it, if you had rather not.

Yours,
Lydia

PS-I am sure that you will be a beautiful bride at your wedding, yet not nearly as lovely as I was.

When I finished the letter, I closed it, placed it with the letter that Mr. Collins had sent my father and clenched them both.

"Is Lydia really in earnest!" I shouted.

Kitty released a sigh. "Indeed, I believe she is. Yet I have known her long enough not to be surprised by it."

"I've known her equally as long as you, Kitty, but it never ceases to be terribly vexing."

"I try not to let it affect me so, for one reason only."

"And what reason is that?"

"It is not worth exerting my energy, nor submitting my sensibilities to it —or compromising my sense."

I shook my head and sighed. "Sense and sensibility. I would rather have Lydia contain one or the other rather than possessing neither. Then again, since Lydia does not know how to practice moderation, she would do them both ill."

I looked at the letters and arrived at the only thing that could be done.

"Drastic measures should be answered in one way only."

I walked up to the fireplace along the wall and dropped both letters into the fire and felt a calm wash over me.

"That form of disposal never ceases to be cathartic." I brushed off my hands and walked away.

❧

"A letter from Mr. Collins and from Lydia in one day," Cassandra Austen said as we sat on the branches of a tree in the woods. Cassandra and Jane Austen had climbed the tree with me while Jane sat on the ground and Mary read while sitting in the grass.

"I apologize," Cassandra continued, "for that is too much grief within so short a time frame."

My sister Jane and Jane Austen chuckled.

"And she really said those things?" Jane Austen asked. "Now Mr. Collins I can readily believe him thinking and writing such ridiculous prose, but even Lydia I did not expect to be so foolish, as careless as she has been before."

"Yes," Jane said, "even that was too much, but Lizzy, you must ignore all that Mr. Collins had said."

"Indeed, you must," Jane Austen concurred. "A perfect match should not be torn asunder because of society's perpetual inability to understand...and of a deluded clergyman's inability to see his own tendency to mistake sanctimonious views with aristocratic ones."

"Mr. Collins is a very refined and earnest young man," Mary said, lowering her book. "You must not accuse him of such hypocrisy."

"How is your book, Mary?" Jane asked, distracting her.

"Very good, thank you."

"And why don't you tell me about it?"

Mary, successfully distracted, began to talk about the contents of her book, yet we soon found ourselves interrupted by approaching footsteps.

Quickly closing ranks, Cassandra, Jane Austen and I jumped down from the tree, and straightened ourselves up. Jane and Mary stood as well, awaiting the stranger, but only to be met by Mr. Darcy.

৩৫৩

"Mr. Darcy!" I exclaimed.

"Miss Elizabeth," he said, "I came to your house to pay a visit, and your mother told me that you had journeyed down this walk with your companions."

I was genuinely pleased. "And yet you have found me."

He smiled gently, yet one look in his eyes had immediately showed me that all was not right with him. He greeted my sisters and friends politely enough, yet I knew that he wished to speak with me alone. And luckily, my sister Jane saw it as well. As we walked back to Longbourn, she managed to influence our friends to walk faster than myself and Darcy while we lagged behind.

"I've missed you," I said when we were out of earshot.

"And I have with you." Darcy exhaled with a sigh. "Is it so strange that I am so dependent on you?"

"Oh, heaven forbid a person who is marrying someone feel such a thing!" I teased. "Really, Mr. Darcy, you are very much not the modern man."

"You tease me?" He laughed.

"Oh yes, I tease you often and will continue to do so."

"That is very good, and as I would want you to."

I glanced up at his handsome profile. "Really, you like my cheek?"

"It is the most real thing in the world, and the most natural. Never stop making me a better man than I once was, Elizabeth, for I shall need your strength often."

"You always were a good man," I said, wishing to offer solace. "You just made mistakes, like the rest of us. And why do you think on your past now? When your present is so promising?"

"And why do you want me to forget it?" He smiled, running his fingers over my hand lightly. "When remembering it might be the best thing for me to do."

His mere presence sent my heart racing. "And how is that?"

"It will keep me from making the same mistakes again."

I smiled at his candor. "I often look on the past in a way that it gives me pleasure, and then leave out the rest. Yet in this case, I can see why this is a lesson that you want to keep learning, but I don't want your guilt to overcome you. You have made errors, which if you recall, you had no choice but to make."

"How do you think so?"

"You were a man of the aristocracy, given much and told not to always admire those who the world has labelled to be below you."

He nodded, agreeing. "This is true, I've been given good principles yes, but was left to practice them in selfishness and conceit. Had it not been for you, dearest and loveliest Elizabeth."

Again, my heart soared. "This is too much praise!"

"Not at all, for it is me making up for all the times in which I hurt you and almost lost you."

"While I have told you not to feel any guilt, I do admit to your talking about it now does give me a wonderful sense of self-confidence."

"Oh, you wicked woman!"

I laughed at that. "Yes. Very wicked."

"Well your wickedness is what shall save me now. I am a better man than the one you first met, therefore yes, let me dwell in my past every now and again, for only that way will I continue to be the better man."

"Just don't let me come home one day and find you flogging yourself like a strict monk!"

Darcy threw his head back and laughed. "Oh, nothing so dramatic."

"And I have made you laugh more than once in one conversation. How have I been able to achieve that?"

"In only the way that you could do it."

<hr />

"Yet, Mr. Darcy..."

"Oh, would you leave me so unsatisfied?"

"Very well," I purred. "Fitzwilliam."

"There it is. There will never be a lovelier sound than when you say my name."

"It is a good name."

"Oh please, it's a terrible name! It has way too many letters in it."

"As if Elizabeth is not a mouthful."

"It's a lovely mouthful." He squeezed my hand.

"And Fitzwilliam isn't?"

"It has a 'z' in it! By god..."

I stifled my laugh and then refocused.

"Fitzwilliam, I have a strange request."

"And what would that request be?"

"Please love me, even when I don't make you laugh. I know it is not something you would think I should ask, yet when a person falls in love with wit, it makes one feel a pressure to always do so. Love me when I am funny and love me more especially when I am not. For humor is not something that can be conjured always."

"You are not strange for making such a request," he responded, much to my happiness, for I worried that he would not understand my fears and apprehensions.

"I have myself seen men who view their wives less like companions and more like constant sources of amusement. Then when she shows herself to be no more or less human than he is and being just as able to fall into not always being interesting, he looks on her as being guilty of some crime. As if she deceived him and is not the woman that he married."

"That is exactly so." I sighed, relieved. "And I am glad that we see things so similarly in this circumstance."

"Then rest assured, I do witness it. It is a common failing of those who enter the married state to regard their spouse in what seems to be a perfect light, when in truth it is a harmful one that is bound to be a weed between them both that will grow to separate them. Therefore, I know your anxieties and to which they are aimed."

"For a man who has never been wed, you seem to be strangely connected with virtues and vices of the married state."

He nodded, pensive. "Being a part of the aristocracy can show me much. And has done so. Yet I daresay that it has had the opposite effect that it usually has tended to. Many have seen the model living of our station in life and adhered to it, yet it has only made me wish to rebel against it in the end. And it is such a tendency of that which has led me here to see you today."

"Do you mean that you have more than a reason just to see me?"

"Yes, and the news will not be to your liking. I must away to London to bring the end of something that will cause us grief."

I felt immediate concern. "Grief, of what sort?"

"Today I have received a letter."

"Oh, for goodness sakes! What is with this day and letters?"

𝕾 4 𝕾

TORN ASUNDER

Darcy told me of the contents of the letter of Lady Dalrympe and I had the impulse to kick a tree.

"Are we forever to not have peace? Does it seem to be something that we are not allowed to have, even after we have come together?"

"It seems so," Darcy said, "and while I do not pretend to not be amused by your reaction, it is not necessary for you need not worry. I shall not let this time, which should be blissful for us, be impaired by my aunt's constant interfering. Especially since some of it is my fault."

"But why must you go to London? Just answer this invitation with the truth and you need do nothing else."

"You don't want me to leave?" He smiled smugly.

"Of course not. It is already difficult that our wedding won't be for another two weeks."

"I agree as well. How did we agree to such a long engagement?"

"A two-month long engagement is not terribly long at all, my love. It just feels so. And remember, there was no out-arguing my mother on that score. For as you've seen, even you aren't a match for her nerves."

He raised one eyebrow. "No one is."

"Yet Darcy, still, you don't need to go to London."

"But I must, and not just to correct this error, but also to get—oh I know that I sound terrible for saying this, but revenge or a reckoning."

29

"What do you mean?"

"Elizabeth, my aunt came to Longbourn and attacked you, declaring that you are not worthy of me. It is bad enough that my pride led to me making so many wrong decisions, but too often you have suffered for them. Yet if I was to stand by and let my aunt think that she can berate you and continued to do so is something that I will not allow to continue. Elizabeth, I must set this right."

"I admire your desire to defend me, but if you go to London and she attempts to try and persuade you to wed her daughter..." I admitted to being quite insecure still on that score, and I feared Darcy ever regretting his choosing me. "I know that you agreed to marry Anne first, Fitzwilliam..."

"Elizabeth, I can assure you, that you need not worry on that score. I am devoted to you and please, let me do this one thing and let me defend you as I ought to have done for so long."

"Then, as long as you promise to return to me," I said with a gentle smile, "I will...*possibly*... allow you to go."

"And I do believe that you are teasing me again." He gave me a warm look and chuckled.

"Of course, I am."

৩৯৩

"Yet I do wish," I added, "that I might be able to go with you."

"You do not think that I have already thought of that? There were moments when I rode here that I wondered if there was some way that I could hide you in my carriage and take you captive."

"While I admire your inclination towards piracy in this case, it would not do. I daresay that my family would notice that one of their four daughters was missing."

"I wish that they were more aloof."

"At the moment, I do as well, but such lack of presence of mind would affect their parenting, and it has already done that too much, I fear."

"I do so love you."

"And I very much love you. Though I don't know where your sudden declaration of your affection just derived from."

"I simply felt like saying it." He gave me a smug look of satisfaction.

"And you were in luck, for I was very much in the mood to say it in return."

Before we came into view of my home, Darcy grabbed me and pulled me behind a tree. Looking into his eyes, I read his thoughts.

"Are you about to kiss me behind this tree?"

"I am."

"And knowing my inclination to always submit to your pleasing attentions, you are looking for me to give into you?"

"I am awaiting a favorable look."

"Hopefully one day, long after we are married, I won't submit to you so easily."

"And hopefully one day, long after we are married, you will realize that there is no point in not submitting to me."

"If you had not reformed, I would have ended up a heartbroken woman."

"Then luckily for us both, I did reform."

"And luckily for you, I still have not learned how not to submit to your influence."

"Yes, lucky for me."

Mr. Darcy then leaned down while I rose on my tiptoes and kissed him tenderly. And while it is a truth universally acknowledged that a kiss is a wonderful gesture and sensation, it is not universally spoken that one can never usually cease at one kiss alone. Therefore, our kiss went from something that should have lasted for only a few seconds to something that continued for a whole five minutes.

⚜

When we were finally able to recover from one another, Mr. Darcy followed me into the house. My mother was wonderful enough to act as if we had only lagged behind the rest of our company because we must've simply not realized that we were walking too slowly. Even I had to appreciate such a gesture and inwardly declare that my mother's skill in the art of matrimony sometimes were fruitful and led to profitable ends.

After we entered to see all my sisters, mother and the Austens sitting down to tea, I thought that Mr. Darcy would immediately wish to take his leave, yet he did not.

He sat down and began to converse with my mother as well as the Austens, who all turned merrier at Mr. Darcy's sudden interest in them. My mother felt a specific compliment at knowing that an illustrious man such as Mr. Darcy was giving her every attention that would be expected if she was of superior rank.

Mr. Darcy also inquired about our desire to put on home theatricals, which was something that I recall him not caring for once, and my sisters and the Austens began to tell him about all the plays that we put on since we were in our late teens—he even went so far as to congratulate Jane Austen on her published novel, *Sense and Sensibility*, which his sister Georgiana had said was a wonderful read.

"I thank you, Mr. Darcy," Jane Austen said, "and I am happy that I had altered it from its original style and format. Would you believe, originally I wrote it as a series of letters that was back and forth in between the characters?"

"Truly?" His interest was real.

"Yes, in truth, despite all our desires to believe that our writing is perfect when we first take pen to paper, it took me years to improve my method. Yet I believe that I have done so."

"Indeed, you have, Jane," I said. "For it is a delightful book." Everyone else in the room echoed my sentiments, except for our mother, who was not a great reader and therefore had not read it.

"Thank you, Lizzy and the rest of you for your kind words. And therefore Mr. Darcy, writing can place a person in such a strange position. Once I was very critical of other books and yet now, as I write and I see that it is so easy to miss-spell a word here, or write one name when you meant another there, it has led me to be less a critic of execution and more of a studier of the feeling and sentiment of the work, for that is where the real skill of the writer is."

"I must confess to not at all despising the character of Marianne in your novel," Kitty said, "though I know by the end we are meant to praise Elinor for her sense and censure Marianne for her sensibility, I confess to seeing much of myself in Marianne, and hating myself is not something I wish to do today, or tomorrow even."

"While sense always ought to be admired," Mr. Darcy added, "sensibility must always secretly be accepted in our hearts because it is the desire to have a profound feeling and to not be afraid to have them.

Georgiana has written to me of her ideas on your characters, the Dashwood sisters."

He turned toward Miss Austen. "While she admired Elinor and recognized her as the best of heroines, she admitted in her heart, that she also had much in common with Marianne and therefore could not despise her at all, even with her mistakes."

"And therein lies the truth behind my book," Jane Austen declared. "Marianne is all of us, any of us, whether she is a character that is how we are within, or how some of us are without, yet a part of her is how we are.

"It is both very good and very bad. Marianne loves her family a great deal and has all the qualities of a devoted sister. And secretly, we wish that we could express how we feel in the same way that she does, openly and without reproof, yet her very virtue of being true to her feelings and allowing to be ruled by sensibility turns that very fine quality into the worst of vices." She looked at each of us. "Therefore, it makes one wonder: where is that fine line that separates sensibility from turning into a sin? And with Elinor, well, she is everything that we hope to be in many ways, but even I—secretly, and this is a wicked thing to say—found her constant sense as being a little cold.

"Yes, I the writer have admitted here and now that I always wanted Elinor's 'Sense' and Marianne's vitality, her spark of life. And I wonder if there will come a time where a young lady can have both?"

"I hope," my sister Jane said, "that we live to see that day."

While Jane Austen began to regale us with her unfinished novel, *The Watsons,* and how she wished that she hadn't abandoned the idea, for now she realized that she might've had a good idea beginning with that one, I turned and whispered to my husband.

"I had no idea that you had learned to see all the greatness in her being a writer."

"Like I stated before," he whispered, "you have made me quite the better man. And I suppose that it is wonderful that the times are changing."

"And may they always do so, for I quite look forward to it." I gave him a coquettish smile.

"Yet," Jane Austen continued, still talking about *The Watsons,* "one day, if I live long enough to return to it, I might go back and finish it. Although," she added with a smirk, "you know perfectly well that I have begun something else."

⚬⚭⚬

When Mr. Darcy had no choice but to leave, I saw him to the gate where his horse was tied up. My mother had Kitty be my chaperone so that I would not be alone and err against decorum, yet I knew the truth behind her real scheme.

If she had sent Jane, Jane would have remained with me the whole time. Yet in sending Kitty, she knew that Kitty was less inclined to follow decorum and not ruin a moment because of the demands of propriety.

Therefore, as soon as Kitty followed us over the threshold, she pretended as if she had broken the lace on her boot and needed to rush inside to repair it.

Ah, thank you, Kitty!

Now being left alone, I walked Mr. Darcy up to his horse.

"And might I ask why you were so keen to remain and speak with all of us in such a pleasant way?" I asked. "Not that I am discouraging it at all, for it made me quite proud of you, yet it just made me curious."

"I had three motives behind my reasons to linger behind as I had done so."

"And what is the first?"

"I wanted to be around you for longer, and a part of me still does not wish to leave for London without you at my side."

Warmth burst through me. "That is a wonderful reason. A part of me wishes that it was the only reason."

"It won't be when you hear the second reason," he said mysteriously.

"And what is the second reason?"

"I realized, that due to my pride and inclination to not converse with people who I don't have a long acquaintance with, I never got to know your sisters and friends, as I almost did not allow myself to know you once. It was time that I rectify that mistake."

"I like that second reason as well and I wish that it was the only other reason you had."

"It won't be when you hear the third reason."

"And what is the third reason?"

"I just realized, now that I am spoken for and am engaged, I suddenly love to be in a room of many women!"

"Oh, Mr. Darcy!"

"Will you hear my reasons for being so?"

"I am ready for the truth."

"Well, when I was not engaged, I felt if a woman paid attention to me, it was because she wished to marry me, no matter how much she didn't love me or was only paying attention to me for my wealth or status in the ton." He brushed his stallion's nose with his palm. "Yet now I am engaged and whenever a flock of women pay much attention to me and enjoy my company, I know they are doing it simply because they wish to be my friend, they wish to hold me in good esteem, it is because—they want to believe in me. No more and no less."

"I love you," I said. "And this time, I just felt like saying it."

"And I love you." He kissed my hand, then climbed his horse and nodded to me. "I will return as quickly as I am able, I shall cure us of any impediment to our marriage, and I swear, Elizabeth, our bond will not be torn asunder."

He pressed his heels against his horse's sides and was off, yet I watched him leave until he disappeared over the horizon.

'We would not be torn asunder,' I repeated his words to myself, 'we would not be torn asunder!'

5

THE TRIUMVIRATE

After a few days' time, Mr. Darcy arrived at his townhouse in Grosvenor Square. As soon as he reached his destination, he had Jefferson meet with the hired help and arrange for everything to be organized.

"Though remember, Jefferson," Mr. Darcy advised, "to let them know that our visit shall not be a long one, therefore they should not buy too much produce or food so that we will not have to throw away any excess."

"Very good sir, yet I must warn you that we might stay a little longer than expected."

"You are thinking of my aunt and how unreasonable she can be?"

"Yes sir. And her continuous schemes of how to potentially detain you."

"Well, her plans shall not work this time, for I have one thing on my side." Darcy gave him a knowing glance.

"And what is that?"

"I have learned that the best way to deal with my aunt is by having strength in numbers."

They heard the bell ring, then after a couple of moments, a maid entered and addressed Darcy.

"Sir, Mr. Bingley is here to see you."

"And there is one of my reinforcements now."

"Bingley!" Darcy said as he walked down the steps and shook hands with his friend.

"Hello, Darcy. As you can see, I received the letter that you sent."

"Sorry if my handwriting was not as even as usual, yet I wrote to you before I left Hampshire and therefore, I was a little hurried."

"I actually enjoyed it," Mr. Bingley replied happily. "For as you might recall, we had an evening debate once on my tendency to lean toward bad handwriting when my thoughts are disheveled while your handwriting remains clean and neat no matter the—matter. Therefore, it was refreshing to see you in such a state. If I weren't so angry with you about being engaged to a woman that I once fancied, I would say that being in love suits you well."

"You are not angry with me!" Darcy sighed with satisfaction. "For while you enjoyed the attentions of Elizabeth Bennet, you were not in love with her."

"I loved...parts of her."

"Bingley, you must never again say that in my presence unless you would want to end your day with a black eye and bloody nose."

Bingley stepped back, affecting surprise. "Well, I must declare! You really are in love!"

"Yes, very much so."

"Darcy, you misunderstand me. I am not angry at your choosing Elizabeth Bennet, for in earnest, she is a wonderful woman and is very much your match. Yet I am angry that you never confided your feelings to me. Instead you debased your own actions by trying to wittingly throw me off her trail so that I would not find her lovely—so that you would not be jealous."

Darcy nodded with satisfaction. "You are right. I was jealous that you and she might fall in love."

"And all of the miscommunication could have been avoided if you had simply been honest with me. Did you not think that I would have been respectful of your feelings?"

"I know that you would have been the best of men, as you always are, Bingley. It was not your virtue that I did not trust."

"Then what was it?"

"It was my pride. I was in love with Elizabeth Bennet since the moment that I got to know her and was attracted to her far before that. Yet I was blinded by my sense of duty that was also mingled with bitterness.

"Bingley, you know my past and how I respond when I am heartbroken. I cannot bear the pain so well, therefore, when meeting Elizabeth Bennet, I was meeting a woman who I felt all the ties that could bind two individuals permanently. Yet I feared to do so in hopes of not only avoiding going against society and the ton, but also avoiding going against my heart."

"Oh," Bingley said, beginning to sympathize with his friend. "You were afraid that she would hurt you?"

"I've been hurt before, and I'm man enough to admit it now. Just as you have been my friend long enough to have seen it happen to me often."

"Darcy, you are not a statue, no matter how much you try your best to look like one."

"I do not."

"Yes, you do."

"No, I don't."

"Yes, you do."

"No, I don't."

"Yes, you do."

"No, I don't."

"Yes, you do!"

"Well then—I am getting better at moving more."

Bingley graced him with a smile. "I can see that, you are fidgeting—and that means that love has worked wonders on you. Yet as I say, you are not stone, but flesh and blood and the things that set back the common man must every now and again affect you and throw you off your stability and into the abyss that is uncertainty.

"You have seen me in love many, *many* times before. Some I have had the misfortune to be out of my own foolish and idle inclinations and others were women who I should never have made the mistake of liking at all. I have been heartbroken before, to the point where I felt as if I could never love again, just as I have accidentally, and blindly broken hearts and I have no excuse for my actions.

He paused in his thoughts. "To be a gentleman is still to be a man, and to be a man is to not be a hero all the time. Sometimes to be a man is to be a hero one day, and accidentally be a villain the next day. All that matters is that the day after you were the villain, did you do your best to fix your errors and save the people from the effects of your foolishness? And that's what makes you the ultimate hero before anything else."

Darcy applauded him. "That was a wonderful speech."

"It also was not mine."

"Are you in earnest?" Darcy laughed.

"Of course, it's not mine. I have become wiser in my older age, but not that wise. A business associate of mine told that speech to his son when he made a mistake, and I just happened to be there to overhear the conversation."

"Your eavesdropping has actually done us both some good."

"Yes," Bingley agreed, "it has taught me that my wickedness can sometimes be rewarded."

"And it has also taught me that I should have always supported your wishes to still be a man of occupation."

Bingley looked at his friend with an arched expression.

"I was not wrong. Love has changed you."

Darcy nodded. "Know that whenever I offered you advice, I thought I was offering the right sort, or what the ton would find acceptable."

"And how do you feel in knowing that you are about to do what they regard as not being acceptable?"

Darcy took a deep breath. "I say that now I know how it feels to be...alive."

Bingley clapped his friend on the shoulder. "Then I am happy for you— except for Lady Catherine still telling everyone that you are marrying Anne."

"Yes, that is quite the impediment, though I very much brought it on myself."

"Yes, and now you must fix it yourself."

"And that is how I shall become the ultimate hero?"

Bingley shook his head. "No, that is simply how you become Mr. Darcy."

⚜

"Well," Darcy said, feeling more confident, "before we undertake this incredible feat, it is imperative that you know that I would never have continued to pursue Elizabeth if I knew that your feelings were ever wholly marked and if you truly had been in love with her."

"I know and you are correct. I myself released her because love was not what I felt for her. Yet I did feel admiration and I would very much like to fall in love with a woman like her if the circumstance does present itself, therefore, Darcy, treat her well, for she deserves it."

"She deserves more than anything I could give her, yet I will do my best. Now come, we have a fate to save me from."

⊗⅏⊗

Darcy and Bingley rode their horses to the Earl of Matlock's home, who was Darcy's Uncle.

Yet soon into their arrival, the front door opened, and Colonel Fitzwilliam exited from the house.

"Forgive me," Colonel Fitzwilliam said with a laugh, "but your entrance into the house is something that I could not wait for."

"I know that I wrote to you," Darcy said, "but were you really waiting for my arrival with much anticipation? Really, Richard, I am touched."

"I had no choice, for as much as letting you walk into a calamity and see you fend for yourself since you were five years old has always been a favorite pastime of mine, I could not help but intervene this time. I must say that fortune really favors you way too often."

Darcy cocked an eyebrow. "Really, what are you saving me from?"

"Our Aunt and cousin Anne, for they are both here."

"What!" Darcy and Bingley exclaimed in unison.

"Oh yes, our formidable Aunt Catherine and dear ill and even more *ill* Anne are here."

⊗⅏⊗

Darcy's discomfort was evident. "Richard, this is not fortune favoring me."

"Of course, it is. Our Aunt Catherine may be many things that are trying to the nerves, yet there is one thing that even she is not prepared for."

"What is that?"

Richard looked between his cousin and Bingley.

"The power of three, Darcy. The power of three."

Darcy nodded as they all continued to enter quietly.

"Watson!" Richard called out.

The butler came forward. "Yes, sir?"

"I need you to do me the favor of not announcing to anyone that Darcy is here, except for my father, and tell him to come straight away. And that we will be in the study."

"Very good, sir."

"Thank you. Oh, and I am sorry for not asking before. How is your daughter doing?"

"She is still in love with you, sir."

"Oh, that is nice. Now carry on then."

Watson went off to relay the message to Mr. Fitzwilliam Sr. and Richard turned to see Darcy and Bingley staring at him, clearly wondering what the butler meant.

"I can be a bit of a rake," Colonel Fitzwilliam explained evenly.

"We noticed," Darcy replied. "But we still love you, Richard."

"Oh, thank you cousin-who-is-engaged-to-two-women-at-one-time."

Darcy waved the title away. "That's a very long heading. Never mind, this is the time to get focused on my mission."

"It's nice to see that I can still make you act like a five-year old, Darcy."

"And it's nice to know that I'm still more handsome than you, Richard."

"No, you're not."

"Yes, I am."

"No, you're not."

"Yes, I am. Oh, for god sakes, Richard! Stop distracting me."

"Ha!" Colonel Fitzwilliam clapped his hands together in triumph. "See, just like a five-year old."

"Oh, for goodness sakes!" Bingley whispered harshly. "To the study, both of you."

The three men then walked to the study together, with Richard and Darcy both arguing about who was the more intelligent one along the way.

჎

When Mr. Fitzwilliam Sr. received the message, he left his wife to sit with Lady Catherine while he went downstairs and found his son, his nephew and his nephew's friend all pacing back and forward, wondering what would be the best course of action.

"Personally," Colonel Fitzwilliam offered in jest, "I still think that you should have listened to me and not have returned to London, for as you know, I am always correct."

"No, Richard," Darcy replied as a joke, "you very much are not."

"Boys!" Mr. Fitzwilliam exclaimed, and then the three men turned to him. "Cease the childhood nostalgic tendencies for a time when your aunt is not upstairs, and we are not in the middle of a family crisis."

"Yes, sir," Darcy said.

"Yes, Father," Richard acquiesced.

"And Darcy," Mr. Fitzwilliam began, "I am happy that you are here. Yet I must still ask, are you certain that you wish to marry this Elizabeth Bennet over your cousin Anne?"

"Of course, I do."

"And there is no way that you shall be argued out of this, I see."

"Uncle," Darcy began, "I know that you haven't met Elizabeth yet, yet when you do, you shall love her."

"This woman really means that much to you?"

"She ought to... she has made me happy."

"Well then, I know that look, and I am not going to stand in your way."

Darcy sighed, happy that his uncle was the sort of man who talked little in regards to emotion, especially if he knew that objecting would do no good. Also, Earl Fitzwilliam was the sort of man who, though he felt that rank and wealth were important factors in response to his sons' marriages, knew that Darcy was a man with such an illustrious station in the ton that he felt that Darcy didn't need to focus on such qualities in a wife—in truth, the Earl of Matlock wished his own sons didn't need to be tied down to such standards in a wife, yet he could not undo fortune. Therefore, if Darcy wanted to marry this girl, then the less that he said on the matter, the better it would be for everyone.

"Yet," he added, "while I accept being quite won over so easily, it doesn't solve the little matter about your aunt being upstairs. She won't be so giving of her consent, especially since you agreed to marry Anne and have gotten yourself into this somewhat."

"And I am ready for her," Darcy replied, standing up straight and proud.

"Though I daresay that she is not fully capable of being ready for my retaliation."

"Is she not?"

"No, Uncle, for she has made me angry."

The Earl of Matlock started.

"Darcy?"

"Yes."

"You don't need to do your best to look any more frightening, for your usual scowl is quite sufficient."

"No, it is not."

Darcy began to walk forward, followed by Bingley and Colonel Fitzwilliam.

"And where do you both think you are going?" The Earl asked.

"For emotional stability," Colonel Fitzwilliam said. "For father, in matters such as these, singularity is not needed, but rather I think it is time for a triumvirate."

❧ 6 ❧

WHERE ONE DOOR CLOSES

T he three men, accompanied by the Earl of Matlock, walked to the sitting room. Darcy breathed out evenly and then they all entered.

They were met with the sight of Lady Fitzwilliam, the Earl's wife and Colonel Fitzwilliam's mother, who was sitting opposite Lady Catherine De Bourgh and her daughter Anne, looking as timid as usual.

"Fitzwilliam," Lady Harriet Fitzwilliam said, standing up.

"Hello, Aunt Harriet," Darcy said warmly. "It is nice to see you again."

"And it is—"

"Oh, my nephew!" Lady Catherine interrupted. "I can see that you're coming here has shown that you have come to your senses. Now while I am very angry with your actions, which have proven to be of the most base and inconsiderate of nature, and not worthy of the name of Darcy, I will overlook all of your mistakes now that you have come to your senses and abandoned that country strumpet who no doubt used her arts and allurements to draw you in."

"Elizabeth Bennet is innocent of any name that you have just called her!" Darcy said, coming forward. "She is the kindest and most wonderful of women, and I will not have you blame her for the crime of seducing me, when the only person who should be accused of committing any crime is I."

"You? Fitzwilliam, what absurdities are you talking of?"

"It's not absurdity to confess to one's crimes. Elizabeth Bennet is

44

blameless and has forgiven every mistake that I have made, and all that I have left to do now is apologize to Anne for my inconsideration to her feelings. For I have abused them even more violently than I have abused Elizabeth's and my own."

Darcy then turned to Anne who looked up at him with sad, watery eyes.

"Hello Anne," he said gently.

"Hello Fitzwilliam," she whispered, dabbing at her nose.

"Anne, my dear cousin, when I offered my hand in marriage to you, I had done so in the belief that I was easing both of our fates, that I had done my duty and had offered you a union that would have satisfied so many in our family.

"Yet I did not think of the happiness of the two people who were most concerned in the matter, which were us. I know very well now that I would have made you a terrible husband. As you would have made an obligatory wife who was caught in a bond that she never wanted. I know that you are not in love with me. Just as I am not in love with you."

"And what, pray tell," Lady Catherine interrupted, her thundering voice filling the room, "does love have to do with this union?"

"It has everything to do with it!" Darcy shot her an impatient glance. "For Anne has the right to be married to someone who loves her, just as I have the right to be married to someone who loves me for who I am."

He turned to Anne. "In writing to you, breaking off our engagement, I was giving both of us our best chance. I ask for your forgiveness, for I had been so much blinded by my grief in losing my father, that I thoughtlessly walked into a duty that I should not have ever felt obliged to perform."

He took her thin hand in his. "I have been a fool, Anne, a terrible fool. And if it has brought on embarrassment or shame, then I apologize once more. And in the future, I will do anything and everything to make up for my actions. All I can say is that I was blinded by my sense of integrity, of doing my duty; it has led to me being a selfish creature for far too long. Therefore, my cousin, will you forgive me?"

Anne was about to open her mouth when Lady Catherine interjected.

"She will not forgive you."

"Aunt Catherine," Colonel Fitzwilliam began, "should we not let Anne speak for herself? For how is she to succeed you as the heiress of Rosing's Park if she is not allowed to have her voice?"

"I agree," Earl Fitzwilliam said. "This concerns Anne and we ought to hear her voice on the matter."

"She need not speak," Lady Catherine cut in, "because this is all not to be borne, it will not be! For this is not my nephew speaking, but the woman who has manipulated him terribly."

"This is me speaking, Aunt Catherine," Darcy replied firmly. "I am simply stating what you don't wish to hear."

"Fitzwilliam, you ought to know, that I am not to be trifled with. But however insincere you may choose to be, you shall not find me so. My character has ever been celebrated for its sincerity and frankness, and in a cause of such moments as this, I shall certainly not depart from it."

"Aunt, why are you listing qualities of your nature that I am aware of, having been acquainted with them for my entire life?"

"Fitzwilliam, are you showing signs of giving me cheek?"

"I love you, Aunt Catherine, but I have been giving you cheek since I walked in the door."

Color rose in her pale cheeks. "This is not to be borne! This union is an alliance of the strongest kind and was one that was made between your mother and me. Since you were a baby in your cradle, we had intended for you and Anne to join together. Yet this woman, this Elizabeth Bennet, who is almost as impertinent as her wretched mother, may have used her unholy charms to disarm you in a moment of infatuation, making you forget what you owe to yourself and to all your family. Mark my words, Fitzwilliam, she has bewitched you and has drawn you in."

"You make my fiancée out to be of a supernatural sort."

"Stop misinterpreting my words. And when I went to speak to her about it, do you know what her mother said to me, how she spoke to me thus? I, a Lady and of leading society in the ton, to be treated like a hag in the street by a woman of such lowly birth with no family, connection or fortune."

"From what I hear," Darcy replied, "she reacted in the only way a mother should react in the presence of a random woman wrongfully attacking the good name of her daughter. She defended her child, and in that way, she is no different than you."

She pulled herself taller, if that was possible. "Do not compare me to such a lowly woman."

"And what makes Mrs. Bennet so low?"

"She is a foolish woman." She looked away, aloof.

"Yes, she is, but a wonderful mother who loves her children—in that regards, she can be viewed as a good woman. And everything that she said to you that day, all that she called you was well deserved.

"I come here now to warn you aunt. You will apologize for your horrible actions. You insulted my future wife and her family in every possible method, and she deserved none of your callousness and bullying. How, Aunt Catherine? How could you, a Lady who is supposed to know better, act in such a disgraceful and shameful manner?"

"I had no choice and still don't," she replied defensively. "I am almost the nearest relation you have in this world, and I am entitled to know all that concerns you."

"My life is my own."

"And my daughter's life is my own concern. You proposed marriage to her and then withdrew your offer like a libertine."

"Then attack me!" Darcy exclaimed. "Berate me, and call me every name in the world, every foul bit of language that you know! Yet never ever defame the woman who has brought out all the best in me!"

His aunt brought her palms down hard on the arms of her chair. "This is not the best of you! This is the very worst. Let me be rightly understood. This match, to which this Miss Bennet has the presumption to aspire to, can never take place. While in your cradles, I planned you and Anne's union, and now, at the moment when the wishes of both your mother and I would be accomplished, in marriage, to be prevented by a young woman of inferior birth, of no importance in the world, and wholly unallied to the family!

"Do you pay no regard to the wishes of your friends? To your engagement to Anne? Are you lost to every feeling of propriety and delicacy? Because honor, decorum, prudence, nay, interest, forbid it. And Darcy, I tell you this now, do not expect for her to be noticed by this family.

"She will be shunned, no matter if she is your wife! If you willfully act against the inclinations of all and marry her, she will be censured, slighted, rejected by the ton, and despised, by everyone connected with you. Your alliance will be a disgrace, her name never mentioned by any of us, for I will make sure that the name Elizabeth Bennet will be stricken from every acquaintance that we have!"

Every word spoken against Elizabeth was like a sting to Darcy's heart. Rising to his full height, Darcy's tone and glare became more menacing than ever before.

"Silence, you evil witch!"

The sentence hung in the air. All looked on Darcy in earnest, for never had he shouted in such a way. Even Lady Catherine was silenced by his wrathful expression.

"You will never again say anything against Elizabeth, who has forgiven me of every fault that I have clearly possessed. You will not berate nor censure a woman who is everything that I have wanted you to be your entire life.

"Aunt Catherine, do you not see how your actions at Longbourn and your actions now speak of a lowly woman on the street who was taught no manners and who is not fit to sit at the table of the humblest peasant? For even then you will not learn how to appreciate those around you. And so, I say again, if you are looking for someone to express your anger on, then you inflict it upon me and me alone. I am the only guilty party here, for it is my actions that have caused this confusion and emotional abuse.

"I have done things with the excuse that I contained integrity, yet all I thought was wrong. Yet no more will I hurt and reject the woman I love, for I have done it enough. And I shall start with asking for Anne's forgiveness again, but in regards to you, Aunt Catherine, if you speak one more word against my dearest Elizabeth, then so help me, I shall...throw a book at you!"

"Did he really just say throw a book?' Bingley whispered to Colonel Fitzwilliam, who nodded in return.

ॐ

"Obstinate, headstrong fool!" Lady Catherine's shrill voice cut through the air. "I am ashamed of you! Is this your gratitude for my constant love of you all these years? Is nothing due to me on that score? No, I have come here this day with the determined resolution of carrying out my purpose!"

"Oh, do be quiet!"

Everyone was silent again for it took a moment for all to acknowledge where that came from, and Lady Catherine was startled the most of all. All in the room turned around and faced the speaker.

"And I meant it, Mother," Anne said, gathering her courage and standing up. "You will be quiet now, and you will let me speak!"

༺༻

At first everyone was too stunned to respond, for Anne, who had been so soft-spoken before, was now doing her best to rise to her full height and when she saw that all were looking on her without threatening to interrupt her, Anne gathered her courage and continued to speak.

"Mother, I know that my Aunt Darcy and you, as well as the late Mr. Darcy, have been planning our union since we were infants, yet that was a foolish thing to do, for you did not take into consideration that we would grow up and have our own inputs on the matter."

She turned to Darcy. "And the fact is that I forgive you, Darcy, for as you said, I did not want to marry you either, and I was most assuredly afraid that I would be forced to go along with something I so much dreaded. And when you proposed, I did my best to be as despondent as possible to make you feel less inclined to go through with the engagement, but you seemed determined to do it despite me giving you no encouragement.

"Darcy, I had always relied on your indifference of me to keep our union from ever coming about, yet when you asked for my hand, I felt that I had finally been forced to give into the fate that I seemed obliged to meet eventually.

She focused on her mother. "Mother, Darcy and I are cousins, and we love each other in the way that cousins do, yet there it ends. We are not in love, never have been, and never will be. And while you think love should not be a factor into our union, I believe that it ought to be, and that I deserve to have someone love me for who I am. I have the right to choose, as does Darcy and we do not choose each other. Therefore, we will not choose each other. And you must be satisfied with it."

"But I—I..." Lady Catherine then looked overwhelmed and turned away from the group. After a moment of silence, she wielded on everyone. "What have I done for the world to be against me so? I, who have given all, who has always shown my attention to you all."

"There is a difference between giving attention out of affection," Anne said, "and always feeling as if you ought to have your way. You consider meddling being a beneficial mother. I am quite determined on this score. Even if Darcy had not broken off our engagement, I would have wanted nothing more than for him to have done so. Now I feel blessed with good fortune and I am content."

"But who will want you now?" Lady Catherine exclaimed. "No man will wish to marry you now that you have been spurned."

"You are wrong," Bingley said suddenly, and then he stood up with confidence. "For that man is me."

"What?" Darcy gasped.

"I am the man who wished to restore the deficit." Bingley smiled at Anne. "And I wish, Lady Catherine, to request the permission to court your daughter, Anne."

⚜

"What!" Everyone in the room exclaimed out of disbelief.

"It is true." Mr. Bingley nodded to Anne and Lady Catherine. "Anne if you would be so much willing to accept my attentions, then I would like to ask permission to court you."

"Permission is granted," Anne said, her cheeks showing a delicate pinkness.

Then Bingley turned to Lady Catherine. "Well, Lady Catherine, do I have permission to court Anne?"

Lady Catherine was flabbergasted, yet after a moment she contained herself.

"Well, I know the history of your family and that is that you have acquired your wealth through trade," Lady Catherine spat out, acting as if Anne's rank made Bingley as the unworthy one, even though Bingley's handsome looks and pleasing manners were enough to satisfy any woman.

"Yet that can be overlooked because you now associate with the highest circles, making you still unworthy of my daughter, yet I will turn a blind eye to it for now. However, don't think I won't make inquiries about your background."

Bingley nodded. "I understand your awareness and thank you for granting me your permission." Bingley then walked up to Anne and kissed her hand. "I daresay that we are now free to pursue our own destinies."

"Yes," Anne said, giving him a warm smile, "yes we are."

As he looked from one to the other, Darcy had to remember to close his mouth or the look of shock might remain forever etched into his features. Yet inwardly he knew that he was not the only one to ask himself: is everyone going mad?

⚜

Lady Catherine sat down, self-satisfied.

"Ah, now it all makes sense," she said proudly. "Darcy naturally you did not want to marry Anne because your friend here fancied her, and therefore you didn't want to get in the way of their courtship. How noble of you."

"I—I, well—however...well, yes."

"Then that was quite selfless of you, to give up an heiress for a woman who is not even half her worth in rank or beauty."

Darcy clenched his fists, wondering how Lady Catherine could even think to compare Anne's beauty to Elizabeth's. However, he remained silent and saw the prospect of peace in being quiet, but he still had one last request.

"Well then, Aunt Catherine, I want your word that you support my engagement and that you will learn to respect my future wife, who I will hear no word spoken against!"

"As you wish," she said, more lenient. "For now, I know the truth and I have nothing to fear. I still would have preferred Anne's engagement to you, but I will find happiness in this new arrangement, so long as I am to overlook every moment of it."

Bingley looked at Darcy, who could see the nervous look in his friend's eye, yet all was agreed to with alacrity.

⚜

As soon as was possible, Darcy excused himself and went to the library for a moment's peace. In the corner, he saw a bottle of scotch on the table with some glasses, walked up to it, poured himself a glass and then drank it quickly. After a moment, he heard footsteps and turned to see Bingley enter the room to look for him.

"Ah," Bingley said, eyeing the glass of scotch. "I see that you and I had the same impulse."

"Bingley," Darcy nearly gasped. "What was that?"

"That," Bingley said, taking a glass of scotch as well, "was brilliant."

"Brilliant? You just offered to court my cousin."

"Yes, I did." He took a satisfied gulp of the amber brew.

"And then she said yes."

"Yes, she did."

"But from what I recall, you've never taken an interest in her."

Bingley took another swig. "No, I didn't."

Darcy was confused. "So, when did your feelings for her come about?"

"Counting today, never."

"What?"

"I'm not in love with Anne at all." He put his empty glass on the side board.

Darcy flinched and then scowled.

"I should appreciate your gesture there, and all that it implied, but though you are my friend and I love you, and she is my cousin and I am not as close to her as you, she still is my cousin. Therefore, if you plan to hurt her, I will take a strike at you—and it will hurt."

"Why do that when this was all her idea?"

"Pardon?"

Bingley gave him a smirk. "Why waste your anger on me, when the idea of me offering a courtship was in part Anne's idea."

Darcy took another glass of scotch and drank it quickly.

"The disgusting and bitter taste of scotch on my throat helps me to remember that I am not dreaming."

"No," Bingley said, "no you are not."

"Well then, Bingley, I am prepared for the truth on all counts and I'll wait till the end to tell if I should be amused."

"Oh, it is quite simple. I ran into Anne at Hyde Park one day, we got to chatting, and I decided to confront the situation about your strenuous relationship. Anne came up with the brilliant concept that the only way to free you both from each other was if her mother found another match that she enjoyed almost as much. Now my family may have gotten our fortune in trade, yet due to your influence, I have risen enough to be regarded as respectable. Therefore, I offered my services on that score."

Darcy listened, dumbfounded. "And you are certain that Anne did not take your offer as being sincere in any way? I don't want you to get into any trouble on my account."

"Not at all. We would let Lady Catherine enjoy the news for a while, then she would hear through rumor and gossip that I was still taking an interest in my father's old trade in textiles, she would confront me on it, I would declare that I wished to maintain it, she would exclaim that her daughter deserved a man who did not have a profession for it was beneath their prestige, and then she would have Anne reject me."

"And what if she doesn't?"

"Darcy," Bingley said knowingly, "I am taking share in making textiles. Think about it."

"You are right." Darcy laughed. "Lady Catherine would despise that!"

"With a passion that would consume her soul."

"Oh Bingley!" In a peak of emotion, Darcy hugged Bingley who laughed at the sudden burst of emotion. "I am so sorry that I once sneered on your aims at maintaining a trade."

"Darcy, it wasn't your fault. You were raised to look down on such things, and such lessons are hard to overcome, yet you have. Take heart then."

"I'll take more than my heart. I'll also take my mind as well."

"Well, back to Anne. We sent missives back and forward to make certain that our plan was well thought out and believable."

"You sent letters? Yet how so, for to send a lady a private letter is prohibited."

"And that," Colonel Fitzwilliam said, entering, "was where I came in."

"Why am I not surprised that you are part of this scheme?" Darcy said, smiling.

"Because it is in my nature to be. When Bingley sent the letters to our townhouse, he addressed them to me, and I would give them to Anne for him."

"You both have undergone many heroics to save my life? Might I inquire what I did to deserve this?"

"What don't you do?" Colonel Fitzwilliam said. "You may not always say the correct things, but whenever I need help to maintain my living, you are generous with helping me avoid the clutches of poverty."

"And when I found it difficult to enter into society due to my background," Bingley said, "you were there to help me and did not forsake me. I daresay it was my turn to be a hero."

Colonel Fitzwilliam laughed, a hearty sound. "And like I said, I knew that you would ignore my advice to stay away. Lady Catherine may be a formidable force, yet as you have now seen, she is no match for the power of three. Now, step lightly," Colonel Fitzwilliam said, taking a glass of scotch, drinking it and then spitting it out. "Good God, why do humans like scotch, for it truly is disgusting. Still I was actually sent to fetch you. My mother has requested to see you. Bingley, are you planning on remaining here till we return?"

"I wish that I could take such time in leisure, yet I promised my sisters that I would come and view their new plans for our sitting room. And by my sisters, I really mean Caroline, and by view her plans, she really means that she wants me just to agree with everything that she says."

"Tell her that we said hello," Mr. Darcy said, "but don't make it sound personal, for I fear that she might take it as a special compliment."

"You're an engaged man, Darcy," Colonel Fitzwilliam said.

"Trust me, Richard," Bingley replied, "that would never stop my sister. For Caroline, nothing is certain until one is dead, and even then, Heaven might still make compromises."

Bingley took his leave while Darcy and Richard walked to the back parlor and Lady Fitzwilliam was sitting there, looking content to see her nephew and favorite son.

"Aunt Harriet," Darcy said, "I am so sorry that you had to witness such a spectacle today."

Lady Fitzwilliam waved away his concern. "Oh, not at all. It had to happen sometime, and it might as well have been under my roof rather than a stranger's."

She stood up and embraced her nephew.

"So, other than being saved from Catherine's machinations by very strange and unforeseen circumstances, how else are you doing?"

"I am doing well, thank you. I am preparing for my wedding, which will be in Hampshire, as you know."

"I'm surprised that you will be married in such a place. I knew that you would never want to marry here in London, but I thought that you would have wanted to marry in Kent for sure."

"Her family would never hear of it. She has quite a large one and it is more convenient for some of my family to travel to Hampshire and attend the service as opposed to them travelling into Kent and then having to stay at Pemberly. It is too inconvenient and costly to remain in an inn."

Lady Fitzwilliam chuckled. "You are a terrible liar. What you really mean is that you wish to be alone at Pemberly with your new bride as soon as you are able, and her family would be in your way."

Darcy hid a smile. "I wish that I was not so obvious."

"But you are."

"Will you Fitzwilliams still come to the wedding?"

"Of course, Darcy, for this is important to you, and someone must be there to represent our family since Lady Catherine has proven to make a decision based on her pride once more. Though, Richard here will still not be able to attend."

Darcy turned to Richard, who looked at his hands.

"Then you are truly not able to go?" Darcy said, feeling crestfallen. "Truly you're being called to the training grounds?"

"Yes, I am," Colonel Fitzwilliam said. "I have gotten a new regiment of recruits that require training in two days' time and by the time that your wedding day occurs, I shall be marching on the Iberian Peninsula, to join our forces with the Spanish and Portuguese military to march against the French. Emperor Napoleon is as he always is, and at it again."

"Will he ever stop?"

"Not likely, he is a little man who I believe must suffer from a large ego, or large insecurity levels."

"Yet your other cousins will be able to attend," Lady Fitzwilliam said smoothly.

"Yes," Colonel Fitzwilliam said bitterly. "For they were not the ones who were born committing the crime of being the younger son in the family."

Lady Fitzwilliam put her hand on her son's and Colonel Fitzwilliam did his best to adapt a lighter and more amused demeanor.

"Aunt?" Darcy asked. "There is something of import that I would like to ask you."

"Yes?"

"I know that you are coming to Hampshire for the wedding, yet is there any way that you may come sooner than you expected? Hopefully you can convince uncle to come as well and also bring Georgiana with you. I really want the Bennets to see that some of my family is supportive of this match."

"Familial harmony is very important, and I have convinced your uncle to do less logical things than that, so I am sure that I can return with you to Hampshire, even if Earl Fitzwilliam is too busy."

Darcy leaned forward and kissed his aunt on the cheek.

"Thank you, Aunt Harriet."

His aunt gave him a calculated look. "She must be some kind of a woman to have convinced you to fall in love with her, Darcy."

"She is everything that I could have hoped for, and more."

Darcy stood up, but Lady Fitzwilliam embraced his hand.

"Oh, and Darcy...remember how you were hoping to return to Pemberly immediately after your wedding, leaving you free to enjoy your honeymoon as you saw fit?"

"Yes."

"Well, I might have some bad news on that score."

Darcy's heart sank. "Bad news?"

"I don't think that you will be able to return to Pemberly, for you might be making a longer trip instead."

"Well, I do plan to go on holiday."

His aunt shook her head. "I don't mean holiday, I mean a certain kind of trip. Your uncle and I have received a letter, from a correspondence that will interest you. We let them know of your wedding and they are most desirous to become acquainted with your wife and get re-acquainted with you."

"Who is this acquaintance?"

Lady Fitzwilliam took out a letter from a box of sewing materials and then handed it to Darcy.

"It's from our fellow Darcys in America."

Surprised, Darcy asked, "The American Darcys?"

"Yes, they reside in Philadelphia and they are very much wishing to re-establish the bond that was once broken."

Darcy opened the letter and began to read on.

After reading the letter, Darcy decided that he would send a missive to the Philadelphian Darcys. Even in the wake of war between both countries, he wanted to see if this acquaintance could bring about some fruitful connections, for it was a fact, commonly known, that rank, and society was not always too stiff in that city.

The American Darcys were more likely to accept his beautiful bride for the wonder that she was and would view her as a novelty. And while tension was building between both countries, they still had not fully decided to go to war yet, therefore peace still reigned between tourists—and who knew, maybe even he needed a bit of a change.

As his stay came to an end, Colonel Fitzwilliam walked his cousin out to his horse, and he noted Darcy's lighter state.

"What is on your mind?"

"I admit to being sad that you could not attend my wedding, and that so much tension has occurred because of my choosing a wife, yet I feel now that the saying is quite true. 'Where one door closes, another one opens'."

❧ 7 ❧

DUTY AND DESIRE

E very day that Darcy was gone felt long and dull. Therefore, when he finally returned to Hampshire and was riding down the lane to my home, I rushed out the house to meet him and practically tackled him once he got off his horse.

"You missed me I see."

"La!" I said. "I barely noticed that you were gone."

He gave me a peck on the nose. "And there is the wickedness."

I slipped my arm through his. "That you love so much. So, how was London? I can see that Lady Catherine didn't try and chain you down to her dining room table. Or did she try?"

"I moved too quickly for her to attempt it. Yet, things have somehow taken a happy turn and Lady Catherine's attentions are now focused on someone else for Anne, and it has altered to everyone's satisfaction. Well, not really to anyone's satisfaction, but well enough."

"Who does your aunt set her sights on to marry her daughter to now?"

"Mr. Bingley."

"Mr. Bingley!" I gasped and brought my hand to my chest.

"Shush! Or your mother will hear that we are out here alone."

"Right, follow me."

I pulled him into the backyard where we began to walk through the trees and out of sight.

He pulled me close. "Oh Elizabeth! I want to ravage you right here."

"That can occur, after you tell me this nonsense about Mr. Bingley and Anne de Bourgh."

Mr. Darcy began to tell me all the details and by the end of it, I had to laugh at how clever and surprising a plot they had used to rid Darcy and Anne of the unwanted nuisance of being forced to accept a fate that he never wished to belong to. Now the shrewdness of the machination was something that I would easily have seen Colonel Fitzwilliam commit, but not one that I thought Bingley capable of. And yet he was. I had to make an internal note to never underestimate Mr. Bingley again, for he was capable of great thoughtfulness—more than the world around him gave him credit for.

⚜

"There is another matter at hand," Darcy said. "I have received word from my family in America."

I looked up at him, surprised. "You have family in America?"

"Yes, there is another clan of Darcys, for they are on my father's side. Some of them are uncles of mine, aunts, cousins, and they reside mostly in Philadelphia and Charleston, Virginia."

"Why do you never speak of them?"

"We don't write to one another often. When I was a child, many letters passed between both families, for the American War of Independence had ended. Yet for some reason, as is the nature of things sometimes, we just naturally fell away from each other."

"Why do they wish to re-establish a connection with you now, of all times?"

"Oh, it is not so sudden. They had been sending letters to my Aunt and Uncle Fitzwilliam for a few months now, and my aunt mentioned our wedding, to which they responded that it would be nice for us to journey to America so that they can congratulate us for our happiness as well as throw a ball for us."

Such a prospect was overwhelming. "Do you think..." I began, worried, "that they will like me?"

"Rank does not mean as much to them and there is a greater chance that they are more open, as well as the fact that all they will know is that you are my wife and they will not have time to form prejudices that they aren't even aware of having."

"Then," I said, squeezing his arm, "this will be a chance for us to have a fresh start, even if it is only temporary."

"Precisely. It will be the perfect honeymoon for us to go on holiday."

"Oh, but Darcy, you have often spoken of Pemberly and how you wish for us to go there as soon as we are wed. I know that it means a lot to you."

"It is also important to me that I have as much of my family like you as possible. Harmony leads to a solid affection between a husband and wife, and well—I don't wish for you to turn away from me because part of my family does not accept you."

"I would never turn from you for such a reason," I stated firmly.

"One can say that, but discord is like a disease and it can turn a love from pure affection to one of pure bitterness and cause distance between the two that were originally brought together. Pemberly will always be Pemberly, and I will always want to take you there, but I know my nature. If I were to take you there after our wedding, I would never want to leave!"

I laughed at his innocent and child-like confession.

"It's true, Lizzy, you have not seen me when I am at home. Somehow Pemberly brings out the best in me. Maybe it is because it is the best in me."

I rested my head against his shoulder. "You are more than a building and I think you are quite wonderful here now."

"It helps me to care about many things and be transformed from a man who is guarded to one who likes to look on all that he is meant to. If you had met me at Pemberly, Elizabeth, I would never have been so foolish as to have indulged in such an inclination of entertaining a marriage to my cousin. You'll see, something about Pemberly makes me more comfortable and therefore, with comfort comes alignment of temper and attitude, which means at Pemberly I seem to almost always make the right decisions."

"I had no idea that your good nature was so dependent on location changes," I replied archly.

"Oh, you're teasing me."

"Very much so. Yet I will look forward to Pemberly, as well as look forward to seeing how you behave in the comforts of your own home. Yet I confess that I too desire to see your family in America. And my reasons actually were like your own."

"My own. How so?"

At first, I was hesitant to tell the truth, but Darcy had been honest with me, therefore it was my duty to return the compliment. I breathed in evenly and then began to confess my fears.

"I still feared that when you went to London, I would lose you," I began. "As I revolved Lady Catherine's expressions in my mind, however, I could not help feeling some uneasiness as to the possible consequence of her persisting in her interference of trying to split us, and therefore becoming successful.

"From what she had said of her resolution to prevent our marriage, it occurred to me that she must meditate an application on you, she might invent a design to influence you to see her point and carry it through, and how you might take a similar representation of the evils attached to a connection with me."

I gazed at the trees, so lush and green; they always calmed me. "I know not the exact degree of affection you have for your aunt, or your dependence on her judgment, but you have a wonderful devotion to your family, Fitzwilliam, enough so that you attached yourself to Anne De Bourgh just to make your father proud. Therefore, it was natural of me to suppose that you thought much higher of her ladyship than I or my mother would. And it was certain, that in enumerating the miseries of a marriage with me, whose immediate connections were so unequal to your own, your aunt would address you on your weakest side. With your notions of dignity and familiar pride, I feared you too would probably feel that the arguments, which to me and my family had appeared weak and ridiculous, contained much good sense and solid reasoning." I paused a moment, and then added, "I was afraid that Lady Catherine would win in the end."

Darcy emitted a low chuckle. "But she has not. And in regards to our love, she never will."

"Now I do believe we are ready for a happy ending, then?"

"Yes, but I have one more bit of news."

"News?" I groaned inwardly. "Why is that always the way?"

"Do not fear, this is good news," Darcy assured me.

"Very well then, proceed."

"At Aginfield, I have brought up some company from town who would like to make your acquaintance."

I was hesitant at this news, for I feared meeting anyone new at the moment due to so much anxiety that comes from awaiting a ceremony that you are hoping to occur without any more interruptions.

"I have brought Georgiana from town."

"Oh!" I cried out, instantly feeling lighter. "Why did you not say before? Of course, I am happy to see her again."

"And she is accompanied by my Uncle and Aunt Fitzwilliam, Earl and Lady of Matlock."

"Oh!" I smiled, although still felt very apprehensive. "Yet what if they don't like me?"

"They want to like you, and they are certain to if you just give them one reason. And that will not be hard for you because you give many reasons all the time."

"You flatter me."

"I know."

"Good, don't ever cease doing it. Well, I admit to being nervous to meet them, but I shall make sure that my courage rises, and I will do my best to make you proud of me."

"Then that is all well. Now, I have no choice but to let you return home, don't I?"

"Of course, you must, or my mother will never let me hear the end of leaving without giving her notice. And just to warn you, she shall force you to stay for dinner."

"It is well, for I wish to learn more about the antics you got away with as a child. She began to regale me with stories about how when you were young, you used to climb trees and then act as if you didn't."

"Ah. Yes, I did used to love doing that."

"When did you outgrow it?"

At first, I thought it would be better to lie, but then I found it more amusing if I told the truth.

"Oh, I never outgrew it."

"Pardon?"

"I said...that I never outgrew it."

"What?"

"Just joking," I lied.

***

That evening, Mr. Darcy stayed for dinner and I could see his comfort around my family growing, and the sentiments were reciprocated.

At some moments, my mother still sat in awe of Mr. Darcy. He was such an illustrious person, so intimidating in some ways that she ventured not to speak to him, unless it was in her power to offer him any attention or mark her desiring his opinion.

Yet with my father, who I worried would not take to Darcy at all, began to engage in witty banter with him, which was something Darcy could easily accomplish whenever he wished to exert himself in that way. They were both such learned and well-read gentlemen that they soon found much to speak about. As such, I had the satisfaction of seeing my father taking pains to get acquainted with my beloved. When my father and I had a moment to ourselves, he soon assured me that Darcy was rising every hour in his esteem.

"I admire all my two sons-in-law highly," he said in jest. "Wickham, perhaps, is my favorite," he added with a wry lift of one eyebrow, "but I think I shall like your husband quite as well as any other rich man who is used to getting his own way."

***

Once more I saw Mr. Darcy to his horse where I was supposed to be accompanied by Kitty, who this time, at the last minute, realized that she had food stains on her face and therefore had to wipe it off.

Yet this time, as Darcy rode off, I realized just how hard his struggle was.

The man I chose to love came from a world that was affluent, distinguished and he was therefore raised to believe that he was right to have some meanness of opinion, a lack of consideration for those the world regarded as lesser in importance, and his devotion was meant to only be bestowed on those the world acknowledged as being his equal. He was raised to look down on women such as me. And he was also raised to be devoted to his family alone.

And now he was changing before my very eyes. He was brave enough to rise against the world that had him believe in erroneous views and theories. He was willing to face the censure of the world and even his own hypocrisy. His constant internal battle with himself to have chosen to love me after he had proposed to Anne was a struggle that would have been enough to confuse the strongest of men, which Darcy was. I at first regretted my memory of when I accused him of acting like George Wickham, yet then I had to acknowledge that it was my honesty that helped him realize his true feelings and confront his fundamental flaws. Now, at the turn of the tide, he had done his best to do right by me as well as himself.

He could have chosen another path, yet he did not. He could have not cared what he had done to me, how he had almost ruined me, yet he saved me and Lydia in the end.

His internal struggle was not an easy one and many would have made the wrong decision in this. The greatest thing in the world that a person could overcome was themselves and their own misconceptions.

Yet Mr. Darcy, who had walked the fine line that was choosing between duty and desire, chose desire and realized that he needn't fear duty as he ought to have—for the truth of his heart was just as important.

8

TENDER MOMENTS IN BETWEEN

The next day, accompanied by Jane, we took the carriage to Aginfield and were met by Darcy and Mr. Bingley, who awaited us eagerly. After Jane and Bingley politely waited long enough for us to have our private discussion, for they must have thought we were speaking words of intimacy, we nodded to them and then we entered Aginfield.

When we came into the sitting room, I beheld a handsome older couple which must have been Earl and Lady Fitzwilliam, who stood when we entered. Yet the first person who said anything was Georgiana, who had been standing all the while.

"Miss Elizabeth!" Georgiana cried, coming forward.

"Georgiana!" I walked forward and embraced her, despite how lacking in propriety that it made me look in the eyes of the Earl of Matlock and his wife. They may have been my fiancé's kin, but Georgiana was his sister, and was going to be my sister therefore I wanted to show her that the bond we would share would always be foremost in my mind before any other in-law that I would receive by this union.

"Ah," Lady Fitzwilliam said, coming forward. "So, you and my niece are already well acquainted."

"Yes," I replied, tossing Georgiana a smile. "I have had the good fortune to have become very attached to my new sister."

Georgiana chuckled in response and then Darcy came forward.

"Aunt and Uncle, this is my fiancée, Miss Elizabeth Bennet, and her older sister, Miss Jane Bennet. And Elizabeth and Miss Bennet, this is my Aunt and Uncle Fitzwilliam, Earl of Matlock."

Jane and I curtsied.

"We're honored to make your acquaintance," Jane said with a smile.

I added, "And we have heard so much about you that it had quite piqued our curiosity of what Earl and Lady Fitzwilliam were truly like."

"And what do you make of us now?" The Earl of Matlock said, stepping forward. Something about his stance and tone gave me the sense that he was challenging me somehow and I looked at Darcy, who clearly sensed the same thing. Therefore, much was at stake in regards to how I responded.

"Nothing at all yet," I said truthfully. "A long time ago, I learned not to make decisions of a person's nature based on a first impression, for one cannot think anything fitting, accurate or just, when they haven't even gotten to know the person as of yet."

For a second there was some silence and even Lady Fitzwilliam did not know how her husband would react, then he smiled suddenly and chuckled.

"That was a very honest and yet logical response without being offensive in any way. That is a very hard thing to do and I must give you all the credit in the world." Earl Fitzwilliam turned to Darcy. "If she continues this way, I believe that I shall like her."

"Oh, for goodness sakes!" Lady Fitzwilliam tutted lightly. "Don't talk about the girl when she is right here, and don't make it so obvious that she is being measured in any way."

"Thank you very much, Lady Fitzwilliam," I said. "And Earl Fitzwilliam, for you both have done me a great service."

"Have they?" Darcy laughed. "Do tell, my love, what do you mean?"

"I mean that you, Lady Fitzwilliam, have defended me, which makes me comfortable, because you wish for me to be given a fair introduction, you care for propriety, and you care for my feelings. This makes me feel accepted. But you, Earl Fitzwilliam, seemed to have a different intention that would appear coarse to some, but was quite intelligent. Your frankness and your willingness to show me that I am being observed and critiqued has actually made me more at ease because now I feel that I can be honest with you, because you have been honest with me."

I lifted my gaze to his. "How can I be afraid now when you have laid your schemes out here for me to see and therefore be ready for? Now, because of you both, I can be comfortable. I can be Elizabeth Bennet."

Earl Fitzwilliam took a few steps forward.

"Well, you are a rare find if ever I saw one."

I attempted levity. "Is that meant to be a compliment, insult or simply an observation?"

"The last thing. You must forgive my frankness, but time is against me."

"How so?"

"You are marrying my nephew in a couple of weeks, and that does not give me much time to find the truth behind the mystery that is you. In truth, unlike you, I don't have the luxury of making a decision over time, but must make decisions based on my first impressions, however limited it may be."

Earl Fitzwilliam turned to Darcy.

"So, is your fiancée always like this?"

Darcy smiled, his dimple showing. "Yes, she is. And there is no imperfection to it."

"You are right, she is perfect for you."

Earl Fitzwilliam's admission made me falter for a second and then my heart began to soar. He clearly was a man who said what he felt and therefore I felt safety with him.

"You believe so?" I said, smiling due to feelings of exhilaration. "Truly?"

"Yes, as long as you stay this way. My nephew is a great man who is fiercely loyal and deserves no less devotion from the woman he chooses. Therefore, let me not have to suffer the disappointment of seeing him wed to a woman who does not love him for who he is."

"Earl Fitzwilliam!" Lady Fitzwilliam all but shouted. "You are this close to making me quite at odds with you, for you have already passed beyond propriety and into the realm of being impertinent."

"These are faults that I risk being exposed to at the moment," Earl Fitzwilliam replied. "For this is a moment where honesty is needed over manners."

"You are unafraid to break the rules of conduct," I said, "to tell me the truth." Then I turned to Darcy and grinned at him. "Now I see where you get your frankness and quest for extreme sincerity from."

"Yes, clearly, but Uncle, I don't want you antagonizing her any longer."

"You need not worry, I have done," he replied. "And I daresay that this fiancée of yours quite understands me, and above all is not made of weak inclinations or lack of courage. Which is good, for she will need both of those virtues to be a proper wife to you."

He turned to me. "Miss Elizabeth, continue to be as you are, and I will continue to think you are the most perfect choice that my nephew has ever made."

Such words were a great comfort to hear, especially after being berated so by Lady Catherine de Bourgh.

"Thank you, sir, and I daresay that you have now made me quite at ease, for encouragement is always a food that nourishes affection."

"Which you knew of, Earl Fitzwilliam?"

We all turned to Jane, surprised that she had spoken, I most of all. Jane usually did not address anyone unless they addressed her first, yet this was not the case.

"Forgive my acknowledging you when I was not to whom you were speaking," Jane continued, "but since you confront my sister so frankly, I cannot stand by and act as if I have no proper feeling as an older sister who should defend her younger one at all costs." She turned and gave him a rather stern look. "You knew that the only way to see if my sister was a perfect match for Mr. Darcy was by this test, did you not?"

"Yes, I did. Well, are all you Bennet girls built of such courage for confrontation? It is refreshing to see loyalty amongst siblings, and it is the eldest's duty to look after the younger ones."

"It is." Jane lifted her chin. "And it is a duty that I bear proudly."

In that moment, Mr. Darcy and I looked on Jane with such wonder, for I never would have thought she had that in her.

"Then I must applaud the family of the Bennets," Lady Fitzwilliam said, "for they truly are of a noble attitude."

"All we can say," I replied, "is that this is a virtue and to others this is a vice. We feel deeply and still believe in having a merriness to us."

"I can see that in earnest, for you make my nephew smile. Well then, I want to approve of you as well, but I cannot do so without having some tea. Since Mr. Bingley's sister is not here, I have been allowed to play hostess for my duration."

"Indeed." Mr. Bingley agreed.

"Therefore, now that confrontation has ended and frankness has ceased along with it, let us all sit down to tea and limit our discussions to talks of the weather and state of the roads. Neutral comments after a serious discussion are always like deserts to a conversation."

We all sat down as tea and cakes were brought out.

⚜

Jane and I stayed for dinner as well, where Georgiana was very voluble and talkative, to my happiness, for it made me feel at ease.

Mr. Bingley also contributed to the conversation greatly, as was his nature and natural talent at doing so. Overall, the evening went by with much success. Yet I felt that Earl and Lady Fitzwilliam favored Jane most of all, for not only was she a stately beauty, but she also had the grace and manners that seemed to belong to someone of the highest circles. That was something that I could never aspire to, even if I were to attempt it all my life.

By the end of the evening, my spirits were high, for I knew that I had found an ally in Darcy's relations now and that it would be enough encouragement for Darcy to never regret his choosing me.

Their affection for my sister and me was solidified when all of them saw us off to the carriages and before I stepped in, Lady Fitzwilliam took me aside.

"I apologize for my husband's behavior," she said. "He is not usually so indelicate, and I promise I shall certainly chastise him for that later."

"No apology is needed. Though I definitely shall never stand in the way of a wife reprimanding her husband, for it is a very necessary thing to do sometimes."

"Yes, it is. I should like to call on your family at Longbourn and become acquainted with your mother."

"She would like that, and you need not worry about sending a letter beforehand. If I tell her when we return, she will be happy to receive you by tomorrow if you like."

"Yes, the sooner the better."

Jane and I entered the carriage and then were off back to Longbourn.

"Thank you for defending me," I said to her.

"You are welcome," Jane replied. "And it felt nice to fight for something...for a change."

"You have your own strength."

"We all do, but I confess that sometimes I envy yours."

Silence fell between us as we continued our journey home.

❧

Upon hearing the news of Lady Fitzwilliam and Georgiana Darcy coming to call the next day, our mother was all a flutter. At first, she declared that her nerves could not survive meeting such an illustrious person without fainting, but then she recovered and made sure that all the cooks and servants knew what they must do by tomorrow to attend to the ladies every need.

The next morning, she sent one of our maids to the marketplace to fetch some special food and cakes, we daughters picked fresh flowers and put them in vases around the house, then Lady Fitzwilliam and Georgiana arrived after midday.

My mother was on her best behavior, and for some reason was very subdued, which must have been the result of being in the presence of an Earl's wife. Thus, I could not have been more proud of her and then when Lady Fitzwilliam began to talk of the current fashions worn in town, our mother perked up, knowing that she could become animated and Lady Fitzwilliam would be content with it, for clothing was something any lady of any station always felt it her right to become over-excited about.

This time Kitty and Mary joined us, and it became very apparent quite quickly that Georgiana missed Kitty, which made sense. Not only were they of the same age, but Kitty, whether her nature pleased a person or not, was a very good sort of girl who was comfortable to be around always.

And now that Lydia lived in Newcastle, there was so much chance for Kitty to be given the proper attention that she needed as well as to be away from the influence of my wild youngest sister. And Georgiana, who had always wanted a sister herself, might probably have regarded Kitty as the perfect match for such a role. Kitty, who now no longer had Lydia for a constant companion, was looking for another friend to replace her loss, making both women looking for camaraderie and willing to step in and play the part for each other.

By the end of the tete e tete, Lady Fitzwilliam overall enjoyed her time and invited us to join her in Meryton in two days' time.

⚜

This peace, this wonderful harmony that reigned over Longbourn should have made me suspicious of an impending doom that I should have foreseen. For the day after Lady Fitzwilliam's visit and the day before our outing, a carriage arrived and there was much ado about something.

I was upstairs when the arrival occurred, and I heard much hustle and bustle, of footsteps rushing to and fro and then I heard my mother's exclamations from the front lawn.

"Oh, my dear Lydia! You are come home at last."

"Yes, of course I have." Lydia laughed.

"Oh dear, how I have missed you!"

"Well, I have been far too merry to have missed any of you!"

I closed my eyes and groaned inwardly. As much as I loved Lydia, for she was my sister, I had hoped that she could not be able to attend my wedding, for the cost and time it took to come to Hampshire from Newcastle should have been substantial enough to be trying to her purse. Lydia's nature was too boisterous, and she was too much of a flirt to ever give off a good impression to Lady Fitzwilliam. And yet, what was more frightful was that Lydia's arrival signified something else; her being joined by George Wickham, her husband.

I braced myself before taking the stairs, for I knew that Lydia would be as bold and thoughtless as ever, with her handsome and horrible husband at her side, smiling, simpering and making love to us all while being false in every way.

I walked down the steps and saw all my sisters and mother hugging her while my father stood rigid, looking down on her with indifference and coldness. It was nice to see that he was not willing to concede into looking like he condoned Lydia's attitude any longer, and I hoped that in seeing his censure, she would feel the loss of ever being able to obtain his good opinion.

I walked out of the front door and there, making a big show, was my sister Lydia Wickham.

❦

And with no Wickham beside her!

"Lizzy!" Lydia shouted. "Well, hello."

"Hello Lydia, you are looking well, and I trust that you enjoy Newcastle."

Lydia groaned. "Oh, it is well enough, but the soldiers here were more to my tastes."

"And they shouldn't be to your tastes any longer," Mary said, "because you are a married woman."

"Oh la!"

"And where is my favorite son, Wickham?" our father asked sardonically.

"Do you hear that, Lizzy? Our father's favorite is my Wickham and not your Darcy. So, what do you say to that?"

"I say that you still have not the ability to detect sarcasm," I replied.

"Indeed," our father added. "That was a lie if ever there was one."

"Let us all get inside," our mother said, "and out of the cold. Now that you are here, Lydia, we are to go to the Phillips this evening. Not that I like going here and there at night. I'd much rather stay at home and rest my poor nerves."

❦

As we entered the home, with Jane following our mother, Lydia chided her.

"No, Jane, you must go lower now, and I before you, because I am a married woman."

"Really?" Mary said, annoyed. "Because I don't see your husband anywhere."

"Oh, don't be so stupid! When marrying a soldier, one cannot expect that he travel over the country every time one of his relatives gets married, you should know."

Mary groaned. "And by that, you mean that he could not come because none of us want him here."

"Mary!" our mother gasped.

"Oh, mother, we were all thinking it."

Our mother placed her hand to her chest. "What has gotten into you?"

"I just don't feel like putting up the charade of liking a man who there is no reason to like."

"You're just mad that no one loves you." Lydia sat down. "Which you make it impossible for them to do so."

"Lydia!" our mother said, her voice stern. "Enough of you both still feeling as if you must reenact all of your sibling rivalries since you both were children. Sit down and be civil, and Lydia my dear, how does married life suit you?"

"Very well, Mama! In Newcastle I have many friends and I am quite a favorite among the officers."

"Funny how you don't mention your husband," Kitty acknowledged, "which I'm assuming was an intentional slip."

"There is no need to mention him for I do love him dearly and I hope that you, my spinster sisters, might one day have half of my good luck. And you should have gone with me to Newcastle, for I could have gotten all of you husbands."

"Thank you for my share of the offer," I said, "but I don't particularly like your idea of how to get a husband. Nor do I like your tastes in their regard as well."

"Oh, you are only jealous of me, Lizzy, for Wickham is quite possibly the handsomest man in England. But Lizzy, have you been fitted for your gown yet?"

"I have."

"Well, I daresay that you will make a lovely bride."

Surprised, I replied, "Thank you."

"Yes, but I wish you all could have been there for my wedding, for I believe that I will still prove the lovelier bride of us two."

And that was when I closed my eyes, then opened them when I realized that my father had stood up and left the room.

"Where is he going then?" Lydia groaned. "To his study already, good gracious! Nothing ever changes here."

❧

That evening, we went to the Phillips. While we had done so, I managed to take our aunt aside and asked her if she was willing to have Lydia come to stay with her for the next day while I had my outing with Lady Fitzwilliam.

For I feared that a new acquaintance being pushed on her so suddenly would not have been to our benefit, as well as that if Lydia were not invited, I would have had to slight my own sister.

Therefore, if Lydia was already engaged in something else, then she could not attend our day of shopping and I could just simply have Darcy tell his aunt of the true nature of my sister and her marriage. I knew that Darcy would know how to tell her such news in a way to still have it not reflect poorly on my family.

Aunt Phillips accepted this scheme quite easily and it was very clear that she knew my real motives, but also was keen to not speak about the true nature of my intentions out loud.

Therefore, the next day came and Lydia boasted of being invited by Aunt Phillips, especially to dine with some officers that had agreed to taking lunch with her and a few other neighbors in Steventon.

Yet she demanded that she could not go alone, therefore she asked our mother to join her, who was upset that she could not join us with Lady Fitzwilliam. But so it all had no choice but to be, for Mary refused to go and our father naturally would not want to move past the threshold of his library.

We took our carriage to Aginfield, met Lady Fitzwilliam and Georgiana there and then were off to shop in Meryton. The day passed along wonderfully, and Lady Fitzwilliam and Georgiana made themselves well-liked by the shopkeepers of the town, for they bought much and inquired about Hampshire and of how lovely of a county it was.

I learned much from our day together. As a child, Darcy and his cousin Colonel Fitzwilliam liked to pull pranks on people and were often chastised for it, but they kept doing so. Darcy went through a part of his childhood where he would try and hide whenever strangers came to visit his father and wouldn't come out of his hiding place until the stranger had gone. I did my best to remember everything so that I could tease Darcy about it later.

"I often don't understand how it works," Georgiana said to me.

"How what works?"

"You teasing my brother. It makes him happy and yet if I talked to him that way, he might be put out of sorts."

"That's the irony of roles and what form of behavior is allowed per one. Between brother and sister, one way of acting is acceptable, yet between husband and wife, teasing each other can actually be beneficial." I winked at her. "You shall see when you fall in love."

She pulled a moue. "I have fallen in love, you know it, and as you also know, it didn't end well for me, did it?"

"You mustn't blame yourself for what Wickham did to you."

"Yet I cannot help but feel foolish for being taken in so easily."

I took her arm. "It is never easy to see such a rake for what he is, for hiding their evil nature is something that they are often very proficient at. That is what makes them rakes. You mustn't be afraid to love again... and trust yourself again."

"I just don't want to make the same mistake."

"There is always the chance that you might make it again. We humans sometimes take a long time to learn from our mistakes."

She paused a moment, and then asked, "Lizzy?"

"Yes?"

"Kitty has told me that your sister Lydia is now here."

"Yes," I replied hesitantly. "Yes, she has come down for my wedding. She actually traveled alone, so you need not worry that Wickham is with her."

"Yes, but it doesn't stop the fact that your sister is now married to the man who I almost eloped with."

I gave her a weary nod. "I know."

"Especially since... I am still in love with him."

I looked up in surprise.

"You...you are?"

"Yes. I am still very much in love with him."

"You must think me stupid and foolish," she whispered.

I had to answer carefully. "Love is never simple. Remember how I loved your brother even after he chose Anne over me at first? It cannot be erased so easily, for I thought of him every day after I thought myself to have lost him forever. And your brother's actions toward me were not nearly as terrible as Wickham's actions were to you."

She played with the ribbon on her gown. "They were erroneous enough."

"Yes, but Wickham hurt you because he didn't care about anyone at all besides himself. Your brother hurt me because he cared too much of his obligation to another. One cared too little and the other cared too much. That is why your brother will never be anything short of a hero, despite all his flaws—because he cares. Yet if my love for him could never be erased so easily, then naturally your love could not be erased so easily either."

Her expression was one of pain. "And it still can't, despite how senseless it is for my heart to feel it. I thought him so chivalrous, so handsome, and he did play with me often when we were children, being attentive and considerate, yet age, ambition, or lack thereof, became his undoing."

She dabbed at her nose with a lace handkerchief. "Now he is nothing more than a libertine that has my heart with him always, no matter how much he abused it. I—I am jealous of Lydia and I... a part of me wishes to hate her on sight."

She turned toward me. "Oh Lizzy, forgive my speech, for I know I must look evil for feeling such things."

I laughed. "Don't worry. You are not saying anything that really unnerves me."

"Really?" Georgiana said, feeling suddenly lighter. "You do not think me wicked?"

"Of course not, Georgiana. My sisters and I have been jealous over one another whenever a man liked one of us, but we secretly liked him as well. It's just the nature of family. Just accept your feelings, then make sure to regulate them and try to avoid them getting the better of you, which they will if you let your sensibilities go unchecked."

She gave me a sisterly embrace. "Thank you, Lizzy, now I feel better and lighter from my confession."

"Remember, you are never alone."

⁂

That night, I came to a decision. Knowing that Lydia was alone in her room, I knocked, and she told me to enter.

She gave me a smug, victorious grin. "You missed a wonderful afternoon! I bet Lady Fitzwilliam was such a bore, for how could she be

76

anything compared to the company of the officers? Many of them still remembered me and we were like old friends seeing each other again."

Instead of ignoring her words, I decided to confront her with the truth from beginning to end.

"You know perfectly well that I had a wonderful time, and that you wish that you could have come and you are secretly acting as if you are more fortunate than I to hide your disappointment."

Her eyes narrowed. "That is a stupid thing to say. You know how much I favor a handsome officer and there are plenty of those to go around. You were just strange for not noticing them."

"I did not care to notice."

"And that is the strangest thing of all."

"Lydia," I said, sitting down, "I am going to be frank with you."

"About what?"

"About the fact that you are not as foolish as you pretend to be."

"Oh, Lizzy, would you stop offending me?"

"No, I will not. Not when I know the truth."

She slanted me a glance. "And what truth is that?"

"That you know perfectly well that the man you love, Wickham, tried to once elope with Mr. Darcy's sister, Georgiana, but Mr. Darcy saved her before it was too late."

"And should she not have? I above all others can understand why she fell in love with him and it only shows even more how much I was the lucky one to have gotten him."

"And it shows that he once tried to do to another woman what he did to you, and that you are not special to him, but he is special to you despite it all."

She raised her nose in the air. "My dear Wickham loves me."

"Your 'dear Wickham' abandoned Georgiana when he realized that he never would get his hands on any of her money. He hurt her, just as you secretly know that he only married you because of all the money that Mr. Darcy paid him."

"Oh, that's a lie!"

"It is not, and secretly, you know it, don't you?"

"Oh, that is..." Lydia laughed and then a second later, her smile faded, and the light left her eyes. Just as I had suspected, the truth was buried deep within her and eventually, after much prodding, it would eventually be revealed to all.

"What do you want, Lizzy?"

"I want you to promise that when you meet Georgiana, you shall do your best to always speak as little about Wickham as possible. And when you see Darcy again, you will not talk of Wickham ever in his presence, for the reason that you are married now is all because of him. Therefore, the least you can do is be kinder to him, don't you think? Be considerate of him, and I will not have you bring him grief because you cannot control yourself."

"I can control myself!"

"Then do it. If you speak of Wickham in front of Georgiana, then how do you think she will feel seeing you, the woman who eloped with the very same man that tried to elope with her? It will cause her pain. Would you want someone to treat you in such an infamous manner? No, Lydia, you wouldn't. And if I must be candid, then I will tell you this now."

I leaned close. "If you are not on your best behavior to the Darcy and Fitzwilliam families, then I will never loan you money, I will never help you when you and Wickham have exhausted your expenses because you live beyond your income, which I am sure is already happening. If you value your future comfort, then you will treat my husband and his sister with the upmost respect."

"But Lizzy?"

"What?"

"I... very well."

"Very good, Lydia, now have a good night rest."

I then left her alone to think on where her best interests lay.

☙❧

The next morning, Darcy came to see me, and my mother was away visiting our Aunt Phillips. Therefore, Darcy and I were left alone to walk in peace. He made his reason to see me apparent very quickly, which was in response to hearing of Lydia's arrival. I assured him that all was well on that score, that he need not fear for Georgiana's sensibilities and though he was not happy that I had to use bribery to obtain my point, he was happy that all was well ultimately.

"Yet," I began, changing the subject, "on another matter, I have something to ask of you."

"What is it?"

"Can you write to your family in America and ask them to let us bring more than ourselves?"

He gave me a quizzical look. "Pardon?"

"I thought it might be wise to bring Georgiana along with Kitty and Jane."

"Really?"

"I know that you are worried over it, but when you hear me out, you might like the scheme."

"What is your reasoning?"

"Well, I know that when we return to Pemberly, we will want time alone and that there might be no room for Georgiana so she must remain in town for a while. Am I correct in thinking this your plan?"

He nodded. "I was thinking it."

"Well, if we go to America without her, then go to Kent without her, then that is too inconsiderate of us. Yet if we take her to America, then she is with us so that when we return to Pemberly, she might want time to herself.

"Also, if we take Jane and Kitty, then we give her some companions while also caring for my sisters. I know that Mary will not want to go because she does not like to travel. And this way we shall be able to actually be alone sometimes."

"That last part makes little to no sense."

I laughed at his puzzled expression. "Hear me out. Say we go to America and we want a few days where we are allowed to travel or spend time alone together. Our company will not be accused of being singular and not social, because we can always ask Georgiana, Kitty and Jane to attend everything in our stead. Your family will be fine with our exclusion, because there will still be some of our party who will always want to include themselves."

He picked me up and twirled me around. "That is...good Lord, Lizzy that is brilliant! Absolutely brilliant. For there will be days there when I will want you for myself, and whenever I need them, our siblings can make up for our absence."

"Precisely. Now, since we are to go to America, it is best that I research a bit of their history. For I do not wish to be presented to your family and make them believe that you made a foolish decision in choosing me. If I know a bit about American history, and am learned on some of their ways, hopefully they shall be flattered."

"You are magnificent in general, woman, but when you really put your mind to it, you are sharper at strategy than Napoleon Bonaparte."

"I should hope so, for he is very often losing his battles—and at any rate, I believe that I am at least taller."

Darcy laughed at this very jovially. We continued to think on our plans and even though there wasn't enough time for them to write us back with an affirmative reply, Darcy believed that if he wrote to tell them who else was coming, they should overall be fine with it.

"I have but one small addition I would like to make to your machinations, my dear," he said.

I gave him a coy look. "What would that be, pray tell?"

"I would like to invite Bingley to join us. For if we ever wish for our sisters to take part of an event in our place, they will have a male chaperone to accompany them. I would have been fine with it being Colonel Fitzwilliam as well, but he is off marching soldiers to the Iberian Peninsula."

"But would Mr. Bingley be up for going back to America so soon?"

"Elizabeth, you know Bingley. He is always up for an adventure."

<hr/>

I told Jane and Kitty of this scheme and they were luckily accepting to this change of events. Verily, they were quite looking forward to seeing America, especially since this might be there last chance if all did result in war, which it clearly seemed meant to.

Our mother was at first excited, exclaiming that nothing could be more wonderful, for she hoped my marriage would throw her remaining daughters into the paths of other rich men. Also with Jane's beauty, she would very soon find an American Darcy who was quite taken with her.

Unfortunately, my father did not plan his next jest well, for he said that if we should perish because of the conflict rising between Britain and America, we were likely to be forced to become patriots or would be shot.

This sent our mother into hysterics and we had to assure her of our safety. For both countries were threatening war but were not prepared for it in full. Also, many Englishmen were still travelling to America and coming back home safe and sound. Our father, realizing the damage that he had done, retreated into his study until our mother overcame her nervousness.

Meanwhile, in the brief time that I had to myself, I did attempt to do research of some of America's recent history, attempting to make good on my wish to impress Darcy's family. I began with newspapers that discussed the current crisis in American, having to do with the tension between the states and Britain. Yet I did not wish to delve too much into that subject, for I knew the details already to why America and Britain were on the opposite sides of another opinion. Therefore, I attempted to learn more about their society and their political history. My progress was slow, I do not deny, but at least my attempt was genuine all the same.

❧

The day before my wedding finally came and Jane and I sat up in my room, wondering how it all could come about.

"Can you die of happiness?" I asked, so content with my fate in life. "Oh, why can't everyone be as happy as I am, and Jane if only there was such another man for you."

"If you could give me one hundred such men," Jane said, "I shall never be as fortunate as you. Till I have your spirit, I shall never have your luck. But perhaps, in time, I may yet meet with another Mr. Brocklehurst who is too impotent to have started another family before I met him."

We both laughed over her comment and spent an hour talking of my good fortune before I went off to say good night to our mother.

"Lizzy!" Our mother said, "Come in! Come in!"

I entered and shut the door behind me.

"What is it, Mother?"

She twisted her handkerchief into knots. "I um... oh dear, now that it comes down to it, I feel nervous."

"Nervous about what?"

"I wanted to do this with all my daughters, but in Lydia's case, I could not for she did not marry here in Hampshire therefore I could not do this. Lizzy, whenever a mother marries off one of her children, it is a strange sensation. It is happiness, and yet it is also very sad. You see, I am happy for you, and I am so proud of all that you have accomplished.

"To marry is one thing, but to marry a man such as Mr. Darcy, who is not perfect, yet still emulates the best in humanity somehow, that is a triumph of the will, and I know that I have not always been the best mother in the world, I see that now.

"Yet I did love you and I only wanted the best for all of you. And you have found it, not by my will, but by your will and yours alone. You have proven yourself to be quite strong and stubborn, yes, but in the best sense."

My mother then began to cry. "And I am happy for you, but sad, for somehow there is nothing as hard as parting with one's children. One seems so forlorn without them."

"Oh Mama..." I said, giving her a hug, "you were a wonderful mother in the end."

She dabbed at her eyes with her wrinkled handkerchief. "Thank you, dear. That was nice to hear."

Such words of love and devotion make all the difference in the world, for these are the tender moments in between the harder memories that you have in your life, that come back to you when time is hardest, and you need the good memories most of all.

❧ 9 ❧

A NOTEWORTHY MARRIAGE

"Mary!" my mother called from my bedroom as I sat there while Hill did my hair. "It's your sister's wedding day. Find some useful employment than just your book!"

"Yes Mama," I heard Mary say and then I heard a creaking sound, which meant that Mary had been enjoying her favorite pastime of reading in the rocking chair.

It was the day of my wedding and the house was all in disarray. Our mother, Kitty and Jane were already helping me when Mary soon entered, looked around and watched the chaos that plagued a woman on her wedding day.

"Don't worry, Mary," I said from my seat. "I know this is not your area of expertise."

"Why aren't you wearing your dress yet?" She eyed my chemise and corset.

"Mama wishes to make sure all of the wrinkles are out of the gown."

"On a wedding day," our mother said, "a woman can never look too perfect. Still I can't believe it! One of my daughters marrying such a rich man as Mr. Darcy!" She fanned herself with her handkerchief. "Ah, my poor nerves."

"It couldn't be helped, Mama. But if it's any conciliation, I would be perfectly happy to not get married, just to spare your nerves."

"Lizzy, do be serious," Jane said, sitting in the corner and watching the havoc.

"Oh, don't you dare!" Mama shouted, not knowing that I was speaking in jest.

"I think Lizzy was making a joke, Mama," Kitty said, coming forward.

The door crashed open, and Lydia entered grandly and plopped down on my bed as if the room was her own.

"Lord, I'm so fat!" Lydia said rashly. "It doesn't matter. I was prettier on my wedding day than you, Lizzy."

"No, you weren't," our father said, entering in the doorway.

Kitty was distracted by something and went over to the window. She turned, her eyes sparkling.

"Lizzy, look!"

I excused myself from Hill, got up and joined Kitty at the window. I followed Kitty's gaze and there standing in the yard was Darcy. My heart fluttered anxiously. He was wearing breeches, boots, a shirt, but his vest was unopened, and he was wearing a long coat over it. He looked up at the window and smiled when he saw me looking down at him.

"Goodness gracious!" Mama shrieked. "What is he doing here and not properly dressed? You're getting married in three hours."

Not paying attention to anything other than Darcy, I threw on a coat over my chemise and rushed out of the room.

"Elizabeth!" Mama called after me. "You must never go out and see the groom before the wedding. Mr. Bennet, stop her!"

My father didn't stop me as I ran past him to see my future husband.

"You forget, my dear," Papa replied drily, "that I'm going blind, so I don't see well, and my hearing is quite shot so I cannot make out a word you just said."

Seeing that he was going to do nothing to further her cause, my mother did the only thing that she could do. She took my wedding gown in her hands and looked it over.

"Ah, we should have added more silk to this gown."

"No silk, Mrs. Bennet, I beg you!" I heard my father say while Lydia snorted, Kitty chuckled, and my mother sulked about her husband's lack of attention to her fashion preferences.

I rushed out of the front door, ran up to Mr. Darcy and hugged him.

"You haven't shaved yet," I joked, running a delicate hand over his face.

"I remembered how much you liked it when I didn't," he answered with a smile.

"I admit that I truly love you when you are at your most rugged." I rubbed his cheek and felt the roughness that I loved so much.

"This will be the last morning that anyone will call you Ms. Bennet."

I smiled up at him. "No, I'm Mrs. Darcy already. In some ways, I always was."

Darcy and I no longer cared for being discrete. We had broken decorum many times over and now that we were so close to being wed, secrecy seemed pointless, therefore Darcy lifted me up and spun me around while we kissed.

When he released me, I giggled like a school girl, so unlike me.

"Is Mr. Darcy so impatient that he couldn't wait to see me at the altar?"

His warm gaze bore into mine. "Yes, he is so impatient. Did you not know the man you married?"

"No, I didn't. I am a very foolish woman."

"And so must he be, to wed a woman who doesn't notice such things."

"Oh, wicked man you are." Then I pushed him away playfully. "And you have no choice but to leave, for how can I get married in my chemise and you get married wearing your stubble?"

"I still just... it is hard for me to believe that this is actually happening. After all the ups and downs, I just wanted to make sure that nothing else would take you away from me."

"We've had our ups and downs, but I don't believe that anything will get in our way this time. Now go! I can see my sisters watching us from the window and I now see that I am setting a bad influence."

"I am a bad influence."

"I love you!" I called as I ran toward my house. "Now go back to Aginfield and make certain that Bingley gets you to the church on time!"

I went back inside, put my wedding gown on and looked at myself in the mirror.

"Goodbye, Elizabeth Bennet. Hello Mrs. Darcy."

And that was all the moments, actions, expressions, glances, reflections and silences that led up to one of the happiest days of my life.

Later, I would notice that the church, though not filled, was certainly full enough to make my happiness complete. There were the Lucases, the Gardiners, the Austens, the Phillips, the Longs, Mr. Bingley, who was nice enough not to force his sisters to come, and the Fitzwilliams along with all my family. Yet as I entered, being led down the aisle on the arm of my father, I beheld Darcy standing there with Mr. Austen, our clergyman and Cassandra and Jane Austen's father.

When I reached the altar, my father released me, sat down and I stood next to Darcy.

Mr. Austen smiled down on us and to think! The same man to have baptized me was the same man who would oversee my wedding—from sacrament to sacrament; he had been there to see it all.

"Dearly beloved," he began, "we are gathered here today, under the sight of god, to join these two in holy matrimony."

The ceremony had begun, he read the ceremonial rites to us and it all seemed to be a blur to me, for all that I beheld was Darcy and I stealing glances at each other as Mr. Austen continued to deliver his speech.

Eventually the ring was given, so were vows and the service soon turned to a close.

"If there is any who believe that there is a reason that these two should not be wed in holy matrimony, then speak now or forever hold your peace."

Very much I thanked God that Caroline Bingley was not present, for I didn't doubt just how far she would go to come in between us. And even more-so I thanked fate that Lady Catherine De Bourgh did not take that moment to barge in and use her boisterous tone to interrupt my happiest of days.

When there was no one who spoke, Mr. Austen continued.

"Then I now pronounce you husband and wife. You may kiss the bride."

Darcy and I turned to each other, I rose on my tiptoes and we kissed.

Elizabeth Darcy now lived!

৩৯৩

Congratulations were expressed all around! Charlotte Collins came forward, but this time was accompanied by Mr. Collins.

"Mrs. Darcy," Mr. Collins said, "might I congratulate you on your most fortunate alliance."

I gave him a most gracious smile. "Thank you, sir. And I am aware that your congratulations must have been a hard thing to offer, considering that you most pointedly remarked that Lady Catherine did not look on this union with a friendly eye."

"Ah, yes! Your thoughtfulness does you credit, my dear cousin."

Upon my honor! He didn't see that I was giving him a delicate set-down but assumed that I was truly thanking him. Obviously, sarcasm wasn't something that he was very good at observing.

"Yet," Mr. Collins continued, "I still feel it my duty, as a clergyman, to wish to bestow peace, bounty and beneficence of all under my flock."

"My dear," Charlotte said delicately, "Elizabeth is not a member of your parish; therefore, I must assume that you regard all in the world as your fellow brethren."

He gave her an obsequious smile. "Quite so, my dear."

Due to all the hustle and bustle, Kitty accidentally came near enough for Mr. Collins to take notice of her. At first, he attempted to ignore her, still clearly bitter at her refusing his proposal, but Charlotte was there to restore propriety.

"Kitty!" Charlotte called. "Wasn't it a wonderful service?"

"It was," Kitty said. "My sister made a beautiful bride, did she not?"

"Aye, she did," Charlotte agreed.

"But you were as well, my dear," Mr. Collins said, patting Charlotte's hand. "Indeed, when I saw you walk down the aisle, I never saw anything so lovely as you."

"Thank you, dear, now—"

"For you had all the fine qualities that one would look for in a wife," Mr. Collins said, clearly trying to wound Kitty. "Serenity, artless manner, economy, usefulness, and a refined manner, which are qualities that many women nowadays are devoid of."

Here, he looked most pointedly at Kitty and though it was my wedding, I was about to cease being polite and chastise him, but we were interrupted as my new husband approached.

"Mr. Collins?"

Mr. Collins bowed, simpering and suddenly looked very subservient. "Might I congratulate you on this happy occasion, I hope that my cousin is well worthy of you, and I should also inform you that your Aunt Lady Catherine was in the best of heath—nine days ago."

Behind him, I saw Cassandra and Jane Austen as they overheard the last comment and stifled their laughter.

"My aunt is always in excellent health," Darcy replied coldly. "For sickness is not something she ever likes to entertain, and thank you for your well wishes, but as to your cousin being worthy of me, not only is she so, but the question shall always remain if I am worthy of her, which I will endeavor to do so. I was just overhearing your list of the fine qualities in your wife, sir, and I could not help but agree. For you have found a wonderful match in Mrs. Collins."

"Thank you, Mr. Darcy," Charlotte said, bowing her head.

"Indeed, yes sir, thank you," Mr. Collins said, bobbing his head like a fish. "My Charlotte and I here seem to be made of one heart and one mind. We seem to have been made for each other."

Behind them, I also saw Maria Lucas, Charlotte's younger sister, roll her eyes.

Darcy nodded. "That is wonderful. It is always a pleasing thing to have such a harmony with one's wife. This is why I always compliment my wife, for being all that is best in me, and her sisters, such as Miss Kitty there. Look at her, *Mr. Collins.*"

Mr. Collins, due to my husband's intense gaze on him which would have unnerved even the most stern and strong of men, felt his reserve and confidence immediately buckle, and he felt all too easily pressured to turn and look at Kitty.

"Such artless manner," Mr. Darcy began listing, "refined with good humor, a willing heart, loveliness and easiness of temper, all can be found in my sister, Kitty. Do not you agree?"

"Well, yes—yes," Mr. Collins stuttered.

"I am happy that you do."

Charlotte was able to steer Mr. Collins away from our company and we all let out a breath as my father appeared beside us.

"And to think that I was almost so lucky as to have him for a son-in-law." Our father chuckled. "Ah, how will I ever recover from the loss?"

❧

In between all of those who attended, eventually I made my way to Cassandra and Jane Austen.

"Congratulations, Lizzy," Cassandra said. "You shall be very happy."

"Thank you, Cassandra, I believe that I shall."

"Oh, you have no choice but to be, for your tempers are so different, it is bound to make life interesting."

"Interesting is a word that is hard to maintain in life," Jane Austen said. "Just be happy if you have a good cook is all that I say. And a good dressmaker. For a good dressmaker is as vital to a woman of your new station as air to breathe."

"Perhaps so. But as long as I don't have to give up my inclination to climb trees, I can cope with such new restrictions."

Stifling a laugh, Jane Austen answered, "I daresay that you can." She then looked around and wistfulness seemed to come over her.

"Jane?" I whispered. "Is something wrong?"

"Oh, it's nothing, Lizzy. I just realized that I am the most selfish person in the world."

I gave her a faux look of shock. "Truly? The most selfish person in the whole world? It's a large world, you know?"

"I should have been thinking about you and your joy, yet instead I was just thinking of how I can't write a wedding scene to save my life!"

At that, I laughed. "What?"

"Oh, Lizzy, you've read *Sense and Sensibility*." Jane shook her head and made a tutting sound. "I just had my characters fall in love, said they got married, but I never actually showed the wedding, and I keep on doing so with my current writings. For some reason, I feel incapable of doing so, just as I choose not to let the story linger after the love is obtained."

We had taken seats near the altar. "Why is that, do you think?"

"I don't know for certain," Jane Austen replied. "Yet all that I assume is that finding love is the point, not the matrimonial ceremony of it. Or maybe it's just because I simply think that weddings are boring to actually write."

We both had a good laugh over that.

"Yet I do think that this wedding of yours, Lizzy, gives me inspiration for me to at least feel that I should attempt to give it a fitting title. I shall therefore say that this was a Noteworthy Marriage, for it seems for the good of all."

❧ 10 ❧

A NEW ROAD

W e had our wedding feast at my Aunt Phillips home, and then Darcy and I spent our wedding night in Aginfield. Lord and Lady Fitzwilliam had relocated to the *Prancing Prince Inn* that was in Meryton after we had settled in Aginfield, for they wanted to give us our privacy on our wedding night.

Naturally Mr. Bingley could not leave his own home, therefore he made himself scarce, gave us the largest and most luxurious room in the house, and made sure that wherever we were, he was not.

Once Darcy and I bathed separately in our different compartments, I received a knock on my door. My servant opened it and I was not surprised to find my new husband there, dressed nicely, but not wearing his jacket.

"I am come to tell you that I have arranged for us to eat dinner in our bedrooms, Mrs. Darcy," he said, enjoying calling me by his name. "If that is agreeable to you."

Mrs. Darcy. How I loved the sound of it! "Of course, it is."

The servants organized a table for us and laid food on it while they stood behind us.

"You may go for now," Darcy said to them, "and we shall call you again if you are needed."

"Very good, sir." They left us alone.

"Do you mind," I said, "since we are alone, if I don't have to stand on ceremony and eat slowly."

"Bet you I can eat faster."

"Oh, I disagree."

I began to eat my fish with alacrity, and he did so as well... at first, and then he put his food down, half eaten and, while wiping his hands, he stared at me.

It made me a trifle nervous. "Why do you look on me so?"

"Because I am still hungry, but not for food."

The beating of my heart filled me. "Oh, and what for, pray tell?"

"Keep eating."

I continued to eat as he stood up and moved behind me. He ran his hands down my shoulders, then he began to undo my gown, sliding it off my sleeves. I aided him by rising up slightly from my chair so he could pull the gown off my legs, letting it lay on the floor like a pool around my feet. Then he unlaced my corset, pulling it off me in full, then began to raise my under-gown up, over my head and I then sat there, wearing nothing but my stockings and garters.

He got on his knees, untied my garters, pulled them off along with my stockings. Then he stood up and gazed down on my nude form.

I shivered with anxious delight. "Might I now be allowed to stop eating?"

"The food? Yes."

Then he lifted me up and kissed me with immense passion that made me feel content in knowing that his desire for me was still healthy and unquenched.

As we stood there kissing, he took some pins out of my hair so that it fell along my shoulders.

"You like my hair!" I said in between kisses.

"I very much do," he murmured against my ear.

Our breaths intertwined. "Is that all that you like about me?"

"Oh, you very well know the answer to that."

As we kissed, he slid his hands down to my chest, then he ran them further down to my stomach, until finally he pressed his fingers deeper in between my thighs, stroking inside of me back and forth while I was lost in his touch.

"I missed this terribly!" I cried, the feeling low in my belly so intense that my knees were weak.

"Upon my honor, woman! So have I!"

Then he lifted me up and carried me over to the bed, laying me down on it. Yet I was no longer a maid, and I felt my courage rising within me as I did not want to remain passive in this circumstance.

"I want to undress you this time," I whispered. "Would you mind?"

"No," he replied, his breathing heavy. "I have just never had the experience before."

"Whatever past you have, I am your wife, and I will be the first woman to undress you then!"

I knelt on the bed and began to unfasten every button on his vest, shirt and trousers. I pulled off his cravat, then his blouse and I looked on him lying there shirtless.

"Darcy, you are perfect."

"Am I all that you hoped to ever have?" he asked insecurely.

"More. You are more."

I then pushed him back on the mattress and pulled off his boots, then I removed his stockings and lastly, I removed his trousers and looked down at him in wonder. I kissed his thighs, then his stomach and ran my hands along his arms and began to bite his ear lightly.

"Have I created a monster?" He ran his hands down my bottom and gave it a squeeze.

"Yes, and she is hungry!"

He rolled on top of me and kissed all along my neck and down over my breasts. Over and over his lips moved and I could not help but cry out as he continued his ministrations, then he lowered his lips further and further as I waited for what he had done to me so long ago.

And then nothing happened!

I raised my head up and looked down at him, only to see him gazing up at me.

"Why have you ceased?"

"Because I'm torturing you."

"You wouldn't dare! You will continue this instant!"

"No."

"Yes, you will."

He chuckled. "No, I won't."

"Oh, yes you will, or I will do the worst thing imaginable."

"And what is that?"

"I will bully you into making sure that we sleep in separate rooms at Pemberly."

"Oh! Well then... I best get to it."

Wrapping my legs around his neck, I was then lowered down, and he began to kiss me in between my thighs. So much feeling, like my blood near to boiling, my breath heaving, my body immediately released, and all tension fell away. I felt as if Mr. Darcy and I, two now becoming one again, were both in the atmosphere, soaring over the clouds and as high as the moon itself.

With every kiss, opening me up and revealing me to all that made womanhood the most fortunate of blessings that were bestowed, he continued tasting the very depths of me and my back arched against the bed sheets as I gasped out. My whole body tensed as I felt myself being rocked to a new height, then all sensations reached an apex—and I was eclipsed by a most wonderful and undefinable excitation.

Darcy then raised himself up, laid his hand down over the spot that he just was kissing and began to run his hands inside of me and my cries of ecstasy continued once more.

Back and forth, he rocked me, and all the while he began to suckle my breasts once more until he knew that I was fully satisfied and awaiting him.

When done his attentions, he rested his body on mine, pressed himself within me and I felt his strength. How I had missed the feeling of us being bound together on this physical and most intimate of emotional voyages. How I loved him!

Back and forth he drove himself into me, getting faster and faster until we both were eclipsed and our bodies and will were both spent.

When done, we lay there on the bed, holding each other, and were husband and wife in full.

❧

We lay in the bed, still naked as we held each other.

"How did we survive such a long engagement before we wed?" Darcy asked.

"My darling, our engagement wasn't over two months long, though I agree that it was long enough. For since we had done it the first time, you have been on my mind in that way ever since. I was in so much agony, for I had wanted you in such a way again."

"Your pain then was equivalent to my own, for I had dreamt of you often. I wanted you in my bed every night with me, and also in some mornings."

I looked into his handsome face. "Do you really wish to confess that you wanted me in such a way every time that we were alone? For you need not fear me knowing the truth of your appetite. I felt the same way."

"Did you? That is a relief to hear."

"Especially whenever you rode up on your stallion. I don't know, but such command you have over it made me desire you so much. I suppose I loved your immense sense of power in regards to self-command and regulation of will."

"You find me sensuous on a horse? Then I must find a way to have you ride with me someday, for that will be a new position that I have never tried before."

"While I admire your curiosity in trying new things with me, I think making love while riding a horse with all of humanity and nature looking at us might be taking your romantic sensibilities a little too far."

I ran my fingers over his chest. "Though I admire your sense of creativity, and I also wish to explore many avenues with you. I would very much not want to do anything which my mother would find out about. I would never hear the end of it."

"True, though a man can dream."

We lay there for a while before he began to speak again.

"I want you to know," he whispered desperately, "that I will be loyal to you, I shall be, Lizzy."

"I know. Your indecision before was not because of wickedness, Darcy, I know that now. It was because you were sad over your father's passing, you were heartbroken and the only consolation you had was the comfort in doing a duty, and therefore when you met me, you became torn between that duty versus a new desire."

I raised up on my elbow to study him. "You were confused, and that mingled with heartache can lead to a man falling apart a bit and committing errors. You are not to blame for being human. And I know you will be loyal, for that is your way."

"Thank you, Elizabeth. Yet, even with all my mistakes, which I know I shall commit more of probably, you must promise me one thing. You must never turn away from me, never shun me, for I will always do my best to be what you deserve."

"I know, and I promise to never look away."

☙❧

Darcy fell asleep before I did, therefore I was able to look at him as he slept. Seeing him there, so blissful, so at peace allowed a serenity to wash over me.

In some ways, our intimacy frightened me, for Darcy showed me often that his happiness was directly connected and dependent on my consistency to stand by him. This was a welcome attachment, but also a frightening one, for it made me wonder if I had the ability to always be so strong? Could I always be there to nurture the best sides of him, and be able to calm and rationalize with the worst sides? Would I be able to always see the light where sometimes there was darkness?

Yet then I took comfort, for I knew, even at his worst moment, he was worth it. He would always be worth it.

And yet—there was a co-dependency to our love, and whenever I needed him, I knew he would be there. We were just two entities that could falter at the same time and use the other for stability once more. Therefore, even though I was not strong enough at all times, I would still do my best to be.

☙❧

Our blissful days at Aginfield were numbered to only three more before we would journey to Portsmouth and embark on our new voyage to America.

Darcy, when it came down to it, was angry that he ever agreed to go to America, for he was enjoying the comfort of Aginfield, and of Bingley making sure that we only had each other for company. He immediately wished to send a letter to our family across the ocean, saying that due to complications, our journey would have to be postponed. However, I was able to argue him out of that inclination, for I told him that we would not only be letting down our distant family, but also be letting down our sisters, who were excited to go to a land that they heard much of, but never had the chance to see.

Darcy left to speak with Jefferson to arrange for his correspondence to be forwarded in his absence. Jefferson was to remain behind, in England, to make certain that the Pemberly estate was still maintained and order was kept.

Mr. Bingley approached me. "And if Darcy hasn't told you, yes, I am coming with you to America as well. And even more wonderful, my sister Caroline shall stay with the Hursts and not be making the voyage with us."

"That is wonderful." I sighed, not afraid to show my happiness that Caroline Bingley would not be able to attend, for though she tried to hide it, I knew that she still fancied my husband.

"But what about this unfortunate business of yours, and of you courting Anne? I'm assuming that Lady Catherine won't be too happy with you separating yourself by an ocean."

He brushed the comment away. "Oh, you need not worry about that! She has already rejected me as a proper candidate for a husband to Anne."

"What reasons did she have?"

"The reasons that come from being of such a rank as she is," Bingley said, taking out a letter and handing it to me. "Go ahead and read it, for I was already going to show it to you and Darcy. She sent it to me a couple of weeks ago—yes, she, a Lady, actually broke decorum and sent me a letter! And I have been free ever since."

I took the letter and began to read.

Dear Mr. Charles Bingley,

You can be at no loss as to understand why I am writing you, I am sure. And even if you wish to attempt to be dissembling of the truth, you shall not find me desirous of speaking in non-truths or falsities, and my character has forever been prided on by others of being frank and containing pure honesty.

I am writing to confront a report of an alarming nature. I have heard rumors, from my dear cousin, the Earl of Matlock, that you, Mr. Charles Bingley, son of a man who gathered enough wealth to make certain that his son could be a gentleman and of no profession, has developed a taste for being in trade—and has even begun to start taking an interest in selling textiles!

While I wish to believe this to be a scandalous falsehood, I instantly wrote this letter to make my stance on this known. I hope you don't pretend to be ignorant of it. I must know, are you still in trade? For if so, then I will demand that, unless you make steps to quit the profession immediately, I shall refuse to allow you to court my daughter, for she, an heiress of noble rank, should not be reduced to marrying a mere tradesman.

I shall await your reply, which I demand to be sent to me with all haste."

Sincerely
Lady Catherine De Bourgh

"And I assume that you replied with a refusal of abandoning your trade?"

Mr. Bingley nodded forcefully. "Oh, I most certainly refused, both for a release as well as my sanity. Why does the aristocracy look down on having a profession so? I am aware that not all of them are so cold and close-minded, but there are too many who are prejudiced against the idea of having some form of occupation."

I agreed. "I cannot get on at all with the notion of finding those who must work as being questionable, especially since those who are wealthy have the tendency to live such—boring lives!"

Mr. Bingley laughed.

"Passing from day to day with only idle activities to occupy your time can be redundant and contains no importance or impact on the world."

"Indeed, the way of the world."

"Mr. Bingley, you and I both know that the world is changing. For only months before now, Mr. Darcy was a man who would never have even married a woman like me. And now he has. Slowly and surely, the world will see that sometimes what is not in fashion, doesn't mean that it is wrong. And those of us who swim upstream are simply not afraid of a challenge."

Mr. Bingley smiled at me and kissed my hand.

"Well, may it do so, but until then, I shall relish in the fact that I have saved my friend of a sticky situation while also now being free again." He raised an arm high, a sign of triumph. "Mr. Bingley has his liberty and is loose upon the world, a single man in a world of pleasant women and company."

I shook a finger at him but couldn't stop a smile. "Don't you dare break any hearts."

"Never, but I in turn, have no worries in being heartbroken myself every now and again."

He continued to regale me about all the things that he had seen the last time that he was in America until Darcy joined us.

"Now all is settled. And it's time to ride over water."

⚜

Our things packed and ready to disembark, Jane, Georgiana, Kitty, Mr. Bingley, my husband and I were in two carriages with our luggage, journeying to Portsmouth, where we were to board the ship called The Victoria.

Eventually we arrived and boarded the ship the next day along with a handful of others who were travelling to visit family in our one-time colonies. The ships anchor was raised, and we set sail along the harbor, prepared to journey down a new road of our lives.

⚘ II ⚘
ROCKY SHORES

I held Jane's shoulders while she leaned over the edge of the ship and began to vomit up her breakfast.

Because neither she nor I had ever been on a ship before, Jane had never learned until that instant that she could get seasick, and she very much did.

We had started our voyage the day before and she was fine for the duration of that time frame, however the next day seemed to have gotten the better of her. Kitty, Georgiana and I helped her below deck while a sailor gave us advice on what to feed her as well as suggesting she stay below.

"It is very amusing," Kitty said as we tended to her while she lay in bed. "Out of all of us, I thought I would have been the one to have gotten seasick, for I have a hard time spinning around for more than a few seconds without getting nauseous. It is so strange that I am fine. I more so look at the sea around us and the rocking of it as a way of nursing me to sleep at night. If anything, it just makes me a little tired."

"I've had experience to help me," Georgiana offered encouragingly, "for I confess that when I first took a sea voyage, Jane, I looked quite as you did, very much green in the face."

"Wait, then... my face is green?" Jane said weakly.

The three of us looked at each other and decided that it would be best to lie. We all assured her that she still looked wonderful and very much in the best of ways.

"I feel as if I am such a terrible imposition." Jane wiped her nose with the hem of her skirt, not like my perfect sister at all! "For here we are and should be happy, and I just brought up my breakfast in front of everyone. I am utterly...embarrassed!"

"There are some natural things that society must forgive quite easily," I offered, "because it cannot be avoided. Such ailments of the body are one of them."

"And besides," Georgiana offered. "Even if they were to get irrationally judgmental, then take heart, for after we land, we shall never have to see these people again!"

"True," Jane answered, settling back with a sigh. "True."

⚜

When we went above deck, some people looked at us and snickered, clearly remembering Jane's unfortunate incident.

"I wish I could spit on them," Kitty said.

Both Georgiana and I agreed.

We were then met by a sailor who was passing by.

"How goes the lady who had to be taken below deck?" he asked, carrying some twain that he was going to weave.

"She is doing well," Kitty said. "Thank you. It's our sister's first time on a ship."

"The sea can upset even the strongest of stomachs; therefore, she has nothing to be ashamed of."

He said this loudly enough for all nearby to hear, and I was happy for it.

"Thank you, sir," Kitty said, and we walked away to join our gentlemen. We found them both chuckling with each other about Jane's state.

"I shall not deny," Bingley said with a laugh, "it was so strange seeing Miss Bennet release her meal into the ocean, for though it was innocent, it was such a comical sight."

"Precisely!" Darcy agreed. "It was so amusing to watch something so beautiful just vomit in that way."

"I agree. Jane's beauty has always made her seem like a statue, therefore it is nice to see that she can be as human as the rest of us. For while her beauty is disarming, there is little to no warmth to it, therefore, seeing her in a state of seasickness has done wonders for my perception of her."

"Oh, quiet you two," Georgiana said, approaching them.

"We can't help it, Georgiana," Darcy said. "That was the most amusing thing ever."

I slapped his shoulder playfully, and then we continued to look out at the ocean as we journeyed over it.

The rest of the journey passed without incident and eventually Jane was able to come to the deck again and overcome her seasickness. At first, she worried about how others would view her, but Darcy and Mr. Bingley were so much imposing when it came to her defense, that no one dared mock her at all.

Eventually we reached the harbor in Maryland, where we were going to break our journey, then book passage on another ship that was going to travel up the Delaware River where we would make berth in Philadelphia.

Once we got off, we made inquiries as to where would be the best place to dine until our next ship was ready to set sail. A couple of the sailors escorted us to the *Jolly Drinker Tavern* where they were going themselves to get a pint of ale.

We parted ways with them when we entered, sat down and ordered some food. As we began to converse, Darcy noticed a couple of men looking at us queerly. I followed his gaze, and then one of them winked at me.

"Is there a reason behind your impertinence that you stare at my wife so?" Darcy stated boldly. At first, I thought of interrupting him, but he was well within his rights to mark the man's rudeness.

"I just could not help overhearing your accent. Are you all from England?"

"Yes, we are. Still that does not justify you staring at my wife."

"Why should I not? Why should you be allowed to keep her to yourself?"

I felt my face flood with heat. I could not believe the man's tenacity and cheek.

"You will repent what you have just said," Darcy said, "and I will forget what you've stated. You've simply had too much to drink. If that's not the case, I will slam your head into that table behind you."

The man uttered a bitter shout. "I am not drunk!"

At this point, all were watching us in earnest. Further down the tavern, I saw the sailors watching the interaction and among them was the sailor who had been kind to Jane.

"I am not drunk," the man repeated, lowering his voice, but still with menace. "I am just simply stating what is right and what is fair. You see, why should I not have your four beauties there? Why should not every man in this tavern have them, when you all in England think it your right to take our sailors as if they are mere animals?"

❦

Then the explanation of his rage became clear. He was angry at seeing us, because of the impressment of sailors on American vessels. For years, due to many British sailors abandoning their posts on our ships due to terrible working conditions and fleeing to work on American vessels, the British Navy legalized impressment.

They would come in contact with American vessels, get permission to board them and if they found their own sailors who had deserted their vessels, they would take them back to their ship for chastisement and return them to their previous post. Collecting naval deserters was innocent enough, but that is the way things always begin: merely innocent. Unfortunately, they almost always take a turn to corruption. Realizing that it was also an easy way to get sailors to fill their empty posts on their vessels, the British began to falsely accuse sailors who never were British, who never defected, as being deserters. The captains of the American ships had no choice but to let the English captain drag his sailors off the ship, impress them, and make them become British sailors.

In many ways this was accusing innocent men of the basest naval crime, and then taking them as captives. It was, in a way, a form of oppression. At first no one noticed or cared about it, but then slowly and surely both countries began to hear of these nautical crimes and tension began to rise. But there were also said to possibly be land disputes to add to the conflict.

Therefore, in regards to tension, history was repeating itself.

ⓈⓍⓈ

And the man, whether he was drunk or not, was standing up now and Darcy was clearly doing everything in his power to contain his rage.

"Do you know what it is like," the man continued, "to be a sailor on a ship, a merchant vessel where all who worked on it were just honest men with families back home... and then to encounter a British vessel, and your captain has no choice but to let them board, for if he doesn't, the British might fire on us?"

He stepped so close we could see the graying hair at his temples.

"So, he does so, content in knowing that all of us are Americans and he has nothing to fear for us remaining under his employ. And then the British Captain boards the ship, inspects all of you, and then looks at the man who is standing just next to you. His name was James Seymour, and he was originally from England, but he had been living in America for years, and just never lost his native accent. I would know, for I had known him even before he became a sea man."

I looked down at my hands and prepared for what was going to be said next. A part of me was quite enthralled by his tale, for it was of woe clearly, and woe can always attract a listener, even if the woe was not one of fiction or fantasy—but was real. And yet, I could tell in his narrative that the poor man, James Seymour, was bound to a terrible fate that no man deserved.

"Then the British Captain told him to speak up, and James did. Hearing that James had an English accent that poor James just never lost, the captain demanded that he was a British Naval deserter and therefore ordered him to work on his ship." The man's demeanor became even more agitated.

"James refused, stating that he never deserted, and that he worked on American vessels for years, and talked of his wife and child that he had back home. The Captain did not believe him, but our captain stepped forward and told him it was true, that James was our mate, fair and square. Both captains began to argue about it, but our captain eventually was forced to concede, and James was dragged off our ship. The rest of us tried to fight for him, but we were held back. Now imagine what it felt like for us, for me, to have to come home, make berth and then when James's wife and children came to see him return home—I had to tell them that he would not return."

"I am sorry for James's tragedy," I said. "And I know what anger you are feeling, just as I know that you are about to unleash your desire for revenge upon my husband in the place of that captain, but he is not him! And he doesn't deserve your scorn, so I beseech you, kindly desist from offending him and feasting your eyes on my sisters."

The man took another drink of his mug and laughed, turning to Darcy and Bingley.

"She talks for you? She has more strength than you then? Is that what you do?"

"Of course, I let my wife speak," Darcy hissed. "It's called being a proper Englishman, and proper is clearly something that you know little about."

Darcy stood up and took a few steps toward the man. "Now you will apologize for insulting me, my wife and my companions, or suffer the consequences."

The man took another drink and suddenly threw his mug at Darcy, who moved out of the way before it hit him. Bingley then stood up to assist Darcy, but the man rushed up to my husband.

I jumped up, wishing to do something but unaware of how to do it, yet my husband seemed to be made of iron and certainty. Easily moving out of the man's path, he tripped the man with his foot, then pushed him into a nearby table.

The man recovered, and then stood up again, ready to rush to my husband once more. However, the sailors from *The Victoria* had intervened and subdued him.

Out of spite and with incredible self-command, Darcy walked over to our table, picked up his mug of ale, took a sip of it, and then he took a coin from his pocket and tossed it on the man.

"A silver piece...for your wounded pride and misplaced notions. And for being the greatest fool I have ever met."

He nodded to us and we all stood up, thanked the sailors who came to our aid and then we left.

At first, we were silent, for we did not know how to talk about it. As we walked along the harbor, Mr. Bingley rolled his shoulders.

"Well, that was the most unpleasant welcome to a country that I have ever had in my life."

And then we all began to discuss it.

Bingley assured us that he didn't have such a conflict at all when he had previously come to America and that his time amongst the locals had always been quite pleasant. When Bingley went off to purchase our tickets for our next voyage, we all began to speak of it with more heated words.

Jane spoke up. "The man was wounded from having experienced a tragedy that had a marked effect on him. He was waiting to find someone to lash out at and therefore, though he was very wrong to attack us, I cannot help but still pity him for his pain."

Kitty put her arm around Jane's waist. "Oh Jane, you are too good. Can you never think ill of anyone?"

"Not in circumstances such as this."

"The man is to be pitied," Kitty acknowledged. "When I have had more time to think about it. And when I say by more time, I mean tomorrow and certainly not today. For today he acted on his sensibilities and I feel it only right that I be allowed to act on mine. It is never right to attack someone because of the actions of another. And he attacked Mr. Darcy and threatened the rest of us. Therefore, I shall let myself be overcome with sensibility today, and only will I find sense tomorrow when I have had time to adapt myself to its persuasion."

"Those are the very mirror of my sentiments," Georgiana said. "I know he is hurting, yet he was very wrong to do so."

"Yes, he was," I said. "A capital offense."

Darcy was silent all the while and I placed my hand on his cheek.

"You and Bingley defended us valiantly," I offered.

"I am sorry that you had to witness such a sight," Darcy said shortly. "I am very much bitter."

"And I am happy in some ways," I replied lightly. "For though I hope the rest of our time in America may go by without such incidents, it was a nice trial for you."

He raised an eyebrow. "A trial?"

"Yes, for it has shown me, that when a woman is offended, you will defend us, and that you are not afraid to defend yourself as well. Such pride is well-placed, and if I may be so bold, is under good regulation—therefore it shows that you have real superiority of mind."

"Are you teasing me in hopes of making me smile?"

"Yes and no. I am being playful, but I mean every word."

My sisters also offered our thanks, and then Mr. Bingley returned with our tickets, telling us that we had four hours until we would be able to board the ship.

The four hours, as long as they felt to be, eventually ended and we boarded the courier ship *The Laconia*. Our luggage was brought on deck, the anchor was raised once more and we were off, sailing north in hopes of a warmer reception, for as of then we had been dashed against the rocky shores of prejudice and contempt.

PHILADELPHIA

As our voyage commenced, my mind was still on the sailor who attacked us, and his tale of the sailor named James Seymour. As it so happened, my mind was not the only one to still dwell on the memory of it.

"I am uncertain," Georgiana said to me in secret.

"Of what part of that unfortunate incident?"

"I know why he was angry. I even know why he unleashed it on us, and he was also loose in the tongue as well due to the consumption of much ale, but I am torn."

I waited for her to continue.

"He attacked us because of his grief, but how did that make him any different than the sea captains who began to impress soldiers? They were hurt from their sailors abandoning them—though the captain probably deserved to be abandoned—and they unleashed their thirst for justice on American vessels. Then that thirst turned to revenge. Now that sailor saw his friend's life get destroyed, he thirsted for justice, unleashed it on us and it turned to blind revenge."

"Hate is a vicious cycle," Jane said from behind us, "which is why I do my best not to feel it, for it only breeds more of the same thing instead of less of it. I do not deny that it's often right to stand up for justice, even to seek revenge, yet it is a tricky thing—a frightening one."

Georgiana looked pained. "Then should we hate him? I know not what to feel."

"No," I said. "Hate will not help you in this instance. We can feel anger, resentment, but not hate. All that we can do...is regret what happened today."

"It has also made it all true," Kitty said. "When in Hampshire, we are so removed from everything, and never see anything up close and therefore it never becomes real to us. It is an abstract and arbitrary thing to just hear about it but never see any tangible proof. Yet now we do have proof, for we have almost seen the effects of the impressment ourselves. We have seen the tragedy and so... now it is all real."

"Oh..." With that reasonable answer, Georgiana seemed satisfied.

"It makes everything else seem so small now. It makes much seem so... remember when our mother was angry when our father took too long to call on a gentleman who came to our neighborhood once? She was afraid that because he didn't, we would not be acquainted with him and lose our chance of catching a husband. To think! She was worried over something like that when this is happening. Now all of it seems so—"

"Small," I answered, "and of no consequence?"

"Precisely."

"Your lives are not small."

We all turned, and Darcy had accosted us quietly.

"Your lives are not small at all," he continued. "You think epic tragedy is the only emotion that has the right to be felt, but it is not so. One does not need to overcome a great injustice to feel as if their life has consequence. Or meaning. Sometimes it's the small things, the everyday deeds of us ordinary folk that is what makes the world *the world*. Simple acts of kindness, or love, of fussiness and vexing each other, causing our families grief over the most trivial of things, being petty or jealous, those small matters have every right to be in the forefront of our minds just as much as the great feats of man. Great sadness should not erase the mundane trivialities, just as the trivial should not overshadow the great sadness."

"Have you always been so wise?" I asked.

"Only recently have I become so."

Our ship sailed along the Delaware River, and time had begun to soften our memories of the *Jolly Drinker Tavern* and soon, all thought had turned to Jane's constant hardening to living at sea, for she was now celebrating her fourth week of not getting sick on board.

❧

"Elizabeth," Darcy whispered.

I was half-asleep, for I had come below deck to take a nap, and now I felt Darcy's hands on my shoulders, gently waking me.

I rolled over, opened my eyes and saw a tense expression on his face which I learned long ago meant that he was over-excited.

"What is it?"

"We are soon to reach Penn's Landing," he said, "which is the edge of the city. We are now at Philadelphia."

"Really?" I cried, rubbing the sleepiness from my eyes and jumping up. "Finally! And where are my shoes?"

Darcy helped me look for my shoes and once we found them, I followed him above deck.

"Mr. and Mrs. Darcy!" Bingley called, waving to us. With him were Jane, Kitty and Georgiana, therefore we met him, along with the rest of the people who were on board and we looked out over the railing.

"It is so large!" Jane said.

"And beautiful," Kitty added.

"I believe," Bingley said, "that when William Penn found the city, he wanted it to be a place of rural and urban city life. Therefore, there is much greenery, but there is also urban expansion. There used to be more trees, but the city has now grown too large and became quickly popular."

"Why did it become so prominent?" Georgiana asked.

"Because of religious freedom," Bingley added. "Philadelphia was one of the very few places, in the entire world in the 18th century, where anyone could come here and practice any religion they chose without being persecuted. That's why it means city of brotherly love."

"When did you learn all of this?" I asked archly.

"I read... sometimes."

I looked out on the city as we neared it and from a distance it looked wonderful, and I hoped that up close it would prove promising.

"Well then, Philadelphia."

❧ 13 ❧

THE JOVIALITIES OF FAMILY LIFE

Our ship dropped anchor, the plank was lowered, and with our luggage, we came ashore. We reached Penn's Landing, the edge of the city and stepped onto Philadelphian soil.

When we looked out at the river, there was another body of land.

"Is that also Pennsylvania?" Jane asked.

"No," Darcy replied, "I do believe that is New Jersey."

"Very much so," Bingley confirmed. "Many legendary things happened over there as well."

All around us were people who came to greet their loved ones who had arrived on *The Laconia*. We worried that we would be barely noticeable in the throng.

"How will they know us?" I asked.

"I am not certain. I was hoping that they would simply call out the name Darcy so that I knew who they were, but unfortunately—"

"Darcy! Oh, there you are, Darcy!"

We turned and a very large and jovial-looking man, with cheeks reminiscent of Father Christmas, came forward. With him was a portly elderly woman who looked equally as cheerful—and though first impressions were a tricky thing—I must confess that I had wished to like them immediately.

"Is that you, Fitzwilliam?" the man said.

"Yes—yes," Darcy stuttered. "And you are cousin Thomas Darcy?"

"Yes," he said, raising his arms in welcome and then embracing Darcy who actually looked small because of this man's girth!

"Oh Fitzwilliam!" Mr. Thomas Darcy said, "I haven't seen you since you were only a foot tall."

"It is amazing thinking of Darcy only being a foot tall," Jane whispered to me.

Darcy clearly was at a loss of how to act on such a warm reception and he was quite taken aback, therefore I knew to come to his aid.

I smiled at our new acquaintances. "I hope that I shall be allowed to be granted some embraces from my new family as well, once we have become better acquainted."

"Oh, Cousin Thomas," Darcy said, happy to be released from the hug, "would you allow me to introduce you to my wife and family? This is my wife, Mrs. Elizabeth Darcy, her sisters Miss Jane Bennet and Miss Kitty, this is my good friend Charles Bingley, and if you recall me, then you must recall my sister—"

"So, this is little Georgiana?" Cousin Thomas gazed fondly at her. "You are the splitting image of your mother. She was a great woman."

"Thank you," Georgiana said as we all curtsied to him.

"And this," Cousin Thomas said, "is my wife and your Cousin Mrs. Emilia Darcy."

We curtsied to her as well.

"Oh, don't be so formal about it," Cousin Emilia said, her gray curls resting below her mobcap. "For Mrs. Darcy said that once we were acquainted well enough, she would like a hug and I am happy to oblige, but I am so wide that I can hug all of you and you all could get a piece of me!"

The four of us chuckled at her openness and Jane, Georgiana, Kitty and I embraced her... and I must say that it did feel surprisingly like hugging a grandmother that we never knew we had.

Georgiana was also a little stiff at first, but she very quickly adapted to this openness of nature while I looked at Mr. Thomas Darcy.

"But I don't understand, if you haven't seen my husband since he was a 'foot tall', then how did you recognize him?"

"Through the miracle of the Darcy traits, I suppose," Mr. Thomas Darcy said. "His father and I were quite close when we were younger, you see, and well his son here, is the splitting image of what his father looked like when he was his age."

"Truly?" Georgiana asked, curious. "Fitzwilliam truly looks like him that much?"

"To the very life! For there is literally no difference in appearance at all. Even the height is the very same."

"Well, my husband," I said archly, "your mother was one lucky woman. I declare that she might've been as fortunate as I am."

"Well then," Mr. Thomas Darcy said, clapping his hands together. "Let us take you to our home, Canterbury Park, so that I can tell you every hidden detail that your father never told you," he added on a sly wink.

Our luggage was carried along by ship hands till we reached Mr. Thomas Darcy's carriage and he luckily had the gift of foresight to have brought a second one with him.

☙❧

Since all the men were in the other carriage, Mrs. Emilia Darcy was able to talk to us of generalities and specifics that come with being an older woman in the very comfort of her life.

"Well," she began, "you are the very loveliest group of girls that I have ever laid eyes on."

"Oh," Jane replied, "thank you but you make us blush."

"Oh, that is very good then, for blushing makes a woman more beautiful."

"So," I began, "I confess that we are quite curious to know about you. You must understand that it has only been recently that we learned that there even were American Darcys."

She waved her gloved hand toward the window. "Oh, there are a multitude of us in America, and we spring up here and there, like rabbits. Especially at the rate that we are multiplying."

"Then you are a large family?" I asked, hopeful.

"Yes, and if you all continue in this vein, you are sure to be popular amongst us. We love vital and amusing young people."

"If that is the case," Georgiana said, "then you are quite different than our side of the family back home."

Cousin Emilia snorted. "Oh! If you are talking about Lady Catherine De

Bourgh, then yes, we are *very* different. Is she still in the habit of refusing to ever mention me?"

I was disarmed at her bluntness at first, but my interest was very much roused.

"I confess," Georgiana admitted, "that she has never uttered anything of you, and very little about Cousin Thomas."

Again, a disgusted sound in her throat. "Of course she hasn't. We hadn't met each other for more than two minutes before it was decided between us that we would perpetually despise one another."

"And what was her reason for disliking you?" Kitty asked. "For I have heard that she can be very disagreeable, and I am assuming that it was she who made the first slight."

Cousin Emilia raised her hands to her chest. "Oh, you know the truth of her. Good! And that will make my arguments on the matter more pleasant. Well, at first it was simply because she disagreed with Thomas for marrying me. She did not think I was 'worthy' enough for him."

"She thought the same thing of me with Mr. Darcy!" I added, happy to not be alone, and even happier to have something in common with the woman whose acquaintance I relied on turning into a stronger one.

"Then that means you are the perfect woman for him!" Cousin Emilia stated bluntly, "Lady Catherine is a woman who has never been right a day in her life, and I daresay never will be. Forgive me for speaking so bluntly, but when you get my age, well my dears, you begin to understand that you lose nothing by speaking the truth sometimes. And by sometimes, I mean most often."

"It is fine," Kitty said, beaming. "I am quite interested in all this."

"And I," Georgiana admitted. "But Cousin Thomas married you all the same."

"Aye, he did, and I daresay that he has never regretted it, nor have I for that matter. And our number of children is proof of that."

"How many children do you have?" Kitty asked.

"Oh, we have nine."

"Nine!" We all chuckled, intrigued.

"Yes, we initially had eleven, but one died in infancy and the other died of pneumonia when he was a child."

"Oh, we are sorry for that," I said with true sympathy.

"It is fine, for though I would have enjoyed the idea of having two more with me, having nine healthy children grow to adulthood and be mostly healthy does satisfy me greatly. That is why it is nice that you are come now."

"And why so?"

"Well, a mother spends so much of her life doing everything to raise her children to become independent adults. Then they do so, and she no longer has them around to depend on. Of my nine children, seven of them are girls. Four of them have married very well, but their husbands all live elsewhere, and mostly in the north and west. My eldest, Samantha, lives with her husband, a Mr. Eastbourne on his estate in New York. Molly, the second oldest lives with her husband in Boston and they are not so wealthy, but they run a shop together."

"Oh, one of our uncles is involved in trade," Jane said, "and the other is an attorney."

"Very good," Cousin Emilia said, looking more content in knowing that we were a family that was a mixture of gentlemen and tradesmen. "For one of my sons married a merchant's daughter and he lives in Philadelphia still. His name is Joseph and you will love him and his wife, for they are such charming people. Then, my other daughter, Deborah, has taken orders and has become a nun."

"Really?" I was truly surprised.

"Yes, and here is the irony of the matter. I am as religious as the next woman, mind you, but when she decided to take her vows, I was actually a little heartbroken."

"Really?" I asked. "Why was that?"

"I know it sounds wicked, yet so it was. Then there is my other and eldest son, Henry, and he is quite the eligible bachelor in Philadelphia. He has his own barouche and Miss Bennet," she said, looking at Jane, "I think he should love to make your acquaintance."

"Oh," Jane said, color rising into her cheeks, "I would like to make a good first impression."

Another snort. "I can't promise you that he will. One moment he is charming and then the next moment he can be out of humor and sullen. I love my children, but I know what they all are."

"And then," Cousin Emilia continued, "there are my other daughters Victoria, Felicity, Helena, and Esther. Victoria lives in New Jersey with her husband and children. When I have sent word that you are all come, she would love to cross the river to meet you.

"Esther married an attorney who lives in Ohio and we haven't seen her for three years."

I was about to ask why but decided against it.

"Yet Felicity and Helena remain in Philadelphia. Felicity is married to a gentleman named Walter Smith and she will see you often. Helena unfortunately was born with brain damage. She can walk and move, yes, but she can't speak well, and she can't process much thought at all, nor sometimes control her movements, therefore she lives with us so we can nurse her. Yet as I had said before, I am so used to having a house full of children, and now they are all gone and in truth, there is nothing as hard as parting with one's children. One feels so forlorn without them."

I flinched at her words. Could it really be so much a coincidence that my mother had once said the very same thing? Life was a tricky thing in that way, it seemed, or filled with irony.

"But now you are here," she said, "and if we get along splendidly, you can help an old woman feel as if her maternal instincts are still of some use.

She turned to me. "Now, Mrs. Darcy, you were the wonderful creature to catch my young cousin, but am I correct that the rest of you are unattached?"

Georgiana and Jane looked insecure, but Kitty didn't see the impertinence of the question—or didn't seem to care.

"Yes, we are not attached to anyone."

"And do you have any prospects back in England? A gentleman who is pining away for you and misses your presence?"

"I confess that there is none," Georgiana said, and Jane echoed her words.

Their confession was met with eagerness and excitement on Cousin Emilia's end.

She clapped her chubby hands together. "That is wonderful news."

"And why do you say so?" Georgiana asked.

Cousin Emilia reached out and touched Georgiana's knee. "I admit that I am being selfish now, but you must understand, I am a woman who has seven married daughters, though one is married to our Lord and another is married to her ailment. Therefore, I have nothing else to do but marry everyone else's daughters off as well."

I replied, "Since you have married off so many daughters, clearly this is an area that you excel in greatly."

"Either that, or I am lucky. Yet in your cases, you have beauty, wit and are exotic for being foreigners. Therefore, if I don't have you three wed by summertime, then it will not be my fault!"

Kitty and I laughed at this, and eventually Georgiana and Jane followed suit.

❧

After we arrived at Canterbury, which was a wonderfully beautiful and large home, clearly meant for a family the size of these Darcys, we descended from the carriage. We looked up at the grandeur of the house, complimenting Cousin Thomas and Cousin Emilia on it.

As we followed them inside while the footmen carried our bags, Jane walked close to me and whispered.

"Lizzy, I can see that you like Cousin Emilia, but do you think it was prudent for you to have admitted that Lady Catherine did not approve of you?"

I shrugged. "She confessed the same thing."

"True, but she very well could have been saying that simply to see how you would respond."

"Usually you are the one to contain generous candor."

"I have, but time has taught me to be cautious when my sisters are involved. I am fine with being fooled in my own life, but with you all, I become more on my guard."

"I am happy that you do, Jane, truly, but with Cousin Emilia, I think we need not worry, for she reminds me of someone who I am surprised you didn't think of."

"Who?"

"Our mother. Think on it and you shall see the comparison. And while our mother has not always been the best woman to me, she is still a comforting presence. Therefore, if we left our own mother back in England only to inherit another one while we are here, then I am not one to reject the offer of it."

"Another mother?" Jane thought on it. "Yes, I suppose that it would be nice to have one here for the time being."

"Precisely. We have a chance to be daughters again, and believe me, Jane, when you marry, you miss that simple state somewhat. Even I miss it, and I am fortunate in my choice of husband. Therefore, worry not, Jane, and enjoy it for as long as you are able."

❧❦❧

The part of Canterbury that we first saw was impressive to behold, and Bingley enjoyed the sight of it while Darcy whispered to me that he enjoyed the look of it, but nothing could ever replace Pemberly in his heart.

"So," I said, "how was riding with Cousin Thomas?"

"Educational. I learned that I am still stiff in company and I still lack the talent of conversing easily with people that I have never or barely met before."

"Should I ask you why?" I teased. "Why a man of sense and education, who has lived in the world, should find it so hard to recommend himself to strangers?"

He smiled and nodded. "I suppose that I am forever bashful."

"We shall be in America for two months complete, my love. You shall have time to become acquainted with them, and then they shall love you."

"And if not, I still have Bingley here to make up for my flaws."

"By all means, your friend is at your disposal, but I think that we should find some ease here, for there is nothing so natural and capable of making one merry than the jovialities of family life."

❧ 14 ❧

A NEW ACQUAINTANCE

W hile propriety commanded us to be shown around the house and given a tour, Cousin Thomas easily saw that propriety could go and hang at that moment, for we clearly would be tired from our journey and would also want to have some peace and quiet. So, Cousin Emilia showed us to our rooms, and I was happy to see that Darcy and I were allowed to have our own room, which I worried would not be condoned.

A servant was ordered to request if we would like some tea, coffee or ale before we rested, and after Darcy and I were brought a pitcher of ale, we both undressed and took a nap, wrapped in each other's arms.

We eventually woke up before dinner time, dressed for dinner and then went downstairs to the Dining Hall. I felt slightly embarrassed that we were the last ones to the dinner table, but Cousin Thomas and Emilia did not seem to care much for standing on ceremony. We all sat, food was brought out and we all began to eat.

"Well," Cousin Thomas began, "as I was saying in the carriage ride here, Mrs. Darcy, your husband's father and I had many an adventure."

"Were these adventures of the comical sort?" I smiled. "Or did you have a scheme for them?"

"Oh, we were mischief makers if there ever were any," he said. "The late Mr. Darcy might have been a little worse because he had a pretty face, and as you know, a pretty face can help a person go a long way."

"You were very handsome, Thomas!" Cousin Emilia cajoled. "It is the way of men to never see their beauty."

"Fine then, I will admit to not being *grotesque*, but Fitzwilliam's father was a handsome devil, just like you are, cousin."

Darcy blushed, and I whispered to him from over the table.

"Now is your chance," I mouthed. "Say something amusing."

Darcy at first looked at a loss and then he gathered up his courage.

"Be careful, Cousin Thomas." He laughed nervously. "You make my father out to sound like a rattle or a rake."

"He was not a rake, that's for sure, but like me, he was a bit of a rattle. He broke a couple of hearts, but that is an evil that almost all of us men are guilty of at some point in our lives. Yet it was not just the fairer sex that we loved to have for company, but we did stranger things. We actually partook in wrestling matches."

"What?" Darcy said, almost dropping his fork.

"Yes, your father and I were quite proficient at wrestling and while at the university, there were always secret wrestling matches going on where the students placed their bets on who would win. Your father and I were two fighters in the multitude."

Georgiana gasped. "I would have never suspected that! Our father was always so proper—so refined."

Cousin Thomas twirled his wine glass. "Becoming a father can change a man. It did with me, therefore it had to do so with him. Also, once with a group of men, we tried to swim the English Channel."

"The actual English Channel?" Bingley asked, then reproved himself. "Then again, there is no other one."

Thomas laughed. "No, there isn't. There were seven of us who tried to do it once, and we had our friends in boats, rowing next to us just in case we had to give up or because we were in danger of any kind."

"And?" Kitty said, on the edge of her seat. "Did any of you actually make it across?"

"Unfortunately, there was a heavy wind that day and the tide was against us, so with every stroke that we swam, we were always being pushed back.

"And I remember, two of our mates gave up after a mile, but your father and I continued to go at it with the others. One by one we gave up, and the only reason he and I continued was because of pride, I suppose."

Cousin Thomas looked at my husband, his expression calm. "You know your father, he had much pride, and since I did not give up, he wouldn't, and since he wouldn't give up, I couldn't either. So, we pushed past the pain and kept swimming.

"Then we got two miles from France, and we were so close, but my body just gave up and I began to spasm in the water, getting a cramp. Losing all motor skills, I began to sink, and I was so frightened... so terribly frightened." He paused, recalling the memory. "Then I felt a hand grab hold of me and I felt your father as he wrapped himself around me and helped me float until one of the boats reached us."

"He did that?" Darcy whispered. "He really saved you?"

"Yes, he did," Cousin Thomas said somberly. "Like me, he may not have been perfect, but one thing your father definitely was, was a hero."

"And our mother?" Georgiana asked. "Do you know much about her?"

"I know," Cousin Emilia said, "that up until she met your father, she never believed in love at first sight. Then she met him, and she changed her tune." She gave everyone a sly look. Darcy looked at me across the table and I knew that he was recalling the first time that we met, for it was in a series of stares where both of us could not stop gazing at each other, despite how it would appear to any who looked on us.

"She did?" Georgiana breathed in deeply, ready for a romantic tale.

"Yes, and when she met your father, she was smitten almost immediately. We all laughed and teased her for it."

"Why?" Jane asked.

"Because falling in love at first sight is wonderful in a fantasy tale, this is all too true, but here in the world, it can often be the worst way that you can determine a true romantic partner. You are judging them by how they make you feel in a moment, and not over how they make you feel for long periods of time." Cousin Emilia became thoughtful. "Yet she was rare, and I suppose if she were to fall in love with someone so quickly, she chose the correct man to do it with. Mr. Darcy may have been a rattle, but he became the best of men for her."

"What a beautiful story," Jane said, almost reverently

"It is the way of this family," Cousin Thomas said. "We love a good story as much as we love happy endings, therefore we make it a hidden rule that we all have to go out and make stories of our own. And one can't do that by being rigid."

"Ah!"

We heard a strange voice from behind us. We turned and there was a tall man standing in the doorway.

"My father is giving the whole 'we Darcy's love a good story' speech again. And that must mean that you are family."

❧

"Henry!" Cousin Emilia cried, standing up. "You sly dog! Coming in all quiet like that."

"You know I love the element of surprise, Mother," Henry said, coming forward. "That way one can always walk in on something that one is not meant to overhear."

"Oh, quiet you," Cousin Thomas said as we all stood up. "Fitzwilliam, Mr. Bingley, and ladies this is our eldest son, Mr. Henry Darcy. And Henry, these are your cousins, Mr. Fitzwilliam Darcy and his sister, Miss Georgiana. And this is his wife, Mrs. Elizabeth Darcy, her sisters Miss Jane Bennet and Miss Kitty Bennet, along with their good friend, Mr. Charles Bingley."

We all bowed and curtsied in turn and Henry looked around at all of us and nodded his head.

"Well, hello, and..."

Then he suddenly turned on his heel and walked away. All of us were left there at a loss, except for Cousin Emilia who shrugged her shoulders and began to follow her son.

"Tell them something, quickly," she said to Cousin Thomas.

"Yes, thank you, my dear." He was obviously annoyed. then he sat down, and we all sat down as well.

"Please forgive my son Henry," he began. "He seems to forget that being five and thirty years old means that he has to overcome his shyness often and learn how to act like a proper new acquaintance."

15

THE AMERICAN DARCYS

"Oh," Jane said, "so he is just simply bashful when meeting new company?"

"That is part of it," Cousin Thomas replied. "Though I often wonder if it might be best that he doesn't talk to you. My son is a brilliant man, and he knows it. Thus, his nature can sometimes lean toward wit and sarcasm, which is often not fully acceptable to everyone who speaks to him.

"Yet he, when you get used to him, is a very learned and good sort of man. I suppose I spawned a man who is more like a cat. He is slow to trust anyone and make new acquaintances, but once he does, he grows very affectionate and becomes a great companion, if I say so for myself," he finished proudly.

"Well," I said, gently, "then we shall excuse him, for being shy among strangers is a very common trait that one should not be so quick to call a great flaw in a person. We have all learned that first impressions can be dangerous things to rely too heavily upon."

"Thank you for that, Mrs. Darcy," Cousin Thomas said, appearing lighter. "For that is all too true. Henry is slow to start, but he always gets there by the end. Out of my two sons, Joseph is the one who loves to meet new people, and is curious about everything, and Henry was always the reverse, not wishing to ever meet anyone, but being fiercely loyal to those he was around."

"Then that is an admirable trait indeed," I concurred.

"Every parent, despite themselves, does have his favorite child, no matter how hard we try to do otherwise."

"Is Joseph yours?"

"On the contrary, my daughters are my pride and joy, but that is often the way that it is with fathers when they have many children.

"If a man loves his wife, then his daughters remind him of her, and if he doesn't love or even like his wife, then the affection that is lacking there can be made up by his love for his children.

"As you see, Emilia and I married for love. It has never done us anything but good—and we are lucky for it. Love does not always lead to happy endings, as it would seem, and sometimes it can lead to being a nuisance, but not here on Canterbury. And my daughters, well, I was also sorry when Deborah became a nun, even though I should be proud. A beautiful nun is always a terrible waste, I think."

Mr. Bingley choked on his food to hide his guffaw.

"Oh, you all were thinking it." Cousin Thomas chuckled. In truth, I could see his point.

"And Deborah was one of the loveliest of my daughters, so it was a little painful. However, Felicity and Samantha were always the most enjoyable and lovely as well, for they had the most wonderful of dispositions—they were lively and energetic. My other daughter, Molly, can be quite loud and boisterous, but I sort of like that as well, no matter how much she gets censured for it, for she is open and artless—long ago I learned that those demure and serene women did not signify that they were sophisticated.

"Experience has simply taught me that they usually are just the best ones at hiding their true nature. With an open woman like Molly, a man knows what he is getting, but with the women that society sometimes praises, a man often finds that he is engaged to one woman, then he marries her and is trapped because she changes utterly into someone else now that she has caught him."

"Thank you!" Kitty exclaimed, but then she remembered herself and quieted down. "Oh, I mean..."

"It is fine dear, as you can see, I love having like-minded women amongst me."

We continued to talk about Cousin Thomas's family when Emilia returned.

"I am so sorry for our son's absence," she said hurriedly, "and I know that his manners at present do not recommend him at all."

"Oh, never mind that," Cousin Thomas said. "I've apologized for him enough for the both of us and now our company here is actually very interested in hearing about the rest of our children... you know, the *ones who actually learned not to speak a sentence and then run away.*"

Emilia tutted at him. "Henry is a good man, Thomas, and you know that."

"I do, but being his father allows me the right to berate him as much as I like and call it love. For love it still is. I was just about to tell them about Molly and Esther."

"Oh, I wish that they lived closer!" Emilia said, happy to change the subject. "They were very like you Miss Bennets and you as well, Georgiana. So full of life and vigor. Naturally, it is the way of mothers to lean toward the sons of her family, for they remind her of their father—"

"I just said the same thing about a father with his daughters," Cousin Thomas added.

Cousin Emilia gave him a warm gaze. "Yes, it can be the way of the world. So, Joseph is my pride and joy and Henry, despite his flaws, has a special place in my heart, but no matter how loud our lives were with all our children in the house, I wish often that they didn't marry.

"Though tomorrow, invitations will be sent to Victoria and Samantha as well to influence them to leave their comfortable abodes in New Jersey and New York and come here for a week or two. I accept that you can never get to know Molly and Esther, but you shall meet Felicity and Joseph when we attend church. And I shall let you meet Helena—when she is ready for it."

"Oh, take all the time you like on that score," Mr. Bingley said. "For that must not be an easy endeavor, but I'm sure that your daughter does the best she can with her condition."

Cousin Emilia nodded, agreeing. "She does, very much so. Now if you don't mind, might I dominate the conversation by telling you all stories of the foolish and comical things that my children did as they grew up, for it is a mother's province to love to walk down memory lane and recall such things."

"We would love that greatly," I said, "for our own mother does it often."

"Oh, bless her then, for she helped you grow accustomed to the musings of us older women."

Cousin Emilia and Thomas then began to regale us with all the stories of their children from when they were toddlers to when they reached their teens.

Joseph, Esther and Felicity were the ones who had the worst episodes of pimples on their faces that they worried would never leave and made them self-conscious.

Molly accumulated many freckles over time, and they covered her face. For the most part, all the sisters were a little jealous of Deborah and Samantha because they had perfect skin, but when Deborah took her vows, they all ceased to be envious of her.

For the longest time, Henry suffered from being short, then when he turned seventeen years old, he grew over six inches, making him around five foot and ten inches. He grew more confident in himself, for before then, he never could even utter a word in the presence of girls and often got tongue-tied and embarrassed himself often. Henry had suffered being easily nervous while Joseph was the one who gathered much of the ease of manner that made him able to recommend himself to strangers.

Both Thomas and Emilia did not have much to say on the people that their children married, however.

"For what is there to say?" Cousin Thomas added. "They were born, they live, our children fell in love with them, they are good enough people, and now they are all married. That's all."

We all got the impression quite quickly just how much Emilia and Thomas were family people who felt bonds very strongly, to the point where they didn't like change. This could be good and bad, but for our sake, I was happy with their natures, for if they liked to bond with family swiftly, then they would embrace us even more.

By the time that the dinner had ended, we learned almost every detail about the nine Darcy children, and then we all sat by the fire in the sitting room, where we told Emilia and Thomas all about our family of Bennets, Gardiners and Phillips. Yet by the end of it, we still wished to not only hear of but see the rest of our cousins, the American Darcys.

❧ 16 ❧

GETTING TO KNOW YOU

W hen we retired for the evening, and Darcy and I were left to enjoy the comfort of each other in our bedroom, he removed his cravat and turned to me.

"Elizabeth, my love, I am so sorry for all that lacking of refinement or propriety earlier."

I kicked off my shoes. "What do you mean? Oh, you are speaking of Henry?"

"Well, yes, but I was mostly speaking of Cousin Thomas and Emilia of course."

"Why?" I was confused, for I was truly perplexed at what offense he could have taken from their behavior.

"They have barely known us for a day and they already told us everything about their lives, without paying any respect to propriety and lacking in restraint."

"Are you indeed in earnest? That is what you complain of? What is so wrong with your cousins being open in nature?"

He continued to undress. "They have no sense of discretion."

I watched him, careful to show no emotion. "We are their family."

"Whom they just met."

"And?"

Indeed, I knew my husband to be reserved and sometimes severe, but this side of the Darcys was precisely the warmth of affection that we needed.

"My dearest, they were just trying to make us comfortable. And for my part, and if you noticed for your sister's part, they succeeded."

"Did they? Elizabeth, you have an artless manner, but you cannot be so blind to not see that their behavior requires more tact?"

I stiffened. "What do you mean that I cannot be so blind?"

"I... you are sometimes too trusting."

"And you can be a hypocrite," I responded.

"What?"

I turned to him, hands on hips. "Yes, they told us all about their lives, but how is that any more lacking in decorum than when you first tried to kiss me in the park when we had never officially met? Or when you practically pulled me into a room to kiss me at the Aginfield Ball and then almost was the ruin of me? What is worse?"

"From what I recall, you enjoyed both of those moments," he said bitterly.

I swung away. "I never said I didn't! I am just pointing out the obvious, which is that you criticize your cousins for one thing that you are also guilty of, but more so. I thought that you had changed."

"What? In the months that you have known me?"

I flinched and was appalled! How could he have said such a thing to me in response?

"That last sentence was so tactless," I muttered, "that it doesn't deserve a response. For the moment, your family has embraced us and shown a very good sort of nature about them that was not only well-meaning, but warm and engaging. I will reserve judgment on them for now, because they deserve better. And they are your family, not mine. Therefore, why am I the one who is being lenient on them?"

I began to take off my dress.

"Now I wish to speak no more for the night," I said firmly. "Let us both go to bed."

"Elizabeth..."

"I said good night!"

I got into my nightgown and slipped into bed. Very soon I heard and felt Darcy slide into bed next to me and then blow out the candle, covering us in the darkness of night.

The next morning, I woke up to see Darcy silently putting on his robe, as a bath was being drawn up for him in the neighboring bathing room.

I rolled over, looked at him, and smiled.

"Were you trying not to wake me?"

He looked up, apprehensive and then his muscles relaxed when he saw that my tone was amicable.

"I know that you need your rest and I was just trying to be accommodating."

"No, you just didn't know whether I would be happy if I woke up or if I would still be angry with you. Admit it?"

He lifted one eyebrow in my direction. "Yes, that is so."

"Well, I have slept through my annoyance, and have you slept through your prejudice?"

"My prejudice?"

"Yes. That is where the root of this inability to tolerate your family lies. You have been trained to regard one thing and one thing only as acceptable in regards to being proper, and when someone acts in a way that is different, you are prejudiced against their nature. And this is not me hurting you at all. I would compliment you every day if you just gave me one reason."

"I know... I am simply ashamed." He tightened the belt on his robe.

"How so and what for?"

"As much as I would not wish to admit, you are correct. I did not act any better than they did when I first met you. If anything, I was worse."

"Precisely, and if you could act such a way, desiring intimacy so soon after meeting a woman, then why is it so strange for them to want to let us know who they are after so short an acquaintance?"

I sat up in bed. "And in my case, how can I disregard them when I am also no better? When you first were about to kiss me in the park, did I push you away? Did I slap you? No I did not. I was actually willing to let a man who was practically a stranger kiss me, because I simply desired him.

"I am not better than you. And when you took me to the library at Aginfield and we became intimate, did I stop you? I could have cried out, screamed or resisted, but I did nothing. I let you and therefore, even though you were the originator, I still went along with it, making me just as guilty of breaking down the walls of propriety."

I scooted to the side of the bed and let my legs dangle. "And we cannot forget that it was I who walked the three miles, in the rain, so that we could become husband and wife even before we committed to a ceremony. Therefore, my husband, who are we to judge them? Especially when all of their manners are harmless?"

He shrugged his shoulders and sat down at my side.

"You are right, I suppose," he said, and I sighed out, happy that he had relented finally.

"Darcy, we are in the presence of your family who are quick and willing to accept you if you give them a reason. You may have your peace—if you can keep it."

He rubbed my leg fondly.

"I am too shy, aren't I?"

"My love, even at your worst moments, you never walked into a room, spoke a sentence, then walked out and didn't bother to care about how it looked on your family. Henry's behavior has proven that whatever your faults, there are much worse people in the world."

"Would you like me to speak with Henry? For though we have not met, I still don't like how he felt he could treat my wife and family."

I chuckled and touched his stubbled cheek. "You need not worry on that score, for I am quite sure that his mother gave him a mouthful. And even if she didn't, I am also certain that Cousin Thomas did."

"Well, I shall recline then, but if he continues in the same vein, then I will speak up."

"And I like that you will, just as I was happy how you defended us when we were in Maryland. Never stop defending us, Fitzwilliam. Just don't close yourself off."

"Aye, I think I can do that."

"Very good." Then we kissed.

"And to think," he said, "I was worried that you would wake up angry."

"I have a notorious tendency to fall asleep with one emotion and then wake up feeling quite another."

Laughing, we kissed again.

That day, Cousin Emilia gave us a tour of her lovely home and grounds, then we also met Helena. Although she was mentally impaired, Helena could speak somewhat, and when she couldn't, she and her mother had a way of communicating through sign language. Helena was too clumsy and disoriented to ever be presented to many strangers as well as to be in company for too long, but she managed to wave hello to us and communicate. She could speak, yes, but very little. Therefore, since she found talking not always easy, she learned sign language as well.

She thought Jane was very lovely and liked the way that Kitty, Georgiana and I looked when we laughed or smiled. I felt sorry for Helena, because her life was a sad one in the end. If she had been born without her disability, she would have been able to do much. For with her disability, she clearly tried to do the best she always could, but her life would always, in some way, be limited.

Cousin Thomas had to oversee some business in town, for he had stock in many companies as well as being a merchant who was involved in trade, which was nice to know, for in that regard, we could recommend trade with our Uncle Gardiner with him. However, if war between our countries were to occur, then there would be no hope for it.

We all sat down to tea after Emilia showed us her home, which though very beautiful, also was very comfortable as well. She then told us that if we liked, we could enjoy some time alone in the library, the billiards room, or enjoy some moments of solitude in our rooms until dinner, for she did not really believe in everyone being forced to remain in the same room all day and bore each other!

"Sometimes a good hostess lets her company choose their paths," she said. "Life has taught me that. If you like, I can have some tables brought and we play cards or charades, but something tells me that after being on a ship for so long where you were always in the presence of others, you need some moments of leisure and calm, rather than structure and rigidity."

"Upon my honor!" Mr. Bingley cried. "Mrs. Darcy, you are extraordinary, and it makes me so glad."

"I see that I have said the correct thing?"

Georgiana laughed, taking in Bingley's eagerness. "Clearly you have."

Bingley spoke up again. "But can you blame my alacrity in response? For that concept, that ever-tedious practice of ours to feel as if we must always have to entertain each other and be in each other's company, when we sometimes want to be left to our own devices can be ever so restrictive."

"I agree," Jane said. "Sometimes I want my moment alone and besides, we all need to write our letters back to our families today and will take hours to finish writing our correspondence."

This was a fine point that we all agreed to, for it was an oversight that we all almost missed.

"Perfect," Cousin Emilia said. "Letters are something you don't wish to get behind in your correspondence. However, make sure that you rest as well, because tomorrow is when we bring you out to see society and the city that is Philadelphia."

꧁꧂

With free time, Darcy sat in the library and addressed some letters that required immediate attention, and I sat at another desk and wrote to our parents, to Mary, as well as to the Gardiners.

It would be some time before we received a reply, for I had to accustom myself to the fact that we were separated by an ocean.

After Darcy answered his letters of business and concerns of Pemberly, we both sat down and wrote a letter to Earl and Lady Fitzwilliam, telling them about the quality of our journey, and we wrote a letter to Colonel Fitzwilliam.

"It is strange, when I think on it," I said.

"What is?"

"Well, Colonel Fitzwilliam is very important to you and I have grown to like him immensely, but none of my other family really knows him. Except for the Gardiners, he has not made the acquaintance of any of the rest of them."

Darcy nodded. "Very true. Well, may he survive the Peninsular War, and come back to us, for he will always help to make the inclusion of your family into our world."

I gave my husband a warm smile. "Yes, he would do that quite nicely."

Once our last letters were finished, it was time for dinner and Cousin

Thomas had arrived home by that time as well. Yet now, we were also joined by Henry, who had gone into town to bring his sister Felicity as well as her husband to meet us.

Felicity Darcy—oh forgive me, Felicity Franklin, for that was her married name—and her husband were a very easy couple to get used to. And this was the first moment where Kitty's initiative truly had worked wonders.

Kitty made a bold choice of assuming that Cousin Emilia's open nature had been passed down to her children, for their parents often told us so. Therefore, when Felicity arrived, Kitty grabbed Georgiana's hand, and then told her to grab mine, and then to grab Jane's and we ran out of Canterbury Manor to meet the carriage.

When Felicity stepped down from the carriage to meet us, our excitement at seeing her made her immediately wish to take to us and she had the impulse to offer us a hug, which was very much a good way of making us all comfortable with each other immediately. Her husband, Mr. Edmund Franklin, also was an easy man to get along with, but he was willing to let Felicity do all the talking, which was wise.

Henry remained lingering in the background, not speaking often, but staring at everyone, at a loss as to how to approach us. Every now and again, his mother tried to include him in the conversation, but his response was also curt and stilted.

During dinner, Felicity and her husband had some news that sparked the conversation up immediately.

"My wife and I have a very important announcement to make," Mr. Franklin said. Felicity stood next to her husband and smiled.

"I would like to announce," she said, "that I am with child!"

The reaction of the room was excitement to say the least, but any reaction that we could give was mute compared to her mother's reaction. She practically cried out in exhilaration in a way that could crack a window.

"Yes," Felicity said. "I have been to the doctor and it is certain that I have been pregnant for two months now."

"Oh, finally!" Cousin Emilia cried, clapping her hands together. "I have been waiting for you to give me a grandchild. I wonder if it will be a girl or a boy. I'll like either one, but it is still fun to think on it."

"I want a boy," Mr. Franklin said. "But Felicity wants a girl."

"Girls are all that I know," Felicity said. "Therefore, having a boy just yet would overwhelm me."

"I'm not so sure about that, Felicity," Henry said, perking up, "you helped raise me."

"Henry!" Felicity gave her brother a fond look. "As an older sister, I could never get you to clean up after yourself, no matter how much I threatened to not let you eat if you didn't make sure things were tidy."

He shrugged his shoulders. "I despise cleaning, that is my sin."

"That is not your only sin," Darcy whispered under his breath for only me to hear.

"But my dear," Emilia said, "you must make sure to take care of yourself and not make any swift movements."

"If my child can't survive my energy when it's within me, mother, then I don't know how it will survive when it is out of me. For while I promise to look after myself, I am so far from objecting to dancing, that I must undergo it at the dance this week."

"What dance?" Mr. Bingley asked.

Felicity turned to her mother, eyebrows lifted. "Oh, you didn't tell them? Yes, there is going to be an assembly dance in honor of Fitzwilliam Darcy's wedding."

◈◈◈

"Pardon?" Mr. Darcy questioned, "Forgive me, I knew that there would be a ball for us possibly, but I assumed that it would take a while for it to occur."

"We love moving quickly here," Cousin Thomas said. "And we can still have a ball after the assembly."

"In truth," Emilia said, gazing around the room, "once you confirmed that you were coming to Philadelphia, we decided to tell all of our neighbors about your marriage and your arrival. Well, we Philadelphians are like any other, and we love any reason to come together and have a dance, though our dancing quarters will not be nearly as illustrious as yours. We then suggested to everyone that if you were of the open and dancing sort, we would love our next assembly to be in your honor, and the next assembly will take place in four days' time."

"So, we figured that we'd butter you up," Cousin Thomas said. "And if you liked us enough, we were going to ask you this evening, but my crafty daughter over there just had to beat us to the punch."

"I only anticipated you by a few minutes, Father," Felicity said with a laugh. "And I think I introduced the idea quite well."

"Well," Cousin Thomas asked, "would you mind our eagerness? Or are you all open to the idea of this assembly?"

"Well, I love to dance," Kitty said, "as does Elizabeth and Jane, don't you both?"

"Yes, we do, therefore we are open to the idea."

"And," I added, "thank you for celebrating our wedding so soon."

"And also" Kitty interjected, "Georgiana is a wonderful dancer."

Georgiana blushed. "I am not the best, but I do love to do it."

"Then all that is left is to look at the gentlemen and pressure them into acceptance," Felicity said, and we all looked at Darcy and Bingley.

"Well, I always think nothing is superior in the world to dancing with lovely and pleasant women," Bingley said. "Therefore, I find there to be no objection to this scheme, for out of the both of us, I am the dancer and Darcy here is not."

❦

"My nephew is not a dancer? How shocking," Thomas said.

Darcy smirked. "Bingley, you misrepresent me to my family. I can dance; I just normally don't do it."

"Oh!" Emilia cried out. "Another man who doesn't like to dance? Henry can dance well, but he also chooses not to."

"To dance requires talking," Henry said, "and I am not the best at making small conversation, Mother, you know this. It is only your love for me that makes you believe that anything I say is worth taking heed to."

"Are you so severe upon yourself?" Jane asked. "You are too hard on your own nature."

"Am I?" Henry questioned, looking at Jane in earnest.

"Yes. For there is so much pressure in supplying a good conversation that is stimulating to its hearers, and therefore sometimes that pressure leads to getting nervous. And therefore, conversation becomes less words spoken between two people and becomes more like a performance; some of us are not meant for the stage."

"That is precisely what I have felt," Henry admitted, clearly happy to find a like-minded person in Jane.

Jane gave him a warm smile. "Then take heart. I used to have a hard time smiling and talking at the same time, because the smiling was always easy, but the talking took some work. And what to talk about took even more work. But with time and effort, one can overcome one's nerves. Do you want to know the secret?"

Henry leaned forward. "Pray tell, what is it?"

"Understanding that conversation is a talent that not all of us are born equal in. If you are not the best at speech, then don't regard it as if it is a sin, but something that life has thrown at you. My sisters actually were very much better at speaking than I was."

"You seem to speak perfectly well," Henry said, and the compliment was clearly intended for flattery.

Color appeared on Jane's cheeks. "Thank you, but for very long, I was terrible at it. People called me serene and demure because I was soft-spoken, when in truth, I was soft-spoken because I was timid and never knew what to say. I could get a person to like me, but never for long before they would turn to the left of themselves and start speaking to another person. I therefore decided to learn how to practice at it, and I did so. I began to speak more, even when I clearly had nothing worthwhile to say."

Henry nodded in agreement. "That is my very problem, I suppose. I only speak when I have something of import to say, but I very rarely have anything important to talk about."

"Importance of a subject varies in proportion to its importance to you. If you woke and you had a strange dream, then speak about it. If you stepped in a puddled and wet your stockings, then talk about it. Our lives don't have to move mountains for us to move a word."

Henry raised his eyebrows. "And the cure of this is just to talk?"

"Yes," Jane answered. "It is the only cure. And accepting the fact that just because everyone is a better talker than you, doesn't make your words any less important. All my life, everyone will always be a greater talker than I am, but my words surely must have some meaning somewhere. Or at least, I like to think so."

"I'm certain that your words carry great weight," Henry assured her.

"Thank you, Mr. Darcy." Jane glanced around the room. "Dear lord, there are many Mr. Darcys in this room at once, that it makes me quite confused."

We all laughed at Jane's joke.

"But still," Jane urged, "try and speak, then forgive yourself even if your words are not the best. As long as you give no offense, your virtue is complete for you have given the person the chance of getting to know you."

❧ 17 ❧

HISTORY REPEAT ITSELF

All throughout the dinner, Henry would steal glances at Jane. Every now and again, Jane would smile back, but she remained looking at everyone equally, and I wondered if I was the only one who noticed this. Yet I was not.

I looked down the table and every now and again I saw Cousin Emilia looking between them both and I could see her mind working as a mother's often would. And she had been correct in her first assertion of her own nature when she met us: she had nothing else to do but marry my sisters off as best she could.

After dinner, we sat down by the fireplace, enjoying our company. Emilia made sure to arrange everything in a way to have Henry sit next to Jane and they both talked quietly to each other while we all pretended not to watch but did so through our peripheral vision.

"Did you notice Henry's attentions toward Jane this evening?" I asked my husband while we were all alone in our bedroom. We had just gotten done being intimate with one another and we lay bare under the sheets while he ran his hand over my thighs.

"Oh, I noticed," he replied. "And it makes me uneasy."

"It makes me uneasy as well, but I want to know what your reasons are for it?"

"Because sometimes people confuse desperation for affection. Jane is not just a great beauty, but she's also a kind and forgiving person. My cousin Henry is—well, I don't even know fully what type of man he is yet —but he seems closed off, reserved sometimes, and is not the best at recommending himself to others. I don't want him attaching himself to your sister simply because he has no one else to do it to."

"Precisely," I agreed, snuggling up to my husband. "Like-mindedness is well and good, but one should not determine affection on the foundation of all that a person has in common with another, but also how to overcome when they are not in harmony with each other."

My love stroked my hair. "True."

"What shall we do?"

"I think it wise to let matters unfold at the moment, for there is nothing that we can do. Your sister and Henry are both adults and therefore there is no need for us to worry on their parts."

"I know, but I still can't help but be worried."

"The worst that can happen is one of them suffers under a broken heart."

"Dearest, you know as well as I do that *that* can be the worst pain of all."

He looked away from me, remembering what self-inflicted heartbreak once almost did to him.

"True and that's why we have to do nothing."

I rose up on one elbow. "What do you mean?"

"Because no matter what we say, they are adults, and they will do what they want to do anyway."

"Oh, you are correct in that way. Let us just make it through our assembly for a start, and then we'll take it from there."

"I am content with that. Which reminds me, remind me tomorrow to show you where I keep my spare pistols in the carriage."

I sat up straight, his words a shock to me. "What?"

"Yes, I keep a spare set of pistols in a carriage when I travel, for protection in case of an emergency. I should show it to you. Later, I'll teach you how to shoot them."

"I am content with that, yet how did you think of that based on the discussion that we were having?"

"Oh, we were speaking of Henry Darcy."

"And?"

"And he reminds me of someone in particular."

"Who?"

"Myself, before I reformed. And you recall, Lizzy, I was not to be trusted once, therefore trusting him is not something I am likely to do."

I nuzzled his shoulder with my nose. "Are you implying that you would pull a pistol on your own cousin if he were to get cheeky with us or turn into a libertine?"

"Yes."

I chuckled to myself, amazed at my husband's potentially drastic measures to protect those under his care.

"You, my husband, are a marvel of a man."

"And you are *my* lady."

༺༻

Instead of seeing the sights, we then spent the next four days either visiting neighbors with Cousin Emilia so that we could get acquainted with them before the assembly or learning some dances that were popular in America that were unknown to us in England.

"I don't see why Fitzwilliam does not like to dance," Cousin Emilia said, watching him practice. "For he quite excels at it."

"It is not something he lacks any talent in," I commented, "but it's his will. I don't know why he doesn't like to dance, for I have never asked him."

"Fitzwilliam!" Cousin Emilia called out to him.

"Yes, Cousin Emilia," my husband answered.

"I was just asking your wife, and she had no answer, therefore I have no choice but to attack you directly. Why do you dislike the amusement of dancing so?"

"I am embarrassed to say."

"You are amongst family here; therefore, there is no need to feel ashamed, no matter how much you think so. We are all friends here."

Darcy gave me a look and I nodded my encouragement, in hopes of him taking my lead. He closed his eyes and flexed his hand.

"Well," he began, "I have often confessed of a certain rigidity of my own nature."

"What do you mean?" I asked, actually surprised with his admission.

"You have heard me boast of my main flaw," he said. "I cannot vouch for my temper, and that I call resentful. My good opinion, once lost, is lost forever. Sometimes that implacability stretches towards myself and creates a self-loathing. When I fail myself in some way, I can sometimes reject a certain part of me. One time, when I was dancing, well... I fell down."

I suppressed my look of surprise. "You did?"

"Yes, it was in the middle of a ball and I fell, tripping over my own feet. I embarrassed myself terribly as well as my dance partner, who spent the rest of the dance looking at me with venom in her eyes. When the dance was done, I ran from that ballroom, ordered my carriage to be brought and my valet Jefferson and I were off. However, I am certain that my shameful episode was the talk on everyone's tongue for the rest of the month. They were too afraid of my father to mock me to my face, yet it was very plain that they laughed about it often and I was exposed to the center of many jokes."

"Oh, Darcy," I whispered. "Why did you never tell me?"

"Because it... hurts to remember it. I fell on my bottom, Lizzy, and every time I sit in a seat or lay in bed, sometimes the memory of that fall and touch of the floor comes back to me and I remember my shame. That's the painful thing about memory; it never lets you go often."

"And that's why you are afraid to dance, because you fear falling again?"

"Yes, only when I am so well acquainted with a person can I dance with them because I grow comfortable, and I am less likely to make a mistake. I am less likely to fall."

Ceasing to care about the lacking in decorum, I breached what was deemed appropriate, walked up to him, took his hand in my own and kissed his cheek.

"Don't fear the fall," I said, "just be angry at those who never cared to watch you stand up again."

Darcy pressed my hand to his cheek.

"Oh, bless me," Cousin Emilia said while Georgiana, Kitty and Jane looked away. "You both are quite besotted! That is so very perfect. And I can't wait for you to stand up together at the assembly on Saturday!"

The assembly was not of any aristocratic heights, but one that seemed to belong to the working class as much to the highest circles.

The dance took place not in an official assembly room, but in a large warehouse room that was cleared out and made to accommodate many. The warehouse belonged to a man named Fitzpatrick, who ran a brewery and ale house. Upon entering, we were not met with many looks and silence, but many looks combined with cheering.

When we had entered, Cousin Thomas announced us, and called out to everyone that his nephew had come with a company of wonderful ladies, and a handsome man who was single and willing to dance. Mr. Bingley's smile at this description made him immediately recommend himself to every young woman in the room.

Many people expressed their congratulations to us, Mr. Fitzpatrick and his jovial wife were introduced to us and then they began the first dance. It was lively, and Fitzwilliam and I were asked to dance the first set, for the night was in honor of us.

"Are you comfortable enough around me not to fear falling?" I said archly.

"I am prepared for anything."

Further down the row of couples, I saw Henry stand up with Jane and Georgiana stood up with Mr. Bingley. Kitty unfortunately did not have a partner for the first dance, and she stood with Cousin Emilia for the first set. But trust in our cousin, for by the very next set, Kitty was asked to dance by a man who Emilia introduced her to.

Also at the dance, we met our other cousin, Joseph Darcy and his wife, Cecilia. We immediately saw why Emilia favored him, for Joseph was a very fine and well-spoken young man, his wife seemed very sweet, and he declared that he would love to dance with all of us cousins before the end of the evening.

However, Henry had asked Jane for a second dance, which she accepted readily, and they were both off to enjoy The Country Dance. Darcy and I wished to sit the next set out while Kitty danced with her partner, and this time, Mr. Bingley was seen dancing with a woman who none of us recalled ever meeting. She had dark brown hair, a few freckles on her face, but her features did have a unique brilliancy to them as well as the fact that she had a very handsome figure.

While Bingley and she danced together, I watched Mr. Bingley's face and expressions. He looked quite engrossed by her company and she was laughing as well. Mr. Bingley was the sort of man who was easily amused and enjoyed a beautiful dance partner as much as the next man. However, there was something different about his expression this time. His eyes rested on her too often to be simple amusement, and he also was very attentive to every word that she said.

At one point, when Darcy and I had danced together, we came close to Mr. Bingley and the woman as they moved along the set and were conversing all the while.

"My father is involved with trade as well," she reported. "And he also has some involvement in textiles."

"That is wonderful. My father used to have a factory here in Pennsylvania and in New York, but I sold them once I acknowledged that I would have no choice."

"No choice?" Then she nodded. "Oh, you mean the oncoming war."

"Yes, warfare has made such connections between us strained once more." He took her through the dance moves.

"And it all becomes a vicious cycle, does it not? For history to repeat itself is always a great nuisance in regards to mistakes being made. Yet for history to be cyclical so quickly? Our Revolutionary War has not even turned forty years old in our memory and here our countries are again. And once more it is for what I regard as very much avoidable."

"Too many political figures that are making decisions based on their pride, Miss Miriam."

"And their prejudice," the woman named Miss Miriam replied, smiling at him. "I've often found that both tendencies, when driven to extremity, can be vices that are forever linked and always falling on top of each other. There! I just related pride and prejudice to stacks of laundry that one throws into the washroom on any given Sunday!"

Mr. Bingley laughed as they danced down the line.

"Now," Miss Miriam said, chuckling, "since I have got you laughing again, which I find to be a perfect reward for the serious mien that I had you undergo at our dance, let us see if I can make you smile for the next few minutes."

"It is an easy task you place on yourself, for I love to laugh," Bingley promised.

"That is a sentiment that I share. The world is so serious that sometimes to look on it with levity is often the best that can be done. I daresay that laughter keeps us sane."

"Just as gravity in moments lead to sobriety and reason. Both states are welcome for a well-informed and well-rounded individual."

Miss Miriam nodded. "Quite right. I often never trust someone who is too frivolous in manner, nor do I trust someone who is too serious. For the one never has the talent to take anything and regard it of importance, while the other thinks being forever grave means being forever smart, and those are the people who are the most dangerous of all."

⚜

"How are they dangerous?" Mr. Bingley asked, confused.

"Because they are men or women who think too much, and therefore believe that they know all. Those are the sort of people who blind themselves. The world has often suffered under the weight of powerful people whose idea of changing the world is oppressing it, because only their view is right. And when you are a woman, it is worst of all. Being in a social setting, amongst other women! We can oppress each other with even deciding who is wearing the better gown!"

Mr. Bingley laughed.

"So, whenever the moment strikes you," she continued, "Mr. Bingley, chuckle, laugh, girdle, and don't let anyone tell you that you are foolish for doing so, and don't care about their critical words! For as long as you recognize a moment's harshness when they do come, you are still wise."

He slanted her a glance. "You cling to happiness?"

"I cling to true happiness," she retorted.

"True happiness?"

Miss Miriam nodded. "Well yes. Haven't you often found amusement in things that the world has looked down upon, despite their innocence? Many of the higher circles despise theatre and look down on actors. Yet not only do I find no sin in the theatrical world, but I find it to be quite an integral aspect to society."

"That is just what I find!" he agreed. "I love theatre. Even when the actors are not the best, I still somehow enjoy the performance."

"Somehow, I do as well, and I am quite lenient on actors not being at their best sometimes, for it must be hard. Therefore, I take the good and not so good. For example, I know an actress and one performance she gave as Juliet in *Romeo and Juliet* was not the best, but she was such a nice woman, and I could not despise her for it, but gave her the benefit of the doubt for her next performance."

"You believe in giving your fellow man second chances?" he inquired.

"I can't help but do so. For second chances are something that almost all of us need sometime. So, do you have a favorite Shakespeare play? I would think that you would prefer his comedies."

"A person would think so, in regards to my nature, yet I love <u>Othello</u> and <u>Macbeth</u>."

"Really?" She looked genuinely surprised.

"Yes, for *Othello* has a frightening villain whose mind we have full access into. Very often with the comedies, the heroes are very much analyzed, and the villains are often just there to supply the crisis. Yet in <u>Othello</u>, Iago is just frightening because we are shown his mind, making him complicated. You never question your distaste for him, but you still feel compelled to watch everything and be enthralled. And with *Macbeth*, well, those three witches are spellbinding. The rest of the play is wonderful, but something about the Weird Sisters will always rest in the subconscious of the viewer."

"Yes," Miriam agreed, "they do hold their own, yet do you know of the superstition to that play?"

"What superstition is that?"

"It is said that the play in some way is cursed. That in almost every production of it, some calamity has happened in the show to give the show a feeling of bad luck. Therefore, the only way to counteract such a curse, you must never say the name of the play. You can never call it *Macbeth*, especially inside of a theatre, and if you do, then the only way that you can lift the curse from yourself and the production, is if you run out of the theatre, spin around several times and then spit."

"You have to spit too?" Bingley laughed. "Truly?"

"Yes, truly. To keep the bad luck at bay."

"Yet if you can't call the play by its name, then what do you call it?"

"It's often called 'The Scottish Play'," she responded.

"Hmm... And what is your favorite of his plays?"

"I actually like watching *As You Like It*, and the Henry Histories. From Henry IV to Henry V and Henry XI. For some reason, I do enjoy those. Oh, and there is a theatre here in Philadelphia, called The Briar that is right now staging a production of *Timon of Athens*."

"*Timon of Athens*?" he repeated, recalling hearing that one. "That is one of the lesser done of Shakespeare plays."

"I know, and that is what makes it exciting. For they are giving something that is so rarely bestowed."

"I should love to see that, I think."

"My family and I are," she replied. "We are not sure when, yet we will when the family is all available enough for us to make an event of it."

"Then perhaps I can meet your family?" Bingley asked, hopeful.

She gave him a generous smile. "Yes sir. I believe that they would love that."

Mr. Bingley had the good grace to realize not to ask her to dance a second time, and therefore asked to dance with me afterwards, and then Kitty next.

"You seem to be enjoying yourself immensely," I said to him when we danced together.

"Yes, I am, Mrs. Darcy. Upon my honor, I feel quite at home here. The manners of everyone here are like those of everyone in Hampshire. Country manners—you know I think them charming. Therefore, I am quite taken with our reception here in Philadelphia."

"One of them in particular, I see." I nodded in Miss Miriam's direction and Mr. Bingley chuckled nervously.

"You need not fear being open with me, Mr. Bingley," I assured him. "For you know that I am not the sort to repeat what is said in confidence. Yet I wish for there to be no walls between us, for you are the bosom friend of my husband."

"True, yes. Her name is Miriam Goldman, and I know that I have erred against decorum in dancing with a woman who I have not been acquainted with officially yet."

I looked up at him, surprised. "Oh, you haven't been introduced?"

"No, I confess that we have not. We simply bumped into each other as we were walking, and you know me, Mrs. Darcy. Sometimes I engage in conversation immediately and forget about propriety until afterwards."

"I daresay that she didn't think of it either, and it hasn't ruined you in her eyes. And I can see that it hasn't ruined her in your eyes as well."

"It has not."

"When our dance has ended, have one of our many new acquaintances here introduce you to her family so that you can continue to speak with her."

"Are you offering encouragement?" He chuckled. "Why Mrs. Darcy, if I didn't know any better, I would say that you are being taken away by flights of fancy and wish to toss me into a romance."

"I wish for you to always be yourself, Mr. Bingley, and the fact remains that you are a man who enjoys taking pleasure in the innocent company of a woman you find attractive."

"I do enjoy the company of women, truly, yet I don't ever wish to be a rattle in any way."

"You are no such thing, Mr. Bingley. You simply enjoy us."

"Precisely." As we danced so, he caught the eye of Miss Miriam and smiled at her. "Perhaps you are correct, and I shall take your advice. I shall find a way to be introduced to her family."

"Very good, for I believe that you shall enjoy that as opposed to just having danced with her now and then simply staring at her for the rest of the evening."

"I have not been staring."

"You have so!" I laughed.

"Oh, very well, you are correct, I have been."

Our dance ended, and before the next set began, and Mr. Bingley would have to find Kitty, he went over to a group of men who he had become acquainted with. One of them took up the charge of introducing him to the Goldmans who were assembled in one corner of the room.

I watched the interaction and Mr. Bingley was all smiles and liveliness with Miss Miriam Goldman, and she clearly felt the weight of his compliment, for she never took her eye off him. Miriam's mother and sister were also happy to make his acquaintance, but I could tell that Mr. Goldman was a little cold to Mr. Bingley and looked on him dubiously.

It could have simply been that he favored Miriam as a child so much that his paternal instincts took over in such a circumstance. I hoped that his coldness would not be too much to the point that he ruined his daughter's chances, but his wife seemed to notice this and made up for her husband's rigidity by being very welcoming to Mr. Bingley.

When I saw that the whole interaction was mostly a success, I was accosted by Henry Darcy, who requested my hand in the next dance. Surprised, I agreed, and then we took to the floor.

"You are actually a wonderful dancer," I complimented.

"Thank you; you dance remarkably well also," he said. "Mrs. Darcy?"

"Yes?"

"I am sorry for my behavior at our first meeting. I now acknowledge that I must've made a terrible first impression."

"Thank you for your apology," I said. "It was well given, but you need have no fear of me holding it against you, for I once believed in first impressions and carried much weight on them, yet now I do not. And the second and third impressions you have given me improve with each attempt of yours."

"Thank you. My cousin seems to have made a fortunate alliance with you."

"Thank you, but seen in many other lights, I have made one as well."

"Yes, my cousin's fortune makes him quite the object of desirability."

I tilted my head and looked at him. "You look at his worth from an economic standpoint?"

"Well, yes. Have you not?"

"Henry, while wealth and consequence must always make one a more appealing attraction in the eyes of society, that should never be the reason for an affection to be formed or felt. And that is not how I viewed him when entering the married state. I was not even made aware of his wealth when I first met him."

"Oh, forgive me, have I given you offense?"

"Well yes, if you must know."

"Do forgive me," he continued. "I am simply so used to women and their mothers always regarding us men in such a way. Looking at the size of our pocketbook over the demands of the heart that we often feel as if we are being bought as opposed to being chosen."

"We women can be in the same position as well," I acknowledged.

"Yes, but for us, to forever be placed under the scrutiny of such characters, to be regarded simply for how much we are worth. Everywhere that I look, I see people scraping, haggling, and seeking out the eldest son in a family and not regarding the younger ones when they found out that they are not likely to inherit as much."

"That is a heavy scene to watch, and I assume that you are speaking from experience, yet you are the eldest son."

"I am the eldest son who has had to watch his younger brother not always get the attention he deserved because I had the greater inheritance. You have no idea how it makes one feel as if I am being sought after because of my worth. My brother was luckily blessed with charm, and it was able to find him a wife."

"Yet there are so many I have met amongst your acquaintances who have married without much care or concern for their spouses' income. If anything, this city seems to be one bent on love matches."

He smiled at my comment. "It is if you are poor or middle class, but we are the Darcys. We are rich, and therefore people often can't see past that."

"Every station in life comes with its own luxuries and its own burdens. You are free from the chains of poverty and having to always worry over your next meal, and therefore you are bitter about the burden that comes with many seeing your wealth before your person?"

He frowned. "You think I am ungrateful."

"I think you have the right to complain, but you also have a right to count yourself fortunate."

"I suppose that I am."

"You are, and yet, for one who complains about people not seeing you for who you are, you don't always make it easy. If anything, you make it harder, for you sometimes run rather than stand your ground and give someone a chance to make a fair impression of you. Therefore, it is quite possible that you ridicule the world for valuing your wealth too high but don't counteract that tendency because that's all that you let them see of you."

Henry did not reply at first, but we kept dancing on.

After a few seconds, Henry then decided to speak up.

"Your sister has been so fortunate to look at me outside of my wealth."

"Jane is the sweetest of characters," I said, "for she has a love for always seeing the good in others and doesn't wish to think ill of anyone."

"That is a very generous attitude. It is rare to find such steady candor and good will in someone, and to have it be so natural."

"Yes, when growing up," I began, "I often wondered how she could ever manage such kindness all the time and wishing to care and consider the comforts of all around her. I always thought that only once I had her goodness, would I be able to have her happiness. Therefore, it always seemed strange that my life took such a turn of fortune, while hers went in a different direction."

"Her life has not ended," Henry said desperately. "And hope always is on the horizon. Especially for one who deserves it."

"Yes, I believe she does deserve it."

I wondered at his words, for they were frightening to me and also welcoming. He was right in that Jane did deserve to be loved, but I was still unsure if Henry was the right man for her to be sought after.

There was a complexity to him, a darkness that might not be compatible with her lightness and serene nature. Jane was of the sort who needed someone who was like her in temper and disposition—who strove to naturally be in harmony with others around her. She would not do for someone who was too bent on always getting his own way, who was in many ways tainted by the bitterness of reality, or who's first inclination was not to see the good in others.

Opposites did sometimes attract, as it had with Darcy and me, but Darcy's and my resilience were similar. Yes, I smiled when he was sometimes solemn, but we were both stubborn, determined, and our courage always rose with every attempt to intimidate us. We had a voice and we used it.

Jane was soft-spoken and she needed someone who supported her softness with ease of their own, and not harshness.

And yet, was there much difference between Henry and Jane and Darcy and me? Of differences being drawn to one another. Except this time there were no obstacles for them. Henry did not have a fiancé; Jane was not left to doubts and rejection, making them both open.

Therefore, in regards to two different natures being drawn to one another, if history were to repeat itself, then it would be best if it was done with them.

❦ 18 ❦

WORDS NOT MEANT TO BE OVERHEARD

After I finished dancing with Henry Darcy, I walked back to my company and saw Mr. Bingley further off, talking solely with Miriam Goldman and both looked very much engaged in each other.

Somehow, I was more comfortable with them bonding with each other than thinking on Jane and Henry. However, as they spoke, I noticed Joseph through the crowd, looking at Mr. Bingley and Miriam—and if I was not mistaken, he looked worried as well as a little distrustful of the scene. His expression was the way Miriam's father had appeared earlier that night. However, I tore my attention away, annoyed with all the observing that I had done that night, for much of it was not my business.

However, as the night progressed and I wished to sit out a dance while Darcy danced with Georgiana, I walked through the crowd to get some punch and I heard Joseph Darcy and Mr. Bingley speaking with each other.

"You seem to be enjoying yourself this evening," Joseph said.

"Upon my honor," Mr. Bingley said. "I have never danced with such pleasanter people in my life and several of them uncommonly pretty."

"You have been dancing with Miss Miriam Goldman, who is a lovely partner."

"Mr. Joseph Darcy, she is the most beautiful creature that I ever beheld."

"Yes, she is, slightly."

"Slightly, come man, admit it, she's an angel."

"She is regarded by some as lovely, but to many she is unsuitable."

"Unsuitable? Yet she has appeared as a lovely woman. What would be the reason?"

"Then...you really don't know?"

"Know of what? Her family is involved in trade, yet that is of no ill consequence."

"Of course not, we all here have trades, yet it is her background."

"Her background?"

"Of course it is highly reprehensible to a man from your position in society, for she is a Quaker."

"What?!"

"Yes, Mr. Bingley, Miriam Goldman is a Quaker."

Quakerism was a religion that I had heard of and knew relatively little about. Yes, I knew of much religious strife that occurred in Europe, and England once wasn't very fond of Quakers to the point where they were practically kicked out of it long ago. Yet in Philadelphia, I did not see what conflicts it could cause, especially since the city was founded by a Quaker... until I looked at Mr. Bingley. His expression dropped from one of brightness to one of doubt and disturbance. He looked at Miriam through the crowd and even his tone had utterly changed.

"I cannot believe it."

"It is true. Her family is one of the main Quaker families in the neighborhood. And she is not a Free Quaker, which makes her off limits."

Mr. Bingley continued to study Miss Goldman from across the room. "What do you mean that she is not a Free Quaker?"

"Well Free Quakers are open to marrying outside of their religion. But some Quakers still prohibit it. Miriam is only allowed to marry another Quaker. Even if your background did not prevent you from abhorring her faith, she is unavailable."

"And how attached is she to her faith?"

"I am not so well-connected to the family, but she is most devout. The only reason that they are even here at this dance—because some Quakers are against events such as these—is because her mother loves dancing and won't hear a word against it."

"And, if Miss Miriam is most devout, she can't marry outside of their religion? There would be tension."

"Yes, there would be. Quakers are lovely people, but mostly ineligible. As I said before, Mr. Bingley, many regard her as unsuitable, for she is."

"Yes," Mr. Bingley said, looking downhearted. "Yes, she very much is."

My shock could not be described. To hear Mr. Bingley, who always wished to see the best in all, though being a man of sound judgment, to quickly submit to finding a woman unsuitable because of her religious difference was positively disarming.

Would a religious difference really be so cumbersome to a man such as Mr. Bingley?

And yet, from what I thought of it, I did see where the conflict would arise. Mr. Bingley's faith and hers were cousins of one another, but the separation was enough to make the distinction keenly felt. Sadly, from an objective light, I suppose I could see Bingley's hesitancy.

However, Mr. Bingley was Mr. Bingley, and I did not consider that he would be so quick to turn his mind and heart away completely from her in such a brash manner. For it was quite distinctly clear that he now looked on her with distaste.

And surely Mr. Bingley did not feel a prejudice against her in general. To wish to remove his presence from her slightly was one thing, but to wish to remove her presence from him so completely was ghastly. How could Mr. Bingley, who was determined to think well of anyone, turn to prejudice?

⚜

Mr. Bingley spent the rest of the evening trying to smile but was slightly out of sorts, while also being guarded and making sure not to find himself in the path to Miriam.

After observing them for a moment, I drank some punch, and wondered over these words that were not meant to be overheard.

❈ 19 ❈

WHAT TO THINK

The assembly had ended, and the night was declared a great success, while everyone in our company returned to Canterbury in good spirits and I pretended to be cheerful as well. Yet I watched Mr. Bingley as well as Joseph.

I was a little bitter for Joseph being so presumptuous, but his nature was as could be expected, and I could not control how he acted. Yet with Mr. Bingley, who was now a friend of mine, I was alarmed at his quickly submitting to the ways of the world that were not correct at all. Yes, the Quakers were once practically expelled from England, but that was so very long ago.

However, I hoped that his reaction was simply the initial one, and as time wore on, he would cease to care about such a trivial difference.

When we returned, we were too exhausted for conversation to be the order of the day; therefore, we all retired to bed. When Darcy and I went to bed, we only had the energy to undress and crawl under the sheets and fall asleep. My last memory was of my promise to tell my husband the next evening.

The next day, Cousin Thomas and Emilia's plans to make us acquainted with the city were resumed and we began to travel around the area, taking in the sights and monuments.

"This is the First Bank of the United States," Cousin Thomas said.

"And it was completed in 1797, built under the direction of treasury secretary Alexander Hamilton."

Georgiana gazed at the building, amazed. "A beautiful building."

"Yes, it is, and it is a symbol of how mostly brick is the building blocks that are used in most designs in Philadelphia. It is our look, and while the marble on this bank adds to it greatly, it is the brick that shows the Philadelphian spirit."

We walked past other buildings and then came upon Carpenters Hall, which was a building that Thomas told us was founded in 1773, and originally was used as a place where the carpenters of the city would gather to show off their work. It was also the sight of the first lending library in the country, founded by Benjamin Franklin. Then Emilia told us also that it was the place where the First Continental Congress met to discuss America gaining independence from England.

My husband, who took great pride in being an English aristocrat, was a little apprehensive at the discussion of this subject matter, but I assured him just how much it was a tension that should be let go.

There was nothing wrong with a country celebrating their independence and being happy they fought for it, even if it was from us. Patriotic pride was a healthy trait to have, therefore, the past was the past to me. Especially since we were in the company of an American family who was connected to us and admired that connection.

Thomas then showed us a house that once belonged to a man named John Todd, who died of the Yellow Fever epidemic that ran through Philadelphia at the end of the 18th century. He went on to tell us about how the Free Black Society in Philadelphia at the time, which consisted of free Negroes, stayed behind to help those who were sick while many politicians left the city, and many of those Free Blacks died helping the victims and now were not given nearly enough credit for it.

Next, they took us to Independence Hall, which was where the Second Continental Congress met and finally declared independence from England.

"Our Declaration of Independence was read aloud back here for the very first time on July 8th, 1776," Thomas said. "I was twenty-three years old at the time."

"Thomas Jefferson wrote it, did he not?" Kitty asked, to our surprise.

"Yes, he did. Your knowledge of that impresses me. Our president right now, Jefferson, was the author of our Declaration. Oh, and that building right next to Independence Hall, is Congress Hall, and it was where George Washington, at the end of his term, handed the presidency over to his successor, John Adams."

"Was George Washington reluctant to give up the presidency?" I asked, very much interested.

"Everyone thought he would have been, for never is it so easy for power to be handed peacefully over to another when it comes to ruling a country." Thomas shook his head and sighed. "And therein lays the miracle. It was *peaceful*. President Washington handed over the presidency to John Adams without reluctance."

"What is it like?" Kitty asked, "To be ruled by a president for a few terms rather than have a king who rules for his entire life?"

"It is refreshing in some ways, because if you don't like the president you have now, then you need not fear, because eventually the president will change in four to eight years."

"Do you have a favorite President so far?" Jane asked.

"I can't say, really," Emilia said, "for they all had their strengths as well as their weaknesses. For example, none of them has still abolished slavery, and that is a flaw that they all carry as a large defect during their entire presidency."

"Then... the abolition is not making progress here?" Jane asked, apprehensive. "Slavery is still strong?"

"Yes, I am sorry to say. It is stronger than ever."

"I am happy that you do not support it," I said.

"A terrible evil it is," my husband echoed my sentiments. "And I wait to see the abolition stretch over England in full. We cannot lie, there is still slavery in parts of our society, and I will be happy when the abolition has fully won."

Emilia heaved a great sigh. "I fear that it might never will."

Next, they took us to the site of the first ever Public School for Girls in Pennsylvania, which was founded in 1754. It was just so strange that this was happening here during the same years that the Americans and the British were joined together and fighting against the French during the Seven Year War.

It was just wonderful to know that while a war was occurring, someone still believed that fighting for young girls' rights to an education was still of great import. Education could often be taken for granted in our times, because the notion of not being allowed to do it once was so much an abstract and archaic idea.

Next, we went to Christ Church, and it was a lovely church. We were led around by the Reverend there who gave us a history of the building. We sat in the pew of a past parishioner whose name was Archer, but that was all that I learned about him.

At last, we were hungry, and we went to eat at the City Tavern that was along Walnut Street.

While there, we ordered turkey pot pies, which were delicious and hearty, for it was very cold and this replenished us as well as warmed us up within.

"Are you enjoying the outing?" Emilia asked. "We are sorry to have thrown so much history at you, but there is so much of it here, that it is hard not to always feel as if one is getting caught up in it."

"Oh, don't worry," Jane said, "for we have quite enjoyed all of it. Philadelphia, on the whole, is a lovely city."

"It makes us feel good when you say so," Thomas said, "for one takes pride in their home, and we hoped that you would like it."

"Now then," Emilia said, clapping her hands together. "After being filled with culture, I thought that it would be refreshing for us to reward your attentions with a night out at the theatre."

"Are we seeing a play?" Georgiana perked up.

"Yes, if that is your pleasure."

"It is." I smiled eagerly. "What play do you wish to see?"

"We have heard report that at the theatre, The Briar, Shakespeare's lesser known play *Timon of Athens* is being put on."

"*Timon of Athens*?" Mr. Bingley gasped, wincing while he spoke.

"Yes," Emilia said cautiously. "Do you not like that play?"

"Oh, no, it's just...it's a play that I never thought I would get the chance to see. But yes—I should very much like to see it, for I have always wanted to see his lesser known works."

"Well then, do you all wish to see it?"

The suggestion was readily agreed to and we all perked up, eager to see this play.

As we continued to talk about the production, I eyed Mr. Bingley, who sat there diligently attempting to look as if he was attentive. Yet I knew that he was not. His mind was on the woman from the assembly, Miriam

Goldman, for hearing the play's name clearly made him recall her. It was apparent that he still thought of her often, but only pretended that he had not, and now she was clearly in the forefront of his mind.

Men such as Mr. Bingley were easy to read, therefore his mood was clearly affected, and I wondered if it would not improve until he entertained the option of speaking with her once more. For either he could not release her from his mind because he felt an immediate attachment, or he thought of her because she was exotic to him and his curiosity was still piqued.

Or it could have simply been that she was a forbidden fruit. He could not have her, and therefore he might wonder what it would be like to have her. Yet with such a course of action, it was so confusing and difficult to determine, that one did not know what to think.

A CONVERSATION ONE WOULD NOT
WANT TO HAVE

Two nights later, we all had dressed in our finest and left for the Briar Theatre. This time however, we were joined by Henry, Joseph and his wife. We made it to the theatre and while we left the carriages, Henry remained close to Jane entirely, and this time, even Darcy paid close attention to it.

"What do you think of this now?" I whispered.

"I think that if they marry, I shall be happy for them, yet their natures are so different, and not in the right sort of way. Difference can be a good quality for a couple to have..."

"As long as those differences complement each other, which there's does not."

"Precisely. Elizabeth?"

"Yes?"

"Thank god I found you."

"And I you."

We all walked into the theatre where Emilia and Thomas had box seats and we sat there, looking at the structure of the building until the lights dimmed, the curtain raised, and the play began.

Very soon it became apparent that the leading actor was a genius! It could not be described, yet this man was clearly meant to be an actor, for every word spoken and every gesture that he made was meticulous but also organic.

"We are sitting here," I whispered to Darcy, "and watching a living legend."

He pretended offense. "Don't say such things to me, for it will make me quite jealous."

I nudged him with my elbow. "That is not what I mean, and you know it."

"I do, but he is not so handsome. Is he?"

"Of course, he is handsome." Georgiana sighed, not hearing the first part of our conversation. "He is without a doubt one of the most beautiful things that I have ever seen."

Instead of not caring one way or the other, he looked at me with a stern and 'Elizabeth, don't you dare think him handsome also' expression.

"His nose is strange-looking," I whispered in his ear. "And his chin is weak, while yours is strong and firm. Also, your eyes are fine, while his lack your luster."

He sighed, content. "Very good. And you must never think any man as handsome as I am."

I chuckled to myself, quite amused at his insecurity and need for me to compliment him and no other. I found it quite adorable.

The play reached an intermission and we went out to the concession stand to get some refreshment. While we were there, Bingley went up to a painting and began to admire it but did not notice the person who stood nearby until she turned to him.

"Mr. Bingley!"

He turned to see Miriam Goldman standing there, looking lovely in a lavender colored gown.

"Oh," Mr. Bingley said, looking hesitant. "Miss Goldman, how are you?"

"I am well." She laughed, in a very artless and open manner. "And I am glad to see you. How are you enjoying the play?"

"It is very entertaining, thank you."

"If you recall, we spoke of it at the assembly while we danced."

"Yes, I do recall."

"And how are you enjoying the leading actor? He's quite the genius, is he not?"

"Yes, he is."

"He is also doing another play called *She Stoops to Conquer* in a month. If your party is interested in seeing it, my family would love it if you all joined us for a night at the theatre. While some in my society look down on the theatre, my family shall always never agree with that part of our community."

Mr. Bingley was exceedingly uncomfortable. "Well...well, I thank you for your generous offer, but I am deciding more and more that I partake in the theatre too much." Then he looked at her most pointedly.

"For a man of my station should not indulge such frivolities, for my rank should be preserved. There are certain standards that society places on us, and I should commit to them. And things that it tells me to avoid, I shall avoid. All things as such."

His meaning, though indirect, was plain and most expressly felt. Miriam did not cry, but I could sense the tears swelling up within her. She bowed swiftly and walked away, rushing past her family and to another room. I saw her mother look between her and Bingley, and then run off after her daughter.

Yet as Bingley stood there, looking forlorn, I felt disappointment rising within me. Being so disobliging was not something I ever would have thought of when attributed to Mr. Bingley, yet it was now.

After witnessing his first reaction to her beliefs at the assembly, I assumed it was simply his surprise that had made him act rashly, yet now seeing how he acted over having much deliberation on the matter, I could not believe it!

Mr. Bingley straightened his waistcoat, which I felt was an indirect sign of his nerves getting to him. He turned, approached us and then he stopped dead, yet he wasn't looking at me, but looking over my shoulder. I looked above me and saw my husband staring at Mr. Bingley with a cold and stern glare, making it all too clear. He had overheard everything as well.

We went back into the box and watched the rest of the play, but I barely paid attention to it, for I kept stealing glances at Mr. Bingley, who also didn't watch the play attentively either. He was lost in thought and feeling an immense sense of guilt clearly.

Eventually the play ended and as we stood up to leave, Cousin Thomas had a wonderful announcement to give.

"I have a special treat for you all. I know the director and producers of the play and spoke with them earlier. They are going to allow us backstage to meet the actors. Therefore, Miss Georgiana, you will meet the actor who you clearly favored."

"I never should have said anything." Georgiana blushed.

"What is the actor's name?" Kitty asked.

"Persons. His name is Parson Persons."

⚬⚭⚬

We were allowed backstage and met with the actors after they had finished getting dressed. I felt apprehensive about meeting them, for after performing a show, they might just wish for solitude, and performers could often be temperamental. Yet the ones we did meet were quite content in seeing that most of us were women, which made sense. It being a Shakespeare play, most of the thespians were male, and for us to speak about enjoying their talent was a boost to their confidence.

However, the director brought forward the leading actor whose height eclipsed even my husband's.

"Ladies and gentlemen, allow us to introduce the leading actor, Parson Persons."

The actor smiled at us, the women in particular, and we bowed and curtsied to him.

"This is the family of the Darcys," the director said. "This is Mr. and Mrs. Thomas Darcy, their son Mr. Henry Darcy. And this is Mr. and Mrs. Fitzwilliam Darcy, Mr. Bingley, Ms. Jane Bennet, Ms. Kitty Bennet, and Ms. Georgiana."

"A herd of Darcys I have before me." He gave a dramatic laugh. "And it is wonderful to make your acquaintance."

"The pleasure is all ours," Georgiana said softly. Parson Persons turned to her and then he started. His expression changed to one of curiosity, wonder, and as if he was struck by a thunderbolt.

"Ms. Georgiana, it is nice to meet you. By any chance, do you know a woman named Harriet Price? She is an Englishwoman, but I'm not sure of what town again. And I can tell from your accents that you must be from the English countryside."

Georgiana continued to blush. "Um... I am sorry, but I do not know her."

"Oh, forgive me, you and she just looked so similar, that for a moment, you reminded me of her."

"Was she a familiar acquaintance?"

He paused, and then answered, "Yes...yes she was."

The actor Parson Persons proved to be most charming and seemed to be a bit of a rake in my eyes, but I was content in seeing that his interest in Georgiana had nothing to do with an attraction to her, but rather it was simply because she reminded him of someone that he did care about. Whoever this Harriet Price was, it was apparent that he felt for her deeply.

After a few moments, we offered our farewells, thanked the cast of *Timon of Athens* once more and then we left for Canterbury.

When we returned there, Henry, who had remained close to Jane throughout the evening, seemed reluctant to leave her side, even though it was time for us all to retire to bed.

Before I had followed Darcy up to bed, I took Georgiana aside and decided that she might wish to speak about Parson Persons a bit.

"I feel so foolish," Georgiana said. "For though he was the handsomest man ever, for some reason, I didn't think as such when we saw him backstage."

Surprised, I asked, "Really?"

"Yes. Call me cold and cruel, but when I watched him onstage, he was like an angel to me. But when I saw him offstage, he was normal, just like any other man, no more and no less. I suppose the fact that he saw another woman in me was why I no longer was affected."

"What do you mean?"

Georgiana sighed and looked away. "Well, I have learned that whenever a person places me on a pedestal, it is frightening because they make me feel as if I am an ideal that I am not, or that they are looking at me for all the wrong reasons."

Her bonnet in her hands, she played with the grosgrain ribbon. "They look at me because they want to see something else and have me become that something else. And I could tell that Parson Persons was in love with whoever this Harriet Price is. I—to my eternal happiness, have learned not to like a man who doesn't fancy me. Wickham was the only mistake that I want to make for quite some time now. After him, I wish for no more flights of fancy."

I clasped her hands in mine. "That is wonderful! He looks charming enough, but I was worried that you would give your heart away to an actor in the name of 'Romantic Sensibility'."

"Oh, I hope to never be taken that far into my own feelings." Georgiana laughed, and then she excused herself.

Feeling assured that Georgiana wouldn't be going off to bed dreaming about this handsome actor, I began to walk up the steps, when I heard two voices arguing on the landing.

"Bingley," my husband said, "be honest with me. What happened at the theater earlier with that woman?"

Bingley did not look at him. "It is nothing."

"It did not appear as if it was merely nothing, and I can tell by your tone that it was not. Charles... you were rude to that woman, disobliging and curt."

Bingley touched the buttons on his jacket. "I simply did not agree to do something that I did not want to do."

"What is wrong with you? You are not acting like yourself."

"Why so? Because I am actually arguing with you? Because I am willing to defend myself at this moment?"

"Are you suggesting that I bully you?" Darcy replied heatedly.

"I'm simply suggesting that you sometimes have a funny idea for what you call giving advice."

My husband narrowed his gaze. "If you are trying to offend me, I shall choose not to fight now, for that inclination to become so easily offensive in manner is proof of you being out of sorts. Charles, this is not you. Something has been tearing at you these last couple of days and I wish to know what. And why did you take it out on that woman?"

He had the decency to look away. "I did not mean to offend."

"And now you are withholding things from me. For I know perfectly well that you danced with her at the assembly, favored her and your attentions to her were so marked that I wondered why you did not wish to call on her at her home the next day. And now, here you are, this very evening, you treated her—"

"The way that you treated Elizabeth when you first met her? With the same amount of rudeness? Why do you speak to me as if you are guiltless at all, when you have treated others worse than I have done so? Why was it aristocratic integrity with you, but with me it is an error? How is that fair?"

"The difference between me and you is that I did not excuse my behavior."

"You did and if you don't recall, I do remember," Bingley added.

"Then if you are acting in such a way, and connecting it back to my own actions, it has made it even more clear than before that you suffer from what I did; you are in the way of being attracted to this Miriam Goldman, and you are not letting yourself be so. Yet if you are going to continue insulting me and using my past actions to justify your own, then this conversation is concluded, and I can have nothing further to say to you."

Darcy began to walk away when he stopped and turned back to Bingley.

"And in case you have forgotten, I realized that I was wrong to treat Elizabeth in such a manner, therefore how can you think I approve of your actions now when I did not approve of my actions before?"

"Darcy," Bingley replied more gently, "it is more complicated than your circumstance."

"If that is what you must tell yourself to—"

"She is a Quaker!"

"What?"

"Darcy, she is a Quaker. And what's more, she's an American Quaker. And therefore, she is withheld from me."

There was a long silence.

"Oh."

"And I am sorry for offending you," Bingley replied. "For you did not deserve it. I have not been myself lately for you are correct... I feel obliged to submit to something that I don't wish to. I wanted to get to know her, but you and I know that it is impossible—and it's hurting me inside. That is why I have been distant of late, despondent, and had just taken my anger out on you. You were able to marry the woman that you at first denied yourself of, and I cannot even get to know this woman."

"Yes," Darcy muttered, "I see your dilemma. And I am sorry for you. Yet you know that there is nothing that can be done."

"Precisely. I have not your luck, Darcy, and I never will."

"I am sorry for it, but Bingley, don't let it ruin you. You are a kind and obliging man. No matter your heartache, don't lose sight of that."

Bingley showed a slight smile. "I shall endeavor not to, and once more,

I am sorry for my harsh words, for I was simply bitter, and jealous of your good fortune."

I began to stomp up the steps to make my appearance known. I heard both men cease their discussion and thus bring an end to a conversation one would not want to have.

✣ 21 ✣

ANOTHER CONVERSATION ONE
DOES NOT WANT TO HAVE

I walked up the steps to see both men red in the face.

"Hello gentlemen," I said lightly. "Don't worry, I can see that I have come in the middle of an intimate discussion on your part, therefore I shall retire while you continue."

"It is of no matter, my love," Darcy said. "All words of import have been spoken and I shall join you. Goodnight, Bingley."

"Sleep well, Darcy and Mrs. Darcy."

"Mr. Bingley." I curtsied.

Darcy and I went into our bedroom.

"Come loving husband and help me take off my gown, for I would prefer your attentions rather than my maid assisting me."

"Of course, Elizabeth."

He helped me undress and then I put on my nightgown while he removed his boots.

"Elizabeth..."

"Yes?"

"My dear, please tell me the truth. How much of our conversation did you overhear?"

At first, I felt very ashamed for being caught in the act and my first impulse, forgive me, was to not tell the truth.

"I..."

"Elizabeth, when you came upon us on the steps, you had the same look on your face that you had at the assembly in Hampshire when you overheard me tell Bingley that you were tolerable but not handsome enough to tempt me."

His statement took me totally by surprise. "You remember how I looked when you said that?"

"Aye, I do."

"And a part of me is still angry at you for saying that about me, for clearly I was handsome enough to tempt you."

"First, I admitted that I was wrong and was a bit of a villain back then. Am I going to suffer for that remark forever?"

I sat down before the mirror to tend to my hair. "Possibly. I am the sort of woman who shall most likely bring it up again just to tease and taunt you for your one-time wicked ways."

"Well, thanks for the warning, and secondly, woman, don't you dare try to distract me from our previous discussion, which was about you overhearing what Bingley and I spoke of."

"Yes, I did eavesdrop a bit."

"Elizabeth, sometimes I never know when I wish to kiss you or scold you."

"First, walking in on a conversation by accident is a common fault of man, and second, I give you full permission to kiss me and scold me after we talk about what I overheard."

"Fair enough. Very well, what part of the conversation do you wish to comment on?"

"Everything, dearest. I wish to talk about everything."

He gave me a patient but warm look. "That's a very broad answer."

"I am a woman who is not afraid to confront an argument from all angles. Surely your time with me at Aginfield Park has shown my sauciness in that way." I pulled my hair over my shoulder to braid it.

"Yes, now continue."

"I can't believe Mr. Bingley, the very Mr. Bingley who has been universally praised for his generous candor and liveliness of temper, along with his happy manners, could be capable of such meanness of opinion."

"Elizabeth, what have I said about complimenting men who were not me?"

"Darcy, stop it!"

"You're correct, sorry."

"And were you not upset with him for excusing his actions by comparing them to yours? That was cowardly of him!"

Darcy nodded. "Yes, it was. For one must never justify one's actions by comparing them to another who was guilty of the same thing. In that way, a person can get away with anything."

"And he thought so. The good and kind Mr. Bingley thought so. And I saw how he treated Miss Goldman as well as you. His treatment of her was abominably rude and I am ashamed of him," I added heatedly.

"While I do not excuse it, I cannot help but understand it."

I put my brush down on the dressing table. "And that is another thing that frightens me, my dear. You actually understand his logic?"

"Of course, I do. But not from being prejudiced against people of Miss Goldman's background."

"Then how, sir? How can you empathize with such an attitude?"

"Because I admit, my brave wife, to fearing the world sometimes."

I turned to face him. "What do you mean?"

"I mean that there are some differences that cannot be overcome, no matter how strong a man's resolve. Say that Mr. Bingley was to indulge this fancy of his, what then? He's marrying a woman who both his and her families will look down on. They might never accept him for being of the Church of England, and his family will never accept her for being a Quaker. We'd have a pair of star-crossed lovers on our hands. And a family can be very successful at destroying a love that two people have for one another.

"You've seen it yourself, Elizabeth, of a family's sometimes intolerable cruelty to someone that they don't find worthy of their relations.

"My Aunt Catherine came to your home and berated you simply because I chose you, and then threatened to ruin you if I were to act on our love. Upon my honor! We are here in America now because I desperately wanted to gain as many relations on our side as a married couple so that I can keep you in love with me for as long as I can."

His comment puzzled me. "What do you mean keep me in love with you?"

"I mean that if my family were to have continued to be cruel to you, I would run the risk of it reflecting poorly on me—and it would make you hate the sight of me. And you may not think so now, but it would always be possible for such hate to spread and sour your desire for my companionship."

"And yet the same could be said for me," I answered with a sigh. "I worried that your aunt's disdain for me would dampen your affection, which I did not want to lose."

"Precisely, and there were not as many obstacles in the way in our case as there are with Mr. Bingley and this Miss Goldman. And with our lesser conflicts, I still had to undergo coming here and willing to move here, if necessary, if the American Darcys would have liked you."

The announcement was a bit shocking. "Move here?"

"Yes, I had to acknowledge within myself the possibility of doing so if it meant that I could keep you. I rationalized that if I sold Pemberly, I could very well set us up here in a nicely-sized home where I would buy an estate, run a farm and continue to make a profit through our tenants and produce."

I gasped and pressed my hand to my chest. "You would have given up Pemberly? For me?"

"I would not have liked to, and it might have weighed on me heavily...but yes, I was ready to do it."

"My dearest husband..."

I rushed to him and we kissed passionately. I then removed my nightgown and stood nude over him and he took my meaning. He wrapped his arms around my waist and kissed every part of me with a voracious appetite. Then I leaned over, unfastened his breeches and pushed him to a chair, after which I sat on his lap and wrapped my legs around his waist. He drove deep inside me and I felt as though we had become one.

He pushed himself into me. Up and down...up and down... as I was rocked along the crests of sensations. He showered kisses on my neck and our bodies were locked in the greatest of marital bonds, and then finally, he spent himself within me, moaning. As he did so, I, too, felt that spinning sensation, sending me skyward and out of control.

"I love you," I said. "And you must never forget that."

"I won't."

I remained sitting on top of him as he cradled one of my breasts in his hand, every now and again pinching my nipples in between the tips of his fingers.

"No one has ever considered such a sacrifice for me before. How can I bear such goodness? It is too much. Darcy, no one has ever made me feel of such importance in the world."

He kissed my forehead. "You have brought me to life. Of course, I must reward that with equally giving all. Yet as you see, Elizabeth, Bingley is a good man, but not of the strongest will. Can you see him always making the ultimate sacrifice in the name of love? Can you see his resolve never faltering in the face of society?"

"I often wish society can go hang!"

"As do I, yet the ton is not going anywhere soon if at all, and Bingley knows this."

"Yes, you are correct. I cannot see him making the ultimate sacrifice, for his temper is too reliant on pleasing others, which is a virtue often, but can be a flaw when it comes to taking a strong stance. He is too easily swayed by the opinions of others sometimes, and not because he cares too little, but because he cares too much."

"Precisely! Marrying someone that might bring him disgrace of any kind is too much for his sensibilities."

I ran my fingers through my husband's dark curls. "And yet he is growing stronger, is he not?"

"In some ways, yes, he is without a doubt a stronger man than he used to be, but in many ways, he does still listen to the advice of others, and can be easily led." He gripped my hand and kissed my palm.

"I admit to at first being upset with you for agreeing with him about avoiding her, but now I see your reasons."

He continued to press kisses against my skin. "Thank you."

"For you were worried that if he continued to follow his heart, then he would grow to hold the very love that he prized in disdain. He would grow to hate the thing that he loved."

He pressed my hand to his cheek. "Yes, and I did it as much for her as for him. No woman should suffer the fate of the man she loved growing to hate her because of matters that were beyond her control. This is one moment where I had no choice but to be cruel to be kind. Moral preferences, though meant to unify, can be a great divider. It would bring a wedge between them, because they cannot be united as one in faith, therefore they would be split in love."

"I still wish that he could be kinder to her. And that life was not so unfair."

"I wish so as well."

"Then what are we to do?"

"Be kind to her if we ever see her again, but never speak of her in his presence."

"I feel terrible about all this."

"This is Mr. Bingley's choice, and either one he makes will be both the wrong and right one. Either way, he has won, and he has lost."

<hr />

The next day, we were all relaxing on the fields of Canterbury. While the men formed a shooting party, we women watched them. Joseph and Henry accompanied Darcy, Mr. Bingley and Cousin Thomas while we ladies watched them at their full form. All the while, Henry would shoot at a bird, and then turned to smile at Jane, who then returned his smile with a gentle nod, but I never noticed any peculiar regard for him. However, Jane was very modest and shy in nature; therefore, I knew whatever feelings she possessed always had the chance to run deep.

Watching the two of them as her son eyed my sister, Cousin Emilia turned to me, for it was I who was sitting the closest to her.

"Besotted," she observed about Henry and Jane. "My son has not looked so smitten since I can't even remember last."

I smiled but did not say anything, for since I knew nothing for certain, I had nothing to tell.

"An excellent match they would make," Cousin Emilia added. "For my son is rich, and your sister is handsome."

"Your son is handsome as well," I said.

"Yes, he is, if I should say so myself, but it is also their natures that make them so much perfect for one another. She is demure, serene, and sensible. She has the graces of a noblewoman as well as the looks of a statue of a goddess. While Henry is a man who needs such a reliable character and a woman who is steady. Also, she is different than the last woman long ago, and that is promising."

I turned to her, sharply. "What do you mean by the last woman?"

"Oh, my son did not have the best of fortune when it came to romance. He fell in love a couple of times, and each time it was with the most unlikely woman imaginable."

Curious, I asked, "What were they like?"

"Lively and flighty women, much like your sister, Kitty. Not that I am offending Kitty at all. She is a very good sort of girl, but for a man like Henry, for such reserve to attach itself to such animated of women who seemed to love to speak and gossip, his taste was very ironic to his temper.

"Yet with Jane, I am quite content that he has done right for himself. Yes, he has made the correct choice this time. May my son find happiness, and may it last this time."

While I wished to give Emilia good news or counsel, I could give her none. I had my suspicions of Henry's growing attachment to Jane, for he made it plain for the world to see. But as Darcy and I had deliberated before, there was a chance that it would be a terrible idea. His mother looked at it from a very logical standpoint, but she was missing something vital: her son sometimes lacked proper manners and lacked grace.

Sometimes, as was the case with my husband, men with such gravity in nature need a woman whose lightness will alleviate theirs, yes, but also who can be firm with them, and show them their errors without being cruel. Jane was not the sort to do that mostly, even though she was growing stronger.

However, I knew now that I could no longer avoid the subject. I would have to see Jane and then be forced to have another conversation one does not want to have. Yet have it I must.

22

SISTERLY COMMUNION

The next day, I heard from Kitty that Jane was in the library, reading, and I went there in hopes of finding her alone rather than being accompanied by Henry Darcy. I was fortunate. There, sitting at a desk with a book in her hand, Jane sat, painting a beautiful picture with the sun shining around her.

"I had no idea that you would take to the library on a beautiful day like this," I said, entering.

"Oh." She smiled when seeing me. "Lizzy...yes I always have so much to do at home; getting the time to read is not easy, but here, I figured that I would make an attempt."

"That is a wonderful intention and I admire your wish to improve your mind by extensive reading, therefore I apologize for interrupting you."

"It is no trouble at all, you know that. So, what do you need?"

I paused to gather my thoughts. "I need to speak with you about something and I need you to tell me the truth."

She gave me a pained expression. "Have I done anything to upset you?"

"Of course not. You never could. Yet I simply need to be honest with you. Jane, I have noticed, as I'm sure you have, that Mr. Henry Darcy has been paying particular attention to you."

Jane looked down at her book.

"He has been very attentive, yes."

"And at first it might have been simply a wish to get to know you, but now it is clear that he is falling in love with you."

She shook her head. "He is not falling in love with me."

"I know that you are modest, Jane, but believe me that he looks on you with much admiration and—"

"Forgive me, Elizabeth, but you mistake my meaning. This is not modesty, but intuition, which I could be mistaken, but I don't believe myself to be. I don't believe that he is in love with me, but rather he is in love with the idea of me."

I sat down in the chair opposite her. "What do you mean by that?"

"I mean that our cousin, Henry, is a good man who doesn't always know how to converse easily with people who he has never met with before. Men such as Henry rarely get far into a courtship because they lack confidence in themselves. However, they also have much pride and will not alter their attitude to accommodate others around them.

"He is too little yielding, not willing to always bend as he ought to, and he believes that my nature will be most likely to withstand his. That, mingled with me appearing exotic to him because I am a new acquaintance, can lead to him thinking better of me, more of me than he normally would."

She lifted her gaze to mine. "He loves the idea of a woman like me, but not me in full. I don't even believe that he sees me for who I am, but only as a woman who he can project his own feelings and intentions on and expect me to echo them."

Her insight surprised me. "You see this in him, how?"

"Because it is the exact same way that Mr. Brocklehurst looked at me."

"Oh, truly?"

"Yes. When engaged to Mr. Brocklehurst, I could not see it because I was in love with him, and still am, but time and much reflection on the matter has shown me all the time that he did not love me for the right reasons.

"He needed a woman who was perfect in all appearance and seemed too safe to love, while the real woman that he loved remained in the background where he could offer his real feelings to her in secret. Well he *did* love me, but he just loved someone else first."

"Then you are still in love with Mr. Brocklehurst?"

"Yes. It is senseless to do so, but the heart can't recover from things so easily. You know perfectly well, Lizzy, that if Mr. Darcy were to have made the wrong decision and married Anne over you, you would not have been able to move on from him so quickly."

"No," I admitted. "I would not have cared for another man for at least a year, knowing my stubbornness."

"It is not stubbornness to be devoted to a man. Some of us just feel so deeply, while others can move from one love to another with alacrity and ease. Neither is more or less fortunate than the other, but only different."

"Yet you see the same sort of affection in Henry Darcy as there was in Mr. Brocklehurst?"

"Since I am not in love with Henry, I believe that I see it clearly."

"Then," I repeated, "You do not love Henry Darcy?"

"I care about him in a way that family cares about family, but I am not in love with him at all. And it is not just my lingering desire for Mr. Brocklehurst, yet it is more than that."

I leaned forward. "What is it?"

"Sometimes a person can't just love someone because that person loves them. The world does not work that way, though we wish that it did. Also, he could not make me happy and I am convinced that I am the last sort of woman who could make him so."

I gave her a gentle look. "Yet he is happy around you."

"He is happy because he thinks he has found a woman who will always accept him for who he is, when that is not what he needs. He needs a woman who loves him even though he is not perfect, and she will need to fight with him often to make him see his mistakes and learn from them. If I were to argue with him one day, he would jump back, shocked. Then his love for me would be at an end and he would be left wondering if I had deceived him."

She put a bookmark in her book and closed it. "He will try to take over my personality, thinking my timidity was blankness where he can write his own personality on, and not always think of my feelings. And I will either spend my life with a man who does not value my sentiments or asks for my input because he assumes that I will always just do as he says, or one day I will try to interject myself too far into a conversation, disagree with him on something and then he will never look on me the same again. The dream he had of me will be broken and only a fragile image will remain in what he once saw."

I gave her the warmest of smiles. "You have grown so wise."

With a slight shrug she answered, "I am a woman who has had her heart broken. It is strange, but it makes one grow wider in perception. The glass has broken, and I saw all the truths underneath it. What is truly comical is how happy I am now."

"You are? Oh, that is very good."

"Yes, you would think I would be sad, but I… well, first, I am happy that I found out the true man that I was engaged to before it was too late. And second, I do not know, but my heart is—stronger than I would have thought. Or maybe, I just wish to go on an adventure. Many adventures. And this feels like the first of many. And I cherish it so much."

She laughed and added, "I think I have stumbled on a different sort of happiness that no one ever explained to me before."

"I am happy that you know yourself, Jane, truly, just as I am happy that you do not consider all the comforts that you can receive just by becoming Mrs. Henry Darcy. If our mother were here, I'm certain that she would encourage the match, yet I am happy that you are choosing to wait for love."

"Thank you, Lizzy, for I am now persuaded that only the deepest love can induce me into matrimony. Therefore, I shall end an old maid and teach you ten children to sew their pillows abominably ill!" She laughed.

"Oh Jane, you need not worry of not finding a love. For you, being five times as lovely as the rest of us and having the sweetest disposition—well, we all believed that the task rested on you to marry well and raise our fortunes in life."

She smiled and touched my arm. "And instead, it fell on you. So now tell me, how does it feel? To be the one to take up my mantle?"

"I will never take up your mantle, for it is too far above me. Yet I can say, if this dream can be obtained by me, then it can be gained by any."

"You don't know your own strength. For too long you were not allowed to see what made you special."

Again, I was puzzled. "What do you mean?"

"Nothing, you need not concern yourself on it."

"Very well, but Jane, you must see that there might be a chance that Henry will one day propose to you."

"I do see that potentially happening."

"Then what will you do?"

"I will have no choice but to say the words that he shall not wish to hear, but never fear, Lizzy. I shall not waver."

"Jane, that is wonderful to hear. Now I am content that you will do what your heart tells you."

"The heart—the one organ that rules the day, even when our head ought to."

I kissed her forehead and seeing that our sisterly communion was at an end, I left her to her book.

❧ 23 ❧

THE VICIOUS CYCLE

The next morning, we received letters from our family. They mostly were from our parents, our Aunt and Uncle Gardiner and one was from our sister, Lydia Wickham. She wrote to me, requesting more money for her and her husband's living expenses—again.

As it happened that I had much rather not give her more, I endeavored in my previous responses to deny her request and put an end to every entreaty and expectation of the kind. Such relief, however, as it was in my power to afford, by the practice of what might be called economy in my own private expenses, I would begin to send them.

It had always been evident to me that such an income as theirs, under the direction of two persons so extravagant in their wants, and heedless of the future, must be very insufficient to their support. This time, Lydia and Wickham, due to lack of finances, had to change living quarters to economize and therefore once more I was being applied to, for some little assistance towards discharging their bills.

Their manner of living, even when the restoration of peace dismissed them to a home, was unsettled in the extreme. I knew that they would always be moving from place to place in quest of a cheap situation, and always spending more than they ought. Wickham's affection for my sister, I also knew, would soon sink into indifference—if it hadn't already.

As for Lydia, I knew her nature and she would cling to her attachment for as long as she could. But one day she would wake up and become sensible of her husband's apathy toward her and see that she had been trapped in a loveless bond. Reality and the truth cannot ever be permanently outrun, and even despite her youth and her manners, she would no longer be able to hide from herself that she was wed to a man who would be a villain in whatever story he claimed to be the hero of.

After we had read our letters, we were joined by Joseph Darcy, his wife, Felicity, and Henry. My sisters, Georgiana, Cousin Emilia, and the lot walked down to St. Mary's convent to finally meet Sister Mary Ignatius, who before she took orders, once bore the name of Deborah Darcy. Yes, she was the one of the American Darcys who had become a nun.

Darcy and Mr. Bingley did not join us however because they had a multitude of letters they had to respond to, concerning business or their estates back in England.

When we entered the convent grounds, we found two Sisters gardening in the front of their domicile, tending to the flowers and garden landscape. When we approached, one of them looked up and she smiled.

"Mother! And Felicity, Joseph! Henry!"

She wiped the dirt from her apron and rushed up to us, smiling and giddier than any other nun that I have seen.

"Oh, Deborah!" Emilia cried, hugging her daughter. I had seen nuns before in my time. Yet usually they were such a solemn folk, devoid of any brightness of character, not often seeing their families and being so open in nature. For some reason, too often people seemed to believe that to take holy orders was to lose any concept of human tenderness for one's fellow man, always making me assume that when one finds their religion, they sometimes miss the point of their faith.

However, Deborah displayed all the affection a daughter would bestow upon her mother. It was to a point where I understood completely why Emilia was sad at her daughter taking orders, for she must have missed having Deborah at home with her.

"Well," Deborah said, smiling at us, "you must be my cousins!"

I returned the smile. "Yes, we are. I am Mrs. Elizabeth Darcy, and I am very pleased to meet you, for I have heard nothing but the highest praise of you."

"Then my mother clearly didn't tell you how I used to pour ink in my siblings' tea all the time so that when they drank it, their teeth turned black."

"I did that a couple of times as well." Kitty beamed.

I groaned, remembering. "Yes, you did, because it was me you always did it to."

"Yes, and it never ceased to be funny to me. Besides you retaliated by always putting jelly in my stockings."

"And that was funnier than anything you could have devised."

"Elizabeth and Kitty!" Jane gasped. "You will make us look positively spiteful in the presence of Sister Ignatius here."

"Oh, you need not worry about that," Deborah said. "For I find sibling pranks as quite the epitome of harmlessness and can be quite healthy. For as long as you mean them no ill will, if you can't do such things to your brothers and sisters, then who can you do it to?"

We all laughed.

"And do me the favor of calling me Deborah," she whispered, "whenever we are not in earshot of another of my Sisters here. I am devoted to my station, but I do miss my birth name."

"Very well," I said. "Well Miss Deborah, these are my sisters Jane Bennet, Kitty Bennet, and my sister-in-law Georgiana Darcy."

They all curtsied to her.

"So, you are all from England?"

"Yes, Hampshire."

"I remember meeting a man from a pleasant town in England that bore that name. Steventon is in it, is it not?"

"Yes, that is where we are from precisely," Kitty said.

"Then you must know someone named Samuel Lucas."

"One of the Lucas boys?" Jane said with surprise. "Yes, we know him, for his sister, Charlotte Lucas, is a dear friend of ours. You actually know one of them?"

"Oh, I knew Samuel Lucas quite well," Deborah said, leading us along the grounds. "He came to Philadelphia with his father, Sir William Lucas, a couple years before I had taken orders. I was quite in love with him."

I put my hand to my mouth and gasped. "What? Truly?"

"What!" Cousin Emilia's cry was louder than mine. "You never told me of this."

"Of course not. I told no one my feelings at the time, for that is when one wants to keep to their own counsel. Yet now that years have passed, I have taken orders, I can confess such things without suspicion or being scrutinized.

"Many think becoming a nun is when you restrict your confessions, and I believe the opposite. We have now given ourselves completely unto our faith, which means now is the time to confess all. How can we connect to humans if we never talk about our own flaws or past experiences? To think otherwise is a hypocrisy that is too often born in this world."

"Sister," Henry bellowed, "you must not speak so."

"Oh, do shut up, Henry," Deborah said. "I daresay that I am making our cousins quite comfortable when you are not."

"Deborah!" Henry groaned.

"Henry!" Deborah snapped. "Grow a sense of humor, for sometimes you are worse than the other nuns here who preach only fire and brimstone."

Their sibling banter was not light.

"Precisely," I concurred, "How can you, with your light and open nature, live in such a place where restrictions seem to be the order of the day? And I do not wish to demean the practice of course, for I have a great respect to it, but you have such a unique and bold nature..."

"That how could I be happy in such a place?" she finished for me.

"Yes," Georgiana requested.

"By loving a good fight. Too many in this world don't know that religion is meant to feel free, it offers morality, yes, and laws, and protects us from the very worst of ourselves.

"Yet it is also there to make us find happiness, accept others no matter how different, smile, be content—we humans are meant to laugh. And if too many in this world forget that, preach of fire and brimstone, of damnation for erring too far in pursuing one's pleasures, then what good do I do if I don't try to fight against them? I am losing that battle, for the strict order of worship is still adhered to terribly, and I know that I will be officially defeated, but I will fight nonetheless—until I am defeated."

"That is a very noble attribute," Jane said, "to fight even when one knows that the fight is pointless."

Deborah shook her head. "The fight is never pointless. And failure to win the fight does not make it so. So yes, I was once in love with your own neighbor. Now you see that I am not so different than the rest of the women who you all know, am I?"

I laughed at that. "No, you are not. Yet I cannot help but be surprised at how small the world can be. For you, here, to know one of the Lucas boys and to have been in love with him is exceptional."

"Yes, that is very interesting. Fate, fortune, and circumstance can be very tricky and intertwined things. But, how is he?"

"He is well. He is still unmarried however."

"That sadly is easier for me to hear, but when he does marry, I shall be happy for him."

"What did happen between you both then?" Georgiana asked.

"Our worlds were too different, I assume. His heart was in England and my heart was here, and I was torn between my love for a married life and my love as a nun. Also, in the end, our differences might have come between us. Love for different things can cause too much of a wedge between two people. Yet don't worry, I did not break my heart. I just will forever remember him as the sort of man who I was lucky to have met once in my life."

๛

Meeting Deborah Darcy—Sister Ignatius—was one of those incredible encounters that one does not often get the chance to have, and it always seemed like a miracle when you did.

There is constant goodness in the world, and people who wield it within themselves perfectly, but they are so rare that it makes their sudden appearance in your life almost unreal or contrived. The Deborah Darcys were the sort of people in the world who you read about existing, but never believed that they did—until you met them. She went on to force Henry and Felicity out of their mannerly shells and tell us about their childhood antics, while also confessing to us one time when she wanted to punch one of her fellow nuns for being mean! Deborah really was a remarkable woman, for who confesses to wanting to strike someone... especially nuns.

When we did part, leaving the convent, Deborah saw us to the carriage.

"You all may come by next Saturday if you like, and make sure to have stories to tell me, and I promise to tell you of the time of when I almost let Samuel Lucas kiss me."

"Really?" Kitty cried.

"Are you serious, Deborah?" her mother questioned.

"Yes, I am quite serious. None of my sisters here can be angry with me for confessing such a thing to my family because of one important detail; they all were in love at one point, and they all still think about it."

"Oh Deborah." Emilia kissed her daughter's cheek. "I miss you all the time."

She touched her mother's cheek. "I'm still your daughter, Mother. Don't worry, I always shall be."

The carriage then drove off as she stood there smiling and waving at us.

"I always shall be!" she echoed.

As I sat next to Cousin Emilia in the carriage, I saw her expression droop the more we drove further from the convent. While everyone else spoke about their happiness in meeting such an amusing woman as Sister Ignatius, who was unlike any nun that we had ever met, I took the noise in the carriage as an opportunity to whisper to Emilia.

"Are you out of sorts, Cousin Emilia?"

"I know it is wrong of me," she whispered in reply. "Yet you see her now and you clearly understand why I did not want her to take orders. I know it is a strange thing to not want such a thing, but Deborah was always made of something not of this world. She can do much good in the church, yes, but she was always the one who I thought would take care of me when I grew too old. She was the one who I thought would see me till I came to an end."

"It must be painful to be parted from her then," I said, offering the best solace that I could think of. "Yet she will be there, that much is certain, and I will say this, you have a remarkable daughter. I never saw such courage in the world."

Cousin Emilia pressed her shoulder against mine. "Oh, bless you, Elizabeth, bless you."

⚜

It was so interesting how different women could be, and how maternity linked them in the end.

Mrs. Emilia Darcy and our mother were both lively and talking women, who had much to say, but that was where the similarity of nature ended.

Cousin Emilia had her favorites, but clearly loved all her children equally, yet seemed to also know their flaws and was not afraid to address this. She also knew that she and her husband were not perfect either, and that there was always room for self-improvement. Also, she was not nervous all the time like my mother and did not possess her meanness of understanding.

But maternity linked them. For like our mother, Emilia Darcy would do anything for her children, and defend them if she needed to. And therefore, like our mother, she suffered under the vicious cycle of having to bear them, raise them to be independent, and then lose them to the world as they had become so.

❧ 24 ❧

BARREN FIELD

W e then went to the Delaware River and began to walk alongside it, looking at the ships.

"Lizzy," Georgiana said, "is it not amazing, we have been here for only three weeks at the most and I feel as if so much has happened."

"Yes, much seems to have. I still cannot believe that Sister Ignatius was smitten with my neighbor. I know that you do not know the Lucases well, Georgiana, but it is an amazing thing. And therefore, when returning home, we shall have many stories to—"

Suddenly as we walked along, we encountered Miriam Goldman, who was walking with her mother, Mrs. Goldman.

"Mrs. Goldman," Cousin Emilia said guardedly when we encountered them. "How are you this afternoon?"

"We are well, thank you, Mrs. Darcy," Mrs. Goldman replied, equally as reserved in manner. "And how are you all doing this day?"

"We are all doing quite well, thank you."

Before uncomfortable silence threatened to reign over us, I turned to Miss Miriam.

"How are you this day, Miss Miriam?"

"Oh," she gasped, startled that I had addressed her. "I am very well, thank you. And how are you..."

"I'm Mrs. Darcy. Yes, we have not been properly introduced, but I have heard your name spoken often and I have heard nothing but the highest praise of you."

"Truly, you are too kind, and I feel sure to disappoint, for whoever gave me these praises might have spoken too highly of me."

"No, I am sure not so, for I heard it all from someone who is not at all inclined to exaggeration. My husband's friend, Mr. Bingley, he danced with you at the assembly and he could not stop talking about your superior dancing and conversation."

"He—he did?" When first hearing Mr. Bingley's name, she looked disconcerted, but when hearing the compliment, her expression lightened, and she looked hopeful.

"Yes, he did. And if you would be so kind, my sisters and I would like to get to know you better. Is there any chance that we might call on you when you are at home?"

"Oh," Miriam said, looking at her mother. "I should very much like that, and I am available tomorrow afternoon, if that be acceptable."

"Thank you. I would be delighted."

Mrs. Goldman gave us her address and then we parted ways.

Later that day, Jane and Kitty confronted me about wishing to become better acquainted with Miriam Goldman, and I told them the truth that I believed she and Mr. Bingley might be interested in each other.

Though I did not wish to fool with fortune and other people's lives by playing matchmaker, I believed that Miss Miriam deserved to be at least given a chance. They easily accepted my reasoning and then all was settled that we would visit the Goldmans the next day along with Georgiana.

However, my meeting with Henry later did not go in the same vein. Later that evening I was getting a book from Mr. Thomas Darcy's library when I heard someone enter.

"Mrs. Darcy, are you in here?" Henry asked.

"Yes, I am," I replied, walking along the bookshelves and facing him. "Does my husband need me?"

"No, I was simply looking for you."

"Oh, well you found me. What do you need?"

"I, this is not going to be easy, but I think that it is necessary for you to hear these words. I respect your judgment, Mrs. Darcy, and your generous candor, but I must request this for your own good as well as that of your husband's friend. I would recommend that, in regards to you calling on the Goldmans, that you send a note cancelling your visit."

I was shocked. "I beg your pardon?"

"Well, my brother, Joseph, and I have been speaking of this and we have both decided that it is not wise for you to become on familiar terms with them, for Mr. Bingley's sake."

Anger rose within me with every syllable that he uttered—and for him to discuss my actions with his brother, then not be afraid to tell me so! What insolence and impertinence!

"Thank you for your advice, Henry," I said coldly. "But I believe that I have the sense to choose my own acquaintances wisely and I find no harm in the Goldmans."

"You must know that Mr. Bingley was interested on that score."

"Mr. Bingley's heart is his own, as my decisions are my own."

"Her differences—"

"Do not make her below my notice," I added, staring him boldly in the face, not willing to be intimidated. "And never shall. If she proves to be a lovely woman, then I will regard her as such."

"I do not defame her person, but she is below us Darcys by a great deal. She is not of our circles or financial sphere. And you best be guided by reason, which you are very much lacking in this circumstance. For you truly don't see what harm it will do to your husband's reputation for you to not consider your acquaintances wisely."

"You accuse me of being blind?" I exclaimed, vexed with him greatly.

"I humbly request that you see reason, Mrs. Darcy, and be guided by the serenity and compliance that rules your elder sister's spirit."

I still fumed inside. "Compliance?"

"Yes, your sister Miss Bennet understands the importance of listening to the superior mind of a gentleman and I ask that you be guided by her single-minded and artless manner. You seem to show a sort of conceited independence, that you will not be guided by another or their wisdom, while Miss Jane Bennet would agree with me with alacrity, for she would see that I know best, while she would not."

"Firstly, you offend me greatly! And you insult her! Both are crimes on your part. And you seem to be confusing single-mindedness with weak-mindedness, and you prefer the second one and call it the first one. Yet my sister is not what you accuse her of being."

"I do not insult her but offer her the greatest compliment in the world."

"By being compliant? Therefore, what you and I regard as a compliment and an insult are quite different. Your very beliefs only show me that you regard my sister's generous views as a negative and call it a positive, then look at my positive attitude and think yourself smart for looking at it as a negative."

I took a few deep breaths before continuing. "A long time ago, I learned not to trust a person who thinks things are what they are not, because those are the sort to look at the world and convince others that the sky is green and the grass is blue, because they can't see that they are in error. Therefore, I ask you sir, what is wrong with you?"

"What is wrong with me?" He was quite affronted. "What is wrong with you?"

"Elizabeth and Mr. Darcy."

We both started, turned and my sister Jane was standing in the doorway, looking back at us.

"Jane?" I gasped.

"Miss Bennet," Henry stuttered and then bowed. "Your sister and I were just—"

"I am aware," Jane acknowledged. "For I have been standing here for quite some time. Now if you would be so kind, Mr. Darcy, I have come to fetch my sister, for *her* Mr. Darcy is requesting her presence in the music room, for he wants her to play some music. And I daresay that his wishes take precedence over anyone else in her life, would you not agree?"

"Of—of course. For a dutiful wife must always be quick to obey her husband, and I am certain that you will agree."

Jane did not favor him with an answer, but only beckoned me to follow her, which I did. When we left the library, and were out of earshot, I turned to her.

"I am happy that you do not love him, Jane. Good god, I am ever so happy that you don't."

"I know. So am I."

⚜

The next day we went to make our visit to the Goldmans, and Mrs.

Goldman, Miss Miriam and her sisters met us eagerly and we all sat down to tea and cakes.

We told them about our lives in Hampshire, what growing up in our household was like, and they responded in kind of what difference it was to be growing up in America after the Revolutionary War.

Mrs. Goldman told us all about what life was like there during the American Revolution, and the hardships of not being able to feed their families. And she had come from a family of loyalists, who had been loyal to Britain when half of the city's inhabitants were patriots.

"Many of us actually were frightened at the idea of breaking away from Britain," she confessed. "It just gets forgotten. My family was against the revolution at first, and we wished to remain British, but then times changed."

The times were naturally hard, and it was quite difficult to be a mother who had to provide for her family at a time where obtaining provisions were almost impossible. She also had a female friend who was a spy against the British during the British Occupation of Philadelphia in 1777, and how she worried what would happen if her friend got caught.

Her stories of intrigue were amazing, and it was nice to hear a fresh perspective in a tete e tete rather than hearing the same old things that a woman does back home and living in a small town.

After our tea, Miriam wished to take a walk in a nearby park and wondered if we wished to join her, which we were happy to do.

Through our preamble along the greenery, Miriam and I conversed very easily, and she proved to be a most wonderful companion. She was open, had lively manners, and seemed to lack an artificiality of any kind while also not ever being rude. She had opinions, while also having the courage to commit to them and not fear someone disagreeing with her.

For my share of the conversation, I told her of my life, ending in my love for Mr. Darcy and the story of how we had come together and found one another.

"That is a wonderful story," she said at the end. "I confess to having once mocked the idea of love at first sight, which you seem to have done. Yet I soon came to realize that I made that assumption based on conceit and pride. For... one time, I laid my eyes on someone, and I felt as if I was stricken by a thunderbolt, and then I understood that I was in error, for it is quite possible. And in your case, I am happy that it did not end in sadness, but the very best of all endings."

"Yes, I am fortunate," I said, and then I dared to take a risk. "What happened to the man who you felt such a swift affection for?"

"Oh, it is not as fortunate as yours. I liked him, but the affection was not reciprocated."

"Did he say as much?"

"No, he did not."

"Then there is always hope, Miss Miriam."

"Thank you, but hope is not something that always can lead to good ends, but I do believe I will smile nonetheless."

"You should smile, for hope is still a good friend to have. It gives one a dream, and dreams do not always come true, but it was nice to have them, nonetheless. For without that hope, life is like a barren field frozen with snow."

25

WHEN LIFE SHOWS YOU THE TRUTH

The next day, Darcy and I were driving in a carriage, looking to go to the marketplace to buy Cousin Emilia and Thomas presents for letting us stay with them. Being alone, it gave me time to tell my husband all that Henry had said to me. When I was done, to say Fitzwilliam was irate was an understatement.

"The insolent fool!" he exclaimed. "To think that he honestly dared to speak to you without speaking to me first is abominable, then to corner you and insult you because of your own infallible guide in matters of morality and then oppress you with his meanness of opinion! Wait till I return to Canterbury when we are done shopping."

"Darcy, please don't trouble yourself on my behalf."

"You are my wife, Lizzy. I have every right to be troubled on your behalf. Would you have me be indifferent to his paltry attack on you? Is it to be endured, it shall not be."

I smiled, for he truly loved me. "I suppose you are correct. I would always want you to defend me and I shall not stop you from doing so. I just wish you to calm yourself so that you do not frighten him in the way that only Fitzwilliam Darcy knows how to."

"Do I look so intimidating sometimes?" He raised one wry eyebrow.

I laughed and nudged his shoulder. "Yes."

We were interrupted by a commotion that was being made in the street and cries were heard. I leaned over and looked out of the carriage window.

"Elizabeth, be careful," Darcy said.

"Oh my god, Darcy, look at this!"

On the street, a Negro woman, along with her children, was being dragged out of a church by a large man. He had a cowhide whip with him, and while she shouted that she was a freed Negro, and not a runaway, the man seemed to not believe her and continued to drag her and her children along the street. Making a quick assumption, based on what I had read before, he seemed to be a slave catcher. The scene felt surreal, for I had never seen such a thing, but only read of them existing. Despite it all, knowing about something and seeing it were two entirely different experiences.

"Yet it is true!" she cried. "I am free; let me get my papers so that I can show you. Do not take my children!"

We stopped our carriage at the sight of this horrific event, but for a moment, I was completely stricken with shock. I moved out of the way so that Darcy could take a look and his expression turned from one of surprise to disgust.

"Blood and 'ounds!" he swore.

The slave catcher then began to brutally hit the woman with the cowhide, and she cried out in agony. There were many people on the street, and they were looking on, but doing nothing.

"Darcy," I cried. "We must stop this!"

"I know," he replied, opening the carriage door and jumping out. As he did so, I noticed a young woman who jumped out of a carriage nearby and began to rush to the slave catchers to help the Negro woman, but my husband grabbed her before she could get closer and be harmed.

"Stay back," Darcy said to her. "I shall make work of this!"

Rushing past her, brandishing his walking cane, Darcy lunged at the slave catcher, struck him across the face, and the slave catcher fell backwards. With the might and force of the strongest of men, Darcy then took up the cowhide whip, and began striking the slave catcher with it. The man cried out, but with each scream, my husband had a reply.

"Are your cries any more valuable than hers? Is your worth of any greater consequence than herself and that of her children?" He brought the lash down on the slaver's back.

"Do you like how this feels?"

The slaver screamed.

"This pain you cry over, now do you see how terrible it is? She's a woman, you devil! She is a mother, and you will never strike her again! Moreover, she is free, and you will not pull her into this terrible life so that you can have wages that you have no right to keep."

My husband whipped the slave catcher more until his blood fell freely down his shirt. When done venting his anger at the man's barbarism, Darcy turned, looked up and addressed the rest of the people on the street.

"You all call yourselves humans? People of God, and yet, and *yet*, you stand by and call this institution lawful. You cry out to England about the impressment and mistreatment of your sailors, of us taking them and having them work on our ships, and yet you do this!"

He strode back and forth in front of the crowd. "How is the evil of my countrymen considered malignant and yet your evil here and now is acceptable! How do you cry out 'oppression', when you allow and encourage such violence upon such persons! I am Mr. Fitzwilliam Darcy, of Pemberly, England, and I call you hypocrites of the worst degree!"

Suddenly a couple of men who were friends of the slave catcher were about to come forward and attack my husband—and that was when my anger would not let me sit still any longer.

I reached under the carpet of the carriage and took out the pistol that Darcy showed me that he kept there if ever in case of emergency. Then I stepped down and brandished it at the two men.

"Attempt to commit violence upon my husband's form, and I shall gladly take your life."

Darcy looked at me with purpose but not with shock, then he turned and addressed the slave catcher and everyone else on the street.

"I know this woman," I declared, gesturing to the Negro woman who the slave catcher was trying to abduct. "And she is no slave! Nor are her children! She works as a cook in my cousin's household and she has done so all her life! Retrieving her is not your right, both morally and legally. Stand down from her, and cease to threaten my husband, or have your life be taken from you!"

It was a lie, yet my husband did not flinch at it, nor did the Negro woman, who saw that it would be best to play along because we were trying to save her. The slave catchers looked between my husband, the

Negro woman with her children, then me, then they moved away and rushed into the multitude, running away.

Darcy turned to the young woman who had gotten down from the carriage to help the Negro woman and nodded to her.

"You were brave to have tried to come to their aid," he said.

"Thank you," the young woman replied. "It is a godsend that you were come by at this time to prove their independence."

"I lied," I whispered, chuckling. "She does not work for my cousin, and I've never seen her in the whole of my life."

The young lady smiled slightly at my confession.

"What is your name, Miss?" I asked.

"I am Harriet Price."

"Harriet Price? I am Elizabeth Darcy. That over there, is my husband Mr. Darcy. And I am pleased to make your acquaintance."

"The pleasure is all mine."

We turned and Darcy walked up to the Negro woman and helped her up.

"Are you well enough to walk?"

"Yessir. Yes, I can walk, but I can even run."

"They will come back for you. Do you have anywhere that you can run to?"

"Yes. I am friendly with a Quaker family who can take me in on Arch Street."

"Fine. There's room in my carriage. I will take you there."

The woman collected her children and Darcy led her to our carriage where he helped her and her children in.

"Your husband is a good man," Harriet Price said to me.

"Yes, he is. He is, and always will be, the very greatest of men."

"Mrs. Darcy," my husband said to me. "If you do not mind, the carriage will be slightly more crowded on our return journey to Chestnut Street."

"I quite understand." I then turned back to Harriet Price. "It is rare to possess such courage, so be happy you have it, and cling to it, Harriet Price. I'll remember that name."

"And I shall remember yours. And his." Harriet Price and I curtsied to each other, then I went to the carriage, Darcy helped me in, and we were off. As we drove along, one of the daughters of the Negro woman peeked her head out of the carriage window and looked at Harriet Price and waved to her as we drove on.

All throughout the ride to Arch Street, the mother thanked us, then she could take refuge with a family of Quakers by the last name of Griscombe and we made sure that she and her family were safe till we took off once more.

Once we did so, I placed myself on Darcy's lap and kissed him passionately.

"You are a hero," I cried. "But then you always have been, haven't you?"

He kissed me passionately and noticed the pistol that I still had on the seat cushion.

"You were about to shoot a man for me?"

"Of course, I would have."

"That is why I love you." We kissed again, with great passion.

Eventually we drove along, continued shopping and then we were on the journey ride home. We began to talk freely of what had occurred.

"The trade is a cancer that should be wiped away from all good society," Darcy growled. "And for people to believe in it! How cruel the world is."

"I agree," I said, shaking my head. "It is not to be born. And yet, yet that woman. That Harriet Price... of all the people on the street, she was the only one to be brave and try and stop it."

"Yes, very rarely do people do the right thing."

"But her name, Harriet Price, I don't know why, but it sounds familiar."

"It's a popular name."

"Well yes, but—I think I know who she was!"

"Who then, for I am quite certain that I have never met her before?"

"Do you remember when we went to see *Timon of Athens* at the theatre, and we met Parson Persons, the leading actor?"

"Oh yes, the one who admired my sister, and I didn't like it."

"He didn't admire her he admired the woman who she reminded him of. And the woman's name was Harriet Price."

"Oh yes, but that doesn't mean that it is the same person."

"The Harriet Price that he spoke of was from England, and the Harriet Price that we just met had an English accent...not to mention that while she did not look like Georgiana exactly, she looked like her enough. Yes, I daresay that we just met that Harriet Price. I don't know what significance that holds, but it is an interesting coincidence all the same."

"Lizzy," my husband said. "When we return to Canterbury, I shall speak with Henry, but I must also speak with Mr. Bingley."

I nodded, understanding my husband's sudden change and determination. He had only then just witnessed what the world would let happen because it turned a blind eye to horror. When life shows you the truth, it marks and separates the empathetic from the apathetic. The empathetic choose to see the truth and fight, while the apathetic continue to let a vicious cycle continue to progress and unwind. And long ago, I learned what my husband was—and apathy was never a vice of his.

❦ 26 ❧

BRAVE ENOUGH FOR LOVE

W e drove on to Canterbury, and when we entered, we came to the house being in quite a stir.

"Elizabeth and Mr. Darcy!" Kitty said, rushing down the steps. "The most terrible thing has occurred. Mr. Henry Darcy has proposed to Jane!"

"He has?"

Breathless, she answered, "Yes, he has."

"Dear lord," I cried. "Please tell me that she refused him."

"Yes, and he has gone to tell his family and now they are speaking with Jane in the sitting room." Kitty's eyes were wide with concern.

Once again, anger welled up inside me. "They are all standing against her? How dare they bully her?"

"Georgiana and Mr. Bingley are there to accompany her, but still you must come directly."

"Blast it, we shall!" my husband said, furious. We followed him swiftly to the sitting room, where we entered to see Jane sitting down, looking very vexed while Mr. Bingley paced back and forth protectively over her and Georgiana sat alongside her. Cousin Thomas and Emilia stood a few feet away, with Henry sitting there looking bitter.

"What is going on here?!" Darcy exclaimed.

"You can calm yourself," Cousin Thomas said. "We simply were wishing to sort this all out."

"And what is there to sort out precisely?" My husband asked sarcastically.

I could see the anger he experienced that day was mingled with his anger at seeing my sister possibly mistreated. "I was told that your son made my sister-in-law an offer of marriage and that offer was refused. Is that correct, Miss Bennet?"

"Yes," Jane said shakily, "it is."

I walked over to her and sat down next to her, putting my hand on her shoulder.

"Well there you have it," I added. "She has refused and that should be an end to the matter."

"It is not an end to the matter," Henry said, turning to Jane. "For these last weeks, I have given you every marked attention, all of which you have received with happiness. Why do you turn away from me now?"

"Maybe this is why," Mr. Bingley said. "A proper gentleman does not act this way."

"And it should not be set down that every lady should be obliged to accept any man who vies for her hand," I argued.

"Yes," Jane said. "I am honored by your proposal, but I cannot accept it."

"And this is all the reply I am to expect?" Henry said angrily. "I wonder at with so little efforts at civility that I am thus rejected?"

"And I might ask with such designs to offend and insult me and my family," Jane said, "that you tell me that you wish to marry me because of my lack of spirit and then berate my sister because she possesses much of it."

Jane looked at Henry sharply. "Do you think anything could tempt me to accept the hand of a man who has hurt and offended a most beloved sister?"

I felt blood rush to my cheeks, for I could see that it was me that Jane was about to defend.

"Yes," Jane said. "I know about how you confronted Elizabeth in the library, practically ordering her to submit to your reasoning when your reasoning is that of a prejudiced man who was trying to coerce my sister. I heard it all. Why would I wish to align myself with someone who would do such a thing? Can you deny it, Mr. Henry Darcy?"

"I have no wish to deny it. I did everything in my power to separate your sister from making a grave mistake and I rejoice in my success." He paced before us.

"Towards her I have been kinder than toward myself. How can you be so foolish as to reject me? For you must surely be out of your senses, and not possessing the rationality that I gave you credit for. When I am the one to degrade myself with this proposal to you? Yes, I very much have not been kinder to myself."

"And kinder than I shall be toward you, you blackguard!" Darcy roared. "How dare you insult Miss Bennet, and accost my wife in private, set her down as if she is a pet at your table, blame her for following her own flawless matters in regards to matters of philosophy and decorum, and call yourself wise while you do it?"

While Henry had ceased pacing, Darcy now began. "I remember the man I once was, Henry Darcy, and I see a pale reflection of that shadow in you. You are an impudent dog and I am sorry for it. How dare you treat Elizabeth in such a way?"

"Anything that I have done is to safeguard the good name of this family," Henry said. "Nor am I ashamed of what I have confessed and of what my own feelings have been, for they were natural and just. Could you expect me to rejoice in having relations who wish to make connections with those who are so decidedly below my own?"

"You are mistaken, Mr. Henry Darcy!" Jane said. "The mode of your declaration only spared me the concern I might have felt in refusing you, had you behaved in a more gentleman-like manner."

Henry Darcy flinched at her implication.

"You do not love me," Jane said. "You love an image. You love that I am someone who you can feel comfortable projecting your own ambitions onto without caring about my own wishes. Tell me one thing you actually know about me? Tell me one, please?"

Henry Darcy looked around, at a loss.

"That is of no import," he muttered.

Jane rubbed her forehead and sighed. "That is of every import. And see, you know nothing of me that doesn't align with yourself. You love yourself, Mr. Darcy, and you love how I fit with you—but it's not love for me that you feel. I've seen real love and it is not what we possess."

"Aye," I added. "Your motive for choosing my sister as your wife was a selfish one, for you believed that if you chose her, you would have a compliant wife who you could move around like a chess piece and never expect her to object to your demands and judgments. That is not love, but an idea of one. One where you believe yourself to think you can have someone who you can control, and not one who you respect."

"Aye," Darcy said. "For if you respected her truly, you would not have subjected her to this circus. And if you respected my wife, you would not have done what you did."

He stopped in front of his cousin. "How can you even think yourself capable of satisfying a woman, Henry, when you never listen to them? Therefore, until you learn to hear them, you will listen to me."

My husband stood his ground.

"You have insulted my wife and were wrong to do so; you will accept my sister-in-law's rejection and learn from it, for until you do, you could not make her an offer of marriage in a way that could have possibly tempted her to accept. For from the very beginning, your manners have expressed to me knowledge of your arrogance, your conceit and your selfish disdain for the feelings of others. And now, it is quite plain that you are the last man in the world who Jane should ever be prevailed upon to marry."

My husband's admonitions made me proud. "Thank you, Mr. Darcy. For I daresay that I could not have said it better myself."

Cousin Thomas stood up and looked between us.

"Henry, Miss Jane Bennet has rejected your proposal with generous candor. And you must accept it."

Henry, looking bitter, bowed curtly and then walked out. Emilia at first began to follow after him.

"Emilia," Thomas said, "let him be alone. For only isolation can heal his wounds."

She tossed her husband a fretful look. "He might do harm to himself."

"He will not. Our son is too proud for that."

Thomas looked at us all.

"I suppose this is entirely my fault," he said. "I gave him good principles but left him to practice them in pride and conceit."

"Then teach him," I suggested. "And remember that he is an adult, and the only person who can change him now is himself."

"Still, it does hurt," he said. "I'm sorry for all this."

I was as well. "I do believe that we have quite overstayed our welcome at this point."

"I never meant to cause any harm," Jane said, standing up. "And I do not wish for a wedge to be caused in between a family. Let my absence from your home be an end to any schism that might occur."

"You need not worry, Jane," I said, "for you have nothing to apologize for."

I stood up and offered Cousin Thomas and Emilia a parcel.

"Mr. Darcy and I would humbly like to offer you these parting gifts that we bought you, to thank you for inviting us to your lovely home and having us feel like the family that we are to you."

Cousin Emilia took the parcel and opened it. It was a set of porcelain dolls that were a family of nine.

"We found it in an antique shop, and it reminded us of your family. And all the good that we saw in it."

Emilia sat down and began to weep. We all excused ourselves and let Cousin Thomas attend to her.

The next morning, all our things were packed, and we rented some carriages to take us to an inn until we could purchase tickets for a passage back to England. Cousin Thomas and Emilia saw us off, along with Helena, who was doing her best to pay attention, despite her disability, but was not able to overcome it. Felicity also saw us off and before we left completely, she hugged Jane.

"Who says that we shall not be sisters in the end?" Felicity whispered in Jane's ear. The rest of our goodbyes were solemn, and we were off, leaving Canterbury. As the estate disappeared behind us, I could not help but be saddened on how something began so promising and all had fallen apart so easily, all at the whim of heartache and misunderstandings.

As we drove along, we turned down a street and Mr. Bingley was the first to notice that we were going the wrong way.

"This is not the road to the inn."

"You are correct, Charles," Darcy said. "It is not."

We stopped in front of a house and Mr. Bingley looked confused.

"What is this place?"

"This is the home of the Goldmans," I said. "Of Miss Miriam Goldman, the woman who you were afraid to face."

At the mention of her name, Mr. Bingley's expression froze.

"What is the meaning of this?"

"It was my idea, Charles," Darcy said. "Elizabeth and I had been discussing it last night and this was the solution that I came up with."

"I don't understand. What are you doing?"

"I'm keeping you from making a mistake. The same mistake that I almost made."

Bingley looked down at his hands, folded in his lap.

"You can tell yourself that you did the right thing," Darcy said, "to justify acting cold toward Miss Goldman, but is that right, Charles? Is that correct? It is not sound, nor is it you. It is me."

Bingley and the rest of us looked at Fitzwilliam in confusion. For how could he be blaming himself for this one?

"Too long I had labored under the weight of propriety," Darcy continued. "And all the while, you watched me do it, you watched me treat others as below me, be disagreeable and disobliging, slighting all in my company and calling myself a gentleman.

"I see now that it might have left the wrong impression on you. Slighting a woman that you feel for is not the Mr. Bingley that the world has come to know. Hurting her because of a difference, an accident of birth is not correct—it is not you! But kindness, openness, willing to approve of everyone that you meet until they give you a reason not to is who you are.

"You are Mr. Charles Bingley, not Mr. Darcy! And the world needs you to remember that. It needs men who don't ridicule others and cast them aside just because of class difference. Time and time again, you have forgiven your taciturn friend here, who always mocked others, but you never lost faith in me. Don't make the same mistakes that I did, and that I almost let ruin my life."

Darcy reached over and grasped his friend's shoulder. "Become Mr. Bingley again, and don't lose sight of that. Forgive me, Charles—for so long you were the better man, and I did not see it. I should have supported every kind gesture you ever made instead of opposing it. You have your goodness now, and no one will take it from you."

Mr. Bingley had begun to weep... for though they were bosom friends, Darcy never showed the magnitude of how important Bingley's presence in his life was. Both men were like characters who were locked in the same journey, it seemed, and their relationship had become co-dependent and very much intertwined.

"Thank you, Darcy," Bingley whispered. "Thank you for everything. You are the best friend I have, isn't that funny?"

Mr. Bingley then got out of the carriage, walked up the steps and knocked on the door of the Goldmans. A maid let him in, and we all sat and waited.

After twenty minutes or so, Mr. Bingley emerged from the house looking happy and Miriam Goldman was with him. She approached our carriage and we spoke a while and she glowed with happiness while Bingley stood beside her. It was clear that a noteworthy courtship was about to begin.

We did not want to leave Bingley in America by himself, yet we knew that we could not remain in the city. Philadelphia was large, but it wasn't large enough for us not to run into the American Darcys, therefore we traveled to New York while Bingley stayed at an inn in Philadelphia and continued increasing his relationship with Miss Goldman.

If Bingley ever wished to come and visit, we agreed to stay there for a month before we wrote to tell him that we must away back to England, whether he was ready to join us or no.

In the meantime, New York proved to be very diverting and enjoyable. While there, I received a letter from Charlotte Collins, who I had written to tell of when I met Sister Ignatius and her confession of her love for Samuel Lucas.

While I was walking in a park in New York City with Jane, I sat at a bench with her, opened the letter and began to read.

Dear Lizzy,

All is well here, therefore I shall not write to you of trifles, but get to the heart of the matter.

I spoke to Samuel of this Sister Ignatius, from when he knew her as Deborah Darcy and nothing else. When he found out that she had taken holy orders, his face practically froze, and he remembered her with perfect clarity. It is such a strange thing, for a sister never thinks of her brother as being in love, yet now I have seen it with my own eyes.

He was in love with her, Lizzy, and he chose not to make her an offer because he was worried that there would be too many differences. If he married her and brought her home, he was worried about how the ton would treat her. Seeing the pains of putting her through that, he ceased having any real designs on her.

Yet—though this is very immodest and since she is a nun, it would be most imprudent of me to do so, my brother has begged me to tell you that if you ever see Ms. Deborah Darcy again, to let her know that he did love her and that there is not one moment of happiness they had that he wants to forget. He also wants to beg her for forgiveness, for he now sees that he has made a mistake. He was a coward and he should not have feared the cruel judgment of the world and demanded the importance of its views higher than the demands of his heart. If he could go back, he would have married her. And he should have been braver.

Well, Lizzy, though I know it errs against decorum, I had to write it, for I have never seen my brother act such a way. And I cannot help but feel sorry for him. Therefore, if you can find it in your heart, tell this woman. I believe she has the right to know it.

Your constant friend,
*   Charlotte Collins*

PS- Jane Austen has begun writing her next book. She is thinking of naming it First Impressions.

I closed the letter and chuckled. *First Impressions* was not a bad title, but I believe that Jane Austen could think of a better one down the road.

After I put the letter away, I resolved it within myself to be brave and write to Sister Ignatius, for she was very much allowed to receive letters in her convent and tell her what Samuel had confessed. Deborah Darcy was a strong woman who would not let the loss of love send her into a spiral of grief. She might feel some internal regret, but she would only let that knowledge of his love for her be like a flame that would burn inside her and strengthen her resolve. It would be a comfort to her, not a bane.

Having come to that conclusion, I turned to Jane.

"How are you, Jane?" I asked. "Truly?"

She chuckled and touched my arm. "You need not concern yourself for me, Lizzy, for I can assure you, I am quite well."

"I must confess to admiring you more than ever. For so long our mother has engrained it within us that we must marry, at all costs. And now you have broadened yourself beyond that and you won't dispose of yourself to just any man who seems like a good prospect."

"How can I? For now, I am quite spoilt."

"How are you spoilt?"

"Because I have seen a marriage where both parties love and respect the other. How can I not compare every coupling of myself with such a superior image as I have seen? How can I not compare it to yours? You and Mr. Darcy found each other, against all odds. You took a risk in letting him in, for he could have quite ruined you, and he took a risk in letting you in, for you could have quite ruined him. Yet through time and space, Elizabeth Bennet and Mr. Fitzwilliam Darcy of Pemberly found each other, and they became something that it seems very few others can touch. I should be jealous of you, but I'm not. I should question why it happened to you and not me, but I do not."

"It may, Jane. It may."

"Perhaps, or perhaps not. For as I have said before, till I have your spirit, I shall never have your happiness. Yet in time, since there seem to be no more Mr. Brocklehursts in the world, I may yet find another Mr. Collins."

We both had a hearty laugh over that.

"But know this," Jane said. "It is very easy for my situation to look as if I have been stricken with misfortune, but that is not so.

"You see, I have just had an adventure—there was no chance for those at home. And a young lady, if she cannot find adventure in her own village, must surely go looking for it elsewhere. And I have now learned to stand up for myself! That is not misfortune, oh no! That means I am now... just bloody brilliant! And I do believe that I am up for another adventure."

Jane laughed merrily and skipped along the walk.

A little over three weeks into our stay, we were greeted by a most wonderful sight: Mr. Bingley had arrived on our doorstep.

He visited us at the inn, was granted entry and met us in our rooms where he seemed fidgety.

"Mr. Bingley," Kitty asked, concerned, "is everything quite all right?"

"Yes, it is, thank you, Miss Kitty."

"Have you left Miss Goldman well in Philadelphia?"

"Yes, quite well, it is just...I have some news and I am quite nervous to share it."

"Well then," I said, patting the seat next to me, "do sit down."

"No thank you, Mrs. Darcy, but standing will help me now, I believe."

Mr. Bingley paced back and forth while we all watched him and then he gathered up his resolve.

"I know that you all think this a fast and speedy decision, yet fast and speedy are my nature and you all know that when I wish to do something, I decide upon it so swiftly, but I feel this to be right."

He paused and took a deep breath. "In the short time that I have known Miss Miriam, I have developed a passionate attachment to her. She and I are so similar, but she also has courage, she has dreams, desires, and we have much to always speak of.

"We see eye to eye on things, but what we see differently on does not frighten us, because our tempers are not the sort to turn away from such a thing. Yes, she is poorer and of a different social sphere, but I do not care. I cannot see myself living with another, loving another, and living without her."

He paused again, and then announced, "Therefore, I have come up here to tell you all, that I have proposed to Miss Miriam, and she has accepted me. I am getting married, and I would like all of your blessing."

I was overjoyed! "Mr. Bingley, that is wonderful news!"

"Oh," Georgiana cried, "I am so happy for you!"

All four of us women threw aside decorum, rushed up to Mr. Bingley and hugged him. He almost fell backwards under our weight, and under the weight of our affection!

Behind us, Darcy stood, ever the presence of aristocratic reserve.

After all four of us released Mr. Bingley from our embrace, Mr. Bingley then turned to Darcy.

He gave him a cautious look. "Well Darcy, will you offer your blessing? Will you support me in this decision of mine, my *taciturn friend*?"

My husband stepped forward and offered Bingley his hand.

"Of course, I do. Well done, Bingley."

"Thank you, Darcy," Bingley said shaking it.

We traveled back to Philadelphia, for we had to attend the ceremony which was to take place in three weeks' time as well as offer Miriam our congratulations.

When she saw us, she rushed up to us and took our hands in hers.

When we asked after her health she laughed, stating that her health did not signify at the moment, but only her happiness.

"Oh!" she exclaimed. "It is too much, how could my life have worked out so? I cannot believe it, but to have such a man to love me so, and to feel this love for him in return, I can scarce believe it, but it appears that fortune has found me!"

The wedding took place and it was one for the ages.

At the ceremony, I sat with my sisters, sister-in-law, and Fitzwilliam in the pews. There were not many at this wedding ceremony, for most of Bingley's relations were still in England, but those who did come were very much happy for the fortunate couple.

As for Darcy and me, both of us looked on the match with a favorable eye, for it was one thing for two people to be brought together because they were so similar, and it was so convenient for them—yet for two people to feel such a strong bond despite their differences was an even more powerful thing.

"Mr. Darcy," I whispered, during the ceremony.

"Yes, Mrs. Darcy?"

"That look that Mr. Bingley gives his bride was the same look that you gave me when we were wed."

"And the look she gives him is the same look you gave me, except you were lovelier."

"And to think, that the only way they found each other was because we decided to make our way to this city."

"Yes, it is a strange thing that so much has happened, all because we were brave. Brave enough for love."

"And we always will be."

"Yes, we always shall."

"Mr. Darcy?" I asked, taking his hand in my own as we sat there.
"Yes?"
"I love you."
"And I love you. Forever and always. I love you."

THE END

Turn the page for a preview of
Pride, Prejudice & New Adventures book III
Desire & Destiny!

Don't miss out on your next favorite book!

Join the Satin Romance mailing list
www.satinromance.com/mail.html

AFTERWORD

Hello, Reader, I hope that you enjoyed Book II of 'Pride, Prejudice & New Adventures'. If you finish this before the third book comes out, then this is just to comment on any questions you may have had after this read.

Question: Why is Jane Bennet not getting married in this book?

Answer: With all of my 'Pride & Prejudice' variations, I always believed that Mr. Darcy and Elizabeth should always get married of course (!) but with Jane Bennet, I had her get married to Mr. Bingley four times, five if you include the book I am currently writing outside of this series. I also had one where she married a Mr. Darcy. As a result, I wanted there to be one depiction of Jane Bennet where she had a different path than usual. Also, by having her not get married at this time, I was able to have her undergo many adventures later on in this series where she is constantly growing as a character. Sometimes it's nice to have a character who shows that after you are in a relationship that doesn't work out, it's fine and often great to take time off and stabilize yourself. That is what Jane Bennet did in this book really. Sometimes a person needs to take time to stand on their own two feet before they make any romantic choices.

Question: What is with the sudden talk in certain places about the historic events that occurred in that time?

Answer: Reader, never fear, the majority of the series shall mostly focus on the actions and thoughts of the central characters. But the fact is that this was a very historical time and all these incidents did occur and could occur. I felt that by confronting all that was happening during the world of 'Pride & Prejudice', it would make the story feel real. Also, people sometimes think such issues should not be talked about in these books, because they weren't always talked about in the novels of the times, but it gets overlooked that often these issues were talked about in period novels. But even if it was not written about, in those times, people could not write about it for fear of offending someone. Yet now, with the times being more evolved, they can be written about. And also, sometimes it gets implied that women did not talk about such issues at the time, but they definitely did. This was the time of the suffrage movement, women were spies during wars, women were abolitionists, and they did many things. It just gets overlooked sometimes. Again, the majority of the series shall focus on the adventures of the Darcy/Bennet family, but every now and again, social issues will get noticed, because they did occur. For me to ignore them just felt strange to me.

I hope that you enjoyed this book, and if not, thanks for reading my book anyway!

THANK YOU FOR READING

Did you enjoy this book?

We invite you to leave a review at your favorite book site, such as Goodreads, Amazon, Barnes & Noble, etc.

DID YOU KNOW THAT LEAVING A REVIEW…

- Helps other readers find books they may enjoy.
- Gives you a chance to let your voice be heard.
- Gives authors recognition for their hard work.
- Doesn't have to be long. A sentence or two about why you liked the book will do.

DESIRE & DESTINY

PROLOGUE

PRIDE, PREJUDICE & NEW ADVENTURES III

I n the pews, we sat, as the ceremony ended.

"I now pronounce you husband and wife," the reverend said, standing before Mr. Bingley and Miriam Goldman. "May you be joined together in holy matrimony. And Mr. Bingley, you may kiss your bride."

Mr. Bingley and Miriam Goldman turned to each other and kissed, while we all stood and clapped for them.

Turning to us, Mr. Bingley beamed, shining from his happiness with his bride standing next to him. Together, with their arms linked, they walked down the aisle to the piano playing the wedding music.

"He looks content," I whispered to Mr. Darcy as he sat next to me. "I wish them all the happiness in the world, yet I daresay that I still looked happier."

"I daresay that you did," Mr. Darcy replied, "For your happiness was infectious, for you made me smile in turn."

"Smiling becomes you—almost as much as scowling does."

"Scowling..." He chuckled, taking my hand in his and kissing my palm. "Yes, that is a favorite pastime of mine."

Later, Darcy said, "Bingley," offering his hand and Mr. Bingley shook it. "Congratulations, and I hope that you and your bride will be very happy."

"Thank you, Darcy." Mr. Bingley smiled. "I do believe I have made the right decision in this case. She is my second self, and I know that our time together was no more than a couple of months, but that was all that I needed."

"Time doesn't always determine intimacy between two people," Darcy acknowledged, "For some, seven years cannot do, whereas for others, seven days can be more than enough. I suppose that if I wasn't certain that she didn't make you happy, I would be anxious for your state. But I have instead seen that she in fact is you, and therefore, I shall hope to find your fortune for the better, as opposed to being ruled over by a mistake."

"Mistake? No, I pray not so. For Darcy—though I say it myself, she is the most beautiful creature I ever beheld. And that is saying much, for you and I both have seen Miss Jane Bennet."

"Yes, you must be truly in love with this woman to determine such a thing."

They continued to speak on while I turned my attention back to the bride, who was surrounded by her family. As she was offered congratulations by them—except for her father who still looked wary— Miriam turned her attention toward me. She nodded to her family, moved through the crowd of well-wishers and approached me.

"Miriam," I said, "oh, forgive me, you are Mrs. Bingley now."

"Yes." She beamed. "I believe I am. Oh, Mrs. Darcy, it is too much! Did you think that it could have ended in such a happy way?"

"I could, and I did." I smiled. "Fortune can favor those of us it seemed least likely to, at first."

"But to have obtained him—it is simply that...he loves me, Mrs. Darcy, he truly loves me. And I am not blind, nor ungrateful."

"I do not understand."

"I know that, despite your pretending to be ignorant of my happy ending, this came about due to your intentions and actions. Mrs. Darcy...Elizabeth, I am not wrong, am I?"

I looked down at my hands and felt the weight of such a declaration, as well as not knowing how to confess my hand in the events leading up to

Bingley's willingness to court her. For if I spoke too much, I did myself too much credit, yet if I denied it, I would not satisfy her curiosity.

"I cannot say that I did much at all," I began, "nor can I say that I did little. All I can say is that I—had faith."

"Faith?" Mrs. Bingley said, smiling. "Yes, it is a powerful thing. Yet you didn't need to have faith in me, nor care if I was the right woman for your husband's bosom friend. However, you did, and I don't know why, but your faith saved my life. I don't know why you decided to help me however I will not soon forget it. And perhaps it's best that I don't."

"You owe me nothing."

"On the contrary, I owe you everything. Mr. Bingley is the best of men, for I have grown to see that, and I always will. I daresay, that you must think that the benefits are all on my side in winning him."

"Not at all," I chuckled, "not at all."

"You do, and in this case, you are right, and I will not argue with you. The gaining of much is on my side entirely."

"Mr. Bingley always has and always will deserve the best of women, and I ask this of you, Mrs. Bingley. You have your goodness now, through him, and while I know that your heart and soul is good, I implore you. You say that you won't forget my helping you now and you suggest a debt to be paid to me. I shall make good on that debt of yours easily. Repay me by being the best woman for him. Mr. Bingley's happiness depends very easily on those around him. Always be there for him, always offer him your love, and stand by him, as he faced the world to stand by you. And that will be enough."

"I shall not make him regret it."

"Then you have made your promise, and you owe me nothing. Be happy to be Mrs. Bingley...be very happy to become so."

⚜

All throughout the wedding feast, all looked content except for Miriam's father, who looked rigid during the entire ceremony. Miriam's mother however noticed this and clearly took charge throughout the day to dominate the conversation whenever she or her husband were addressed.

"Do you notice his stiffness?" Kitty asked me, whispering under her breath. "Her father looks downright miserable, poor soul."

"There is nothing poor about his soul but misplaced pride," I sneered. "He is bitter."

"About what, do you think?"

"The differences between his daughter and Mr. Bingley. Naturally he would not have wanted his daughter to marry so far outside of her class..."

"And therefore, only felt pressured to give her hand to Bingley," Kitty finished, "Due to Mr. Bingley's good name and wealth."

"Precisely."

"Well then," Kitty sighed, "I do hope he gets over it. And I would be very annoyed if he doesn't."

I began to laugh.

"Have I said something foolish?" Kitty asked.

"Perhaps, yet it was still fascinatingly funny."

"What are you both laughing about?" Jane asked, sitting near us.

"I was saying something foolish," Kitty explained. "Nothing out of the ordinary."

⚜

After the wedding and feast, Mr. Bingley and Miriam joined us at the inn we were all staying at in Philadelphia. Once we reached our bedroom, I could not contain my glee and I overwhelmed Mr. Darcy and tackled him. Laughing, he fell on the floor while I remained on top of him.

"And might I be so bold?" Mr. Darcy asked. "What is the meaning of my wife overwhelming me so?"

"Well," I started, "I could begin with the fact that I am proud of you."

"What have I done to deserve your appreciation of me?"

"You encouraged Mr. Bingley to follow his heart. Do you have any idea how strong of a notion that was?"

"I did not want him to make the same mistake that I almost had done."

"I forgave you for that long ago. Will you not, Mr. Darcy, ever forgive yourself?"

"Of course, I will not," he said, kissing me. "I was unfair to you, Elizabeth, and I believe that I owe it to myself to improve always. Though I do believe that being on the other side of the world, away from the pressures of the life and society we have been obliged to walk among, has improved me tremendously."

"Then," I said, "You have no improper pride, and you truly are the best man I have ever known."

We kissed once more.

"And you, Mrs. Darcy, taste better than my mother's pudding."

"Your mother could cook?"

"Of course not, yet we still called it her pudding all the same. It was really the cook's pudding, but with the money that we paid her, she was fine with not gaining the credit. I was at first hesitant, Lizzy, with encouraging his marriage to Miriam."

"She is now Mrs. Bingley, dear."

"Yes, she is, and I was hesitant, for we knew so little about her. Yet Bingley is a grown man and therefore able to make his own decisions. With my nature, I would've once objected to it."

"It is a tricky and dangerous business, Mr. Darcy, to try to influence the fate and decisions of others."

"Yes, it is. I never would have learned that, had it not been for you, dearest and loveliest Elizabeth."

"And I have one more reason for tackling you to the floor in such a rash manner," I said, brushing my lips against his.

"And what is that, pray tell?"

"I just...wanted to embrace you."

"And that, I daresay, was all I needed to hear."

He lifted me up and carried me to the bed. "Mrs. Darcy, I am prepared for anything. For I knew that fate brought me much when it delivered you to me."

"I daresay that I am a lot of trouble."

"Perhaps, yet you are worth every bit of it along the way."

❦

After our bodies lay under the covers, spent from the exhaustion and satisfaction that goes hand in hand with being intimate, we remained in each other's embrace, feeling the joy of our skin being pressed against one another and becoming one.

I looked up into Fitzwilliam's face and I saw a troubled expression.

"And..." I sighed, running my hand down his nose and cheek, "What is that look for?"

"Can you not guess my thoughts?"

"Of course not, for they are locked away in here," I said, touching his forehead, "and that is stronger than any safe."

"Elizabeth...we remain here in Philadelphia and I wish to be happy."

"Oh."

"Do you see?"

"Yes, I do. We are so near your cousins and yet so far away from them all the same. United by being in the same city but separated by disagreement and misplaced pride. Family strife is a damned nuisance, Fitzwilliam!"

"Yes, it is," he chuckled. "A part of me is content to leave for England without speaking to them again. For Henry to even think he could address you thus, and what is even more gruesome was his inability to accept Jane's refusal of his worthless hand! Dear lord, Lizzy, I deserved for you to have rejected me often in the past, yet I hope that if you ever did, I would have taken it more like that of a gentleman than he did."

"I hope you would as well," I added, "yet Henry is a Darcy and, if I might say so, the Darcy pride runs deep, just like the Bennet prejudice runs even deeper. I believe that if I had not fallen in love with you as blindly as I had, I would have loved to have fought with you for everything you had done. I daresay my desire for you kept me from resisting you, even when you deserved it, you wicked man."

"Yes, but do you think, under the same circumstances, I could have acted like Henry?"

"Under the same circumstances, we humans are capable of anything. Yet, I tell you now, resist implacable resentment now, Fitzwilliam. The Darcys here have so much good in them, so much happiness and domestic felicity. Do not let your anger for one ruin your resolve in admiring the rest."

"Henry Darcy's parents condoned his behavior at first."

"And my parents condoned Lydia going to Brighton and look what happened. Now she's married to Mr. Wickham, who we both know by all counts will hurt her eventually, all because my parents thought they *were right*. Parents seem to have a blind spot in regards to their children. I acknowledge, even when we have children, we shall be guilty of that crime."

"I hope we need not fear on that score," Fitzwilliam added, "yet that is not something we need to think on for quite some time. I still am getting my *husband legs* in this rocky ocean that is called marriage. Could you imagine me being a father when I have not even found my *paternal legs*?"

"I believe that you would be a great father. You already look after many under your care with diligence. You protected Lydia, Jane, and you even protected me in the end from all your notions of family loyalties. Any man who can defeat himself has it within him to possess perfect paternal skills."

"You flatter and criticize me all in one."

"And I have the right to do so, for I am your wife!" I laughed.

⊛

"Oh, you have that right, do you?" he continued, rolling on top of me, leaning down and kissing my thighs while running his hand over my breasts. "You use that excuse too often," he chuckled, kissing me.

"And I always will. Dear me, Fitzwilliam, how I desire you always."

"Oh, do you?"

"Indeed. And you best desire me as well, forever and always, or I shall be greatly annoyed."

"I could never annoy you."

"If you stopped loving me, you would."

"And like I said, I could never annoy you."

"Well then, before I fall into you then, for I believe myself to be always at your mercy—except for the circumstances when you are at mine—we must remember the purpose of our discussion. Fitzwilliam. We loved our time here in Philadelphia and we loved most of our time with your cousins here."

"Tis true, we did. I found bliss here with you. You might even say that I stole it while I was here with you. I left our problems over on the other side of the ocean. Even at our bitterest times here, between getting verbally attacked for political problems and having to savagely attack those ruffians, I still felt a purity here. I felt—quite content with the freedom we found."

"And having something to fight for while no society to fight against."

"What do you mean?"

"You hate not being free."

"You're correct. I want to be liberated—I want...to not be judged always. And I wish for the world to not look upon me always and look to either praise or to criticize. Elizabeth, for so long I lived my life under the strict and firm gaze of many prying eyes, who wished to know all that was within me, not because they cared, but because they desired the life that I had. They desired an image—and not reality."

⚜

"Then why me?" I persisted, quite intrigued by all that he was confessing.

"I do not comprehend again. You are being wonderfully elliptic tonight, you know."

"Why did you choose to fall in love with me?"

"I chose nothing, remember? I did my best to reject you, no matter how much you deserved more than my paltry behavior, for I was quite the worthless libertine. No, no, no. You were brought to me, despite my stubbornness. I could not help but fall in love with you."

"Yes, but you had to have seen many beauties in your time. Many who must've enticed you. What about me was different?"

"The fact that you are different—and you are not afraid of me."

"Is that it?" I chuckled.

"And you love to laugh."

"Many women do."

"And it's often a fake laugh. Yet yours is real. That is it!"

"How so and what is?"

"Lizzy, you were *real*. From the first time I saw you at Almacks and you poured me wine, then when you gave me flowers in the park, you were genuine. You were—the truth. I had never met a woman who could encompass such veracity in her countenance while also being light, carefree in her disposition, and optimistic in nature. Your habits and manner lighten my own. Therefore, whenever I looked away from you, I would become lost, and when I chose to reject you, I fell even further."

Darcy rolled me over and began to kiss my back while running his hands over my bottom, massaging me over and over while I moaned into the pillow. He raised his lips, removed my hair off my neck and began to kiss the back of it.

"You must not lose your love for me, Elizabeth," he whispered desperately.

"I won't."

"Then all is well."

"Fitzwilliam?"

"Yes," he replied, raising himself up while his hands stopped moving.

"Oh no!" I sighed, "you can still listen to me while your hands still perform their work upon me."

"Of course," he laughed, continuing to run his hands along my body. "Now, what was it we were speaking of again?"

"Of your family, we were speaking of your family," I whispered, eyes closed and allowing myself to enjoy his touch. "And my fears of you turning from them forever because of one harsh encounter. I do not think we should lightly abandon them and forsake a part of the family who we have had so many good moments with. Whether it is through a letter or by wishing to see them again, we should not leave for England without speaking to them once more. And who knows? Maybe we might need them to help us in the end."

"I cannot see how that is possible, yet stranger things have happened."

"Aye, they have. After all, I am friends to a woman writer who has just published a book named *Sense and Sensibility*. Therefore, all is possible, isn't it?"

"Yes. Everything is. Fine then, I shall submit to your counsel—for the moment—yet, I do not wish to see them just yet. We should write them a letter."

"Shall I write it, or you?"

"You had better do it. I'm afraid if I were to do so, then I would say something offensive."

⚜

Dressed in my robes, I sat at the desk and finished my letter while Fitzwilliam lay in our bed. When I finished, I read it over and then turned to him.

"Well, shall I begin to read it?"

"I am ready for it."

I cleared my throat and began.

Dear Cousin Thomas and Emilia Darcy,
Many a day has gone by where we look on our memories of our time

spent on Canterbury with fondness, for we found much happiness in your company. Just as we have found in coming to America, yet as you know, our fortune in coming across the ocean to these lands was not always for the good or even the acceptable. We have been met with anger, prejudice, racial and social injustice, and yet, rather than deter us from loving the land, we are still endeared to it. Philadelphia has been the greatest of places, and your company made it so. Therefore, as we look on with all things, we choose to refuse to let our memories of tension erase any memories of being content. We grew to love you, our American cousins, and we did not wish to part under such ill terms. May we all, despite the anger that Henry Darcy has, not sever all ties. We shall always look on him as family, if he remembers that we are his. And we urge him to look on my sister's rejection of him not as the ending of a story, yet as the chance for him to make a new one for himself. With one rejection in one quarter can lead to an acceptance from another one more suitable. Another woman will come along, and my sister's actions will allow him freedom to find her. Which he shall. We are soon to leave Philadelphia, for we had returned to see Mr. Bingley wed Miriam Goldman, and now she is to travel with us back to England, where we must acknowledge now will not only be separated by ocean, but by the threat of war. We wish to not lose your love and understand that you have not lost ours. And you never will.

Yours, etc.
   Mr. and Mrs. Darcy of Pemberly.

I turned back to Fitzwilliam.

"Well, does that suit?"

"Yes, very well."

"I can assure you, Fitzwilliam, this is all for the best. For we may never know, but something tells me that if we maintain the connection, they might aid us in some way in the end."

"You do not wish to burn a bridge?"

"I do not know if I have achieved that. All I can say is that I do not wish to build a wall."

"I am very good at building walls."

"Yes," I laughed, "and I love breaking them down in reply."

We rang for Jefferson, who Darcy gave the letter to and had him send. Once Jefferson left, I turned back to Fitzwilliam.

"And on another matter, you must tell me how a man like Jefferson came to be in your employ, and why you trust him so much."

"That is a discussion for another day."

"Why not this one?"

"Because I will only tell you when you have known him long enough to forgive him for anything."

"Was he a villain once?" I asked, intrigued.

"He might have been in some ways, yet he was also a hero in many others. Yet the duality of his nature is not something that I must own to knowing all of."

"Then we shall have something to talk about in the future," I laughed, "And I promise not to tell Cassandra and Jane Austen that part of the story."

"Thank you, Elizabeth, that is a great comfort."

ABOUT THE AUTHOR

Ney Mitch has been a long-standing Jane Austen enthusiast, having written forty novels that were inspired by her various works. Since stumbling on Miss Austen's books after graduating from college, she has always dabbled in Austen inspired literature, ranging from writing works for teens to adults. Originally, her desire was to adapt Jane Austen's writing in a way to help young adults connect with her, however over time, she has spread her aims to other genres and styles.

Having received her BA Degree at Desales University, she is a writer, both literary and dramatic, as well as being a Historic Reenactor.

 facebook.com/courtney.mitchell.589

 twitter.com/CMMitchelPsyche

 pinterest.com/shebaanna

ALSO BY NEY MITCH

WITH SATIN ROMANCE

Pride, Prejudice, & New Adventures

Rapture & Rebellion

Fortune & Misfortune

Desire & Destiny (coming soon)

Memory Series

Moments of Moments Past

Moments of Moments Present

Moments of Moments Future (coming soon)